IN HER DREAMS

JENNIFER LYNN

ISBN: 978-1-4834-9068-7 (sc)
ISBN: 978-1-4834-9067-0 (e)

Lulu Publishing Services rev. date: 12/11/2018

I dedicate this book to my incredible children,
you both bring so much joy to my life.
I love you to the moon and back.
A huge thank you to my amazing family
for their constant support and inspiration.
To my wonderful husband...twenty-one years was not enough.
I miss you with every breath.
Come visit me in my dreams.

PROLOGUE

1154, HOLY LAND

S weat dripped down his forehead, stinging his eyes. Ignoring the urge to remove his visor and cast off his chain mail, he shook his head and focused. With a gentle shove the narrow door popped open. Smashed pottery littered the floor. Remnants of somebody's breakfast lay abandoned on the table and a few sleeping palates were piled in the corner.

Nothing. Whoever was here had already fled.

Disappointment grew in his chest. He had to find her. She was here, somewhere.

He nudged his horse forward paying little attention to the chaos surrounding him. Screams from the wounded and dying resonated along the high walls of the castle's inner city. Nothing was going right today and he was beginning to lose all hope.

His men were in charge of searching the southwest quadrant and they were almost done. So far there was no sign of Ramsey...or her.

From the sounds of it, Robert's men were tearing the place apart. Not what they had been told to do. The peasants were to be left alone. Unfortunately, the castle's inhabitants had fought back and Robert had given the order to kill.

Now, bodies littered the streets and the stench of death was enough to make even the strongest of men gag.

They were running out of time and Royce knew it.

Leaning forward in his saddle, he pushed open another door with his sword. A movement near the entrance startled him and his horse reared up. Instinctively he brought his sword down, stopping just in time when he saw a child's face.

A woman screamed, scrambled forward and grabbed the boy by the arm, dragging him back. Bile filled his throat. "Dammit," he cursed softly. He needed to pay attention.

He called up the street, "Search every door. We can't leave until we find-"

"My Lord." One of his men was cantering towards him. "We found him. He's with Lord Robert and they're heading out."

Him? Not her? His heart clenched. "Anyone else?" He kept his voice firm. There was no room for weakness.

"No sir."

He gritted his teeth. He'd been so sure she was here today. Frustration filled him. There was nothing more he could do now. He gave a terse nod of his head. "Move the men out."

"What of the people, sir?"

"We're done here." He turned his horse. "Leave them."

"But Lord Mortimer gave the order to burn it."

Sure enough, the nauseating smell of seared flesh reached his nose. With a curse, Royce glanced up the street at his men who were still methodically searching each entrance off the alley. Raising his voice, he gave the command, "Tell the men the city has been fired. There's not much time, get them all out while you can."

His man nodded and turned away.

"Sir-" his squire's urgent shout echoed down the alley. Royce swung around to see the lad in a full gallop waving his arm in a frenzy trying to get his attention. Barely able to control his lathered horse the boy waited till he reached Royce's side before whispering urgently, "I think I've found her."

His heart skipped a beat. "Where?"

"The square, near the well," his squire said. "She's-"

Royce didn't wait to hear the rest. His horse jumped from the pressure of his spurs and gave an indignant squeal as it took off down the cobbled lane.

Great plumes of black smoke began pouring into the streets blocking his vision and burning his eyes.

The earlier bustling market center was now devoid of life. Bodies lay at odd angles everywhere. From ahead he heard children scream and then a woman's cry.

A cry he recognized. Panic seized him. He prayed he wasn't too late. With a final kick, his mount tore around the last corner, slipping and struggling to keep upright.

He saw her immediately. She was protecting a group of children. Covered in dirt and blood the visible patches of her white dress a beacon calling him. God, he hoped she wasn't hurt.

A soldier was walking towards her, his weapon raised getting ready to strike. She pushed one of the children behind her and raised her arm to block the blow.

Anger boiled up inside. NO. The single word erupted from deep in his chest. He couldn't lose her now. His horse gathered itself and jumped forward in response to his kick.

She shoved the child behind her. Somehow, she had to save them. The others in the room hadn't been so lucky. She'd managed to get this family outside and down to the well, but now they were trapped.

The boy's mother had taken the first blow and was lying on the ground at her feet. She hadn't been able to stop the monster. He'd laid open her neck with one long sweep of his sword and now he was descending on her.

Out of the corner of her eye, she saw the knight and horse come barreling around the corner. His lathered mount slid on the blood slick stones before righting itself. Smoke and flames licked the walls behind him, making it look as if he was coming straight from hell.

A ringing started in her ears. She saw his mouth open and he yelled something she couldn't hear. He pointed his sword at her as his mount jumped forward.

He looked like the devil himself, and one way or another, she knew she was about to die.

She turned back to face the soldier as he swung his sword, instinctively throwing up her arm trying to shield her face.

That's when she woke up screaming.

GHOSTS

Up until a year ago, I was the kind of girl who
said, "I don't believe in ghosts."
But if I were to believe in them, then there are plenty of people
I would be happy to have visit me in my dreams.
My mother for one, she died when I was four.
I understand I have her eyes.
My sister, Audrey, for another,
she drowned on the eve of my fourteenth
birthday in a horrible car accident.
I idolized her.
She was a beautiful, vibrant sixteen years old and
the day we buried her changed me forever.
Last spring my father joined them both.
He died on a Thursday, just shy of the eighth anniversary of my
sister's death and two weeks before my twenty-second birthday.
It's been nearly a year and ever since then I've
been plagued with nightmares.
His death stirred something in me,
awoken someone if you will.
Now, I can't help but believe something
or someone joins me in my sleep.
And it's not my loved ones.
~Anna

CHAPTER 1

PRESENT DAY
DEVON, ENGLAND

Anna Harrington accepted a glass of champagne off of the tray from a passing waiter and glanced around in satisfaction. The benefit was in full swing and her job for the night was done. Castle Drogo was as beautiful as the committee had promised and lived up to its reputation as one of the most dramatic castles in Devon. The party was a success. Not that she'd had anything to do with the plans. All that had taken place without her. She'd only written the checks.

As the only living relative of her grandparents' estate, Anna had flown to England earlier this week to introduce the collection of antiques they had donated to the museum in Essex.

Her Uncle John hadn't wanted her to come but hadn't been able to stop her either.

"Your father and your grandmother didn't get along," was all John would say.

Anna's friend Kate, and lately the biggest pain in the ass, waved to her from the other end of the ballroom motioning her over. Kate lived in Essex with her husband and their two-year-old daughter, Lily. Ever since she had arrived three days earlier, Kate had been ferrying her around town, getting her ready for this shindig in the hopes that she could *find herself a fella*, as Kate liked to put it. Hmmm...Maybe staying with her hadn't been the best idea after all, Anna considered.

Gritting her teeth, she picked up the train of her white dress and weaved through the crowd towards Kate and her latest "catch."

"Anna, this is Neil Beck," Kate said with a wink. "He's a barrister from London."

Russet haired and stocky, Neil Beck was not the best-looking specimen in the room and not one she particularly wanted to get to know any better. Be nice Anna, she reminded herself.

The gentleman clicked his heels together and bowed over her hand, his lips lingering on her wrist. Ignoring the urge to snatch her hand back, Anna replied smoothly, "Very nice to meet you Mr. Beck."

"Neil," he encouraged. Straightening, he grinned broadly revealing a mouthful of gum and twisted teeth. Her own smile faltered.

"Your friend was just telling me you might be staying on?" Neil said.

Anna raised her brows at Kate. "Was she?"

Kate bit her lip playfully, "I was just telling Mr. Beck that you were considering moving back in to your grandparents' estate."

Anna narrowed her eyes at her friend. "As much as I would love to extend my trip Mr. Beck,"

"Neil."

"Neil. I'm afraid I have to get back to work. I run an antique shop in New York City with my uncle."

"Oh? Where abouts? I'm quite fond of the "Big Apple" and travel across the pond frequently on business."

"In the Chelsea neighborhood, The Hollow Rose," she said ready to be done with this conversation. Deepening her smile, she reached to take Kate's arm and drew her away. "We'd love to have you stop in any time," adding over her shoulder, "It was so nice to meet you, Mr. Beck."

"Neil," he corrected to their retreating figures.

Anna waited until they were out of hearing range before tilting her head and whispering, "Naughty Kate. Stop."

"Come on, it's fun."

"Fun for who? Certainly not me. Just because you're married, doesn't mean I'm ready."

"Baloney. You're ready, you just need to get your head out of the clouds and *find a fella*."

"*Find a fella*," Anna repeated with her in perfect unison.

Kate made a face, "Have I been bad?"

"Yes, and you must stop. You're driving me crazy."

"I'm just so excited to have you with me," she hugged Anna's arm before turning serious. "You must admit, England's been good for you. You're so much better here." They walked out of the ballroom to a long hallway lined with portraits. Stopping in front of a mirror, Kate turned her to face it. "See, no more circles under your eyes and your dimple has returned."

Anna examined the woman starring back at her and wrinkled her nose. Ugh. There were still circles under her eyes. Kate had just done a really good job of covering them up. She sighed. Not enough make-up in the world. She'd let Kate play dress-up on her all afternoon, agreed to the concealer, the foundation, and the blush but put her foot down to the shimmering smoky eyes and false lashes.

"They'll make your green eyes pop," Kate had stated dramatically, displaying jazz hands.

"I don't want my eyes to 'pop'," she had replied unable to hold back a laugh. Kate had finally given up and concentrated on her hair.

Anna tucked a fallen strand of her recently cut and now perfectly styled hair back into Kate's Cinderella up-do and joked, "I don't know how you did it, but I do look pret-ty fabulous." She playfully batted her eyes into the mirror and struck a pose. "Gorgeous...even without the smoky eyes."

"Come on, you know what I mean. Take me seriously," Kate pressed. "When I saw you at Christmas you were in terrible shape. Now look at you, you've got your sense of humor back and you're all sparkles and sunshine." She wriggled her shoulders. "So, it's either Mr. Neil Beck in there or, may-_be_, it's the fresh English air."

"May-be," Anna smiled, "It's my friend." She didn't want to say the obvious. Last week had been the anniversary of her father's death. If she were being truthful, she would admit she would have done anything to get out of New York at the time. This trip was just a convenient excuse and one she seriously never thought she'd accept.

The very last place she expected to be was a town away from where she grew up and three miles from the river that took her sister's life nine years ago.

Her last memory of England had been a dreary rainy Sunday in April. Since then she'd done what her father had taught her, bury and forget...bury, forget and pretend it never happened.

But since his sudden death last year she couldn't pretend anymore. She'd had trouble sleeping. Her vivid dreams had taken a turn for the worse. Horrible nightmares plagued her nights and haunted her days.

Unable to cope, she quit the fencing team and dropped out of college last fall, promising her uncle she only needed some time. "Now I can help you full time at the shop," she reasoned.

"I don't need help at the shop and you work there enough. You are already behind. You've barely got one year left, Anna," he had begged. "Don't give up."

But time hadn't helped. She felt in limbo, like she was living some kind of half-life. At least until she stepped off the plane in London. Kate was right, she _was_ happier here. But not complete.

Turning away from her image, she started to grab Kate's arm to go back inside when something caught her eye at the end of the hall.

"Oh my God," she clapped a hand over her mouth, suppressing her surprise. "I don't believe it."

She took one step, then another and before she knew it she was hurrying down the hall, the sound of her high heels echoing off the walls. Three large glass cases stood at the entrance to the outside terrace. The first held a half suit of armor in silver. Unpolished and darkened with age, the suit was still impressive in its size and the marks it bore from battle.

"Good lord," Kate came up beside her. "Did that *fella* live?"

Warmth spread through her as she touched the glass. "Yes," she giggled. She suddenly felt ridiculously happy. "At least I think so. This guy stood in our front hall for years. I can't believe he's here. I'd forgotten."

"Forgotten what?"

"Forgotten how much I loved this *fella*," she said using Kate's terminology.

Kate bent to read the information tag on the front. "Wow, pretty old, 1154 and from France. You guys go way back."

"Yeah, and that," she pointed to the next glass case. "That was Audrey's *fella*. He came from the thirteenth century I think. See the difference in craftsmanship and style?"

"Beautiful," Kate admired. Stepping on to the next case she squinted, "What about this guy? It says early 1200's"

Anna turned to the last case and froze, the smile dying on her face. The flute of champagne slipped from her fingers and crashed to the floor, startling them both.

Kate's head whipped around, "Anna?"

She couldn't respond. All the moisture had left her mouth as she stared at the mannequin warrior. As if possessed by magic, the simple breast plate and face mask over the thick chain mail filled, coming to life. Eyes as black as night stared back at her and the gloved hand began to move. She stumbled back in horror.

"Jesus," she choked. Her chest felt like it was being squeezed in a vice. "I-ca-n't-bre-bre-ath," she managed, waving a hand in front of her face.

"What?" Kate took a step towards her.

She stumbled back.

"Anna? Honey?" Kate touched her shoulder. "You're scaring me. You've gone sheet white. What is it?"

"It's-just, I recognize him."

"Him? You mean that suit of armor? Is it something from your grandparents' house?"

"No," she managed. She shook her head. "I've got to go," she said clutching her stomach. If she didn't get out of here soon, she was either going to lose her lunch or faint.

"What?" Kate reached out to her, confusion on her face. "Go where?"

"Bathroom. Give me a minute." She waved away Kate's help. "I just need a minute. I'll be right back," she whispered before spinning around on her heel.

"I'm getting Steven. I'll meet you in the bathroom" Kate called after her. But Anna had already turned the corner. Going right by the ladies' room, she headed for the front door.

Both valets were gone. Somehow, she found her keys and her car. Before she could stop herself, she was maneuvering out of the narrow parking space and headed towards the exit. With barely a thought she hit the gas gunning the engine into the night.

Castle Drogo is built on the highest point in Dartmouth National Park. On her way up to the party the view had been charming, sunlight danced through the trees hiding the steep treacherous roads and hairpin turns. Now in the darkness the headlights from her tiny rental bounced off the shadows reflecting a more sinister sensation.

By the time she hit the first turn, rain began to fall. By the third turn it was a torrent. Even with the windshield wipers going full blast, it was nearly impossible to see the road. She knew she should stop, but there was no place to pull over.

She was just starting to breathe a little easier and feeling ridiculous for leaving when she came to a particularly steep curve. Shifting to slow down, she put both hands on the steering wheel to turn when a man stepped in front of her car. Instinctively, she wrenched the wheel the other way to miss him.

What the hell was he doing out in this mess?

But her last thought was lost as her car careened off the road and over a small cliff. The airborne car hit the river so hard it threw her forward, slamming her into the steering wheel. The last thing she remembered was water rushing up to meet her, and then darkness.

CHAPTER 2

"Anna."

Slowly coming to, Anna tried to focus. Someone was calling her name. Air, she needed air. She was trapped in her car and it was filling up with water.

"Anna. You must wake up and get out."

She turned to look at the passenger side of the car and the man who sat beside her. The lights in her dash flickered casting a red glow over the familiar face.

"Dad? Is that you?"

"Yes, sweetheart."

"What happened?" He looked so real she couldn't concentrate. She wanted to reach out and touch him, but his next words stopped her.

"Get out, Anna. Get out."

"What?" She asked confused. Startled by his presence she forgot where she was. The lights on her dash blinked once and went out. She screamed. Panic set in. "Wait...I can't see anything. Dad!" She groped the door until she found the handle and pushed. The door wouldn't budge. "The door's stuck. Help me, please."

"Get out, Anna," his voice became frantic. "Hurry. You don't have much time."

Her fingers were frozen and barely cooperating as she slid them to the window lever and fumbled to turn the crank. Ice cold water rushed in filling the car and bringing her to her senses.

She had to get out of here. Now.

Releasing her seat belt, she pushed herself up and squeezed through the window. By the time she reached the surface, the current captured her and swept her downstream. Fighting her crippling fear, she swam towards the outline of shore. Her skirts catching and tearing on branches below. She could just make out a rocky outcrop ahead of her.

With more strength than she realized she had, she kicked and managed to catch on to a boulder as she brushed against it. But trying to pull herself up with icy hands and an exhausted body proved too much. She was quickly sucked under again and dragged farther downstream. Thrashing with all her might, she came back up and grabbed a branch sticking out in the water just as she was passing it. With sheer determination she held on and worked her way to the shore. Taking deep gulps of air, she pulled herself farther away from the river, and then turned over and threw up.

Cold. She was so cold. She tried to sit up, but pain radiated through her skull. Her lungs felt like they were on fire. Everything hurt. Can't think-just need sleep.

Was she dead? No, death didn't smell like that. Or maybe it did. She cracked open her eyes trying to determine the source and stared at a very dead, very bloated large rodent lying stiffly beside her.

"Ugh." Vomit rose in her throat and she rolled over releasing the contents of her stomach. It was mostly water. Still it hurt as much coming back up as it did going down. She must have swallowed half of the river last night.

With a groan she pushed herself to her feet and stumbled up the bank anxious to get away from the rotting corpse. Her body protested, but the smell was worse. God that hurt, she mused, forcing herself farther away.

Her legs hurt, her torso hurt, her arms hurt and her head was pounding so hard it was making her lightheaded and dizzy. She ran her hands up the side of her face to the knot on her forehead. Sticky wetness. Blood? Hopefully, it wasn't fresh. She sighed relieved to find the blood dark against her fingertips.

Gingerly she made her way over to a hollowed-out log and collapsed with a grunt. Looking down at her muddy, tattered dress. Disbelief filled her. What the hell had happened last night? How could she freak out like that? Running out in the middle of a party? The car, the man in the road, the cliff… "Jesus, Anna," she said out loud. "You idiot. Kate is going to kill you."

She slid her feet out from the shreds of her ruined gown and wiggled her toes, praying nothing was broken. No pain thank god. She pulled her skirt up to her knees and quickly put it back down unwilling to see the scrapes and bruises coloring her body. Instead she did a mental check list, bending and flexing her way up as she ticked each body part off testing for damage.

Feet, bruised, bloody but operational, check.

Ankles, check.

Knees, ouch, check.

Thighs, check.

Body, ugh, sort of…ribs kind of hurt, but you can breathe so check.

Arms, she glanced from side to side, stretching and turning. Hard to tell with the dried mud. Blood oozed from a cut on her wrist. It hurt but nothing she couldn't handle. She ripped the bottom hem off her gown and wrapped her wrist. Check.

Hands, the nails were a mess, dirt and dried blood filled every crevice but not too painful.

Check, check, check.

She'd lost her shoes, her watch, one earring and Kate's necklace. Sorry Kate.

"Looks like you're gonna live Anna," she muttered.

And pretty damn lucky considering the cliff she went over last night. What in God's name had a man been doing out in the road in the middle of a rain storm like that? She hadn't noticed a car and he hadn't looked hurt, but maybe he'd had an accident too. If so, then surely, he'd tell someone about her car going off the cliff, right?

Taking a deep breath, she stood up. "Come on, now. Don't panic," she gave herself a pep talk. "This is a fairly well hiked area. You'll come across someone soon."

Pushing up from the log, she cautiously threaded her way through the woods away from the river. Her thoughts touched briefly on the vision of her father.

Had that really happened?

No, that had to be her imagination. Tears filled her eyes. She choked them back and forced herself to concentrate. How far down river had she come last night?

A mile? More? Had anyone found her car yet?

God, Kate was probably going crazy by now.

Her stomach growled in protest adding to her misery. "Dammit," she said out loud giving voice to her frustration as she navigated her way around some small shrubs. She needed to be careful with her footing. She pushed aside a few dangling branches wrapped with new growth and came into a large clearing. Thick spring grass spread like a carpet before her. Tiny blue flowers waved in the sun. She stopped dead in her tracks. Déjà vu hit her smack in the face.

She knew this place.

It was just like her dream.

Holy shit.

Her heart skipped a beat and then accelerated to unbearable.

"I'm dreaming," she whispered trying to calm down. "It's a dream." Her toes curled into the wet grass. "Don't panic", she reassured herself. She fingered a leathery leaf before pulling it off the vine. It sure felt real.

But it couldn't be, could it? Those dreams were not real. She'd plunged off a 30-foot cliff last night and survived, right?

No, she thought making up her mind. This was not a dream and those dreams were not real. So what if this place reminded her of something.

"Not real," she said with force and continued forward.

"Not real," she said again a little more quietly as movement near the tree ahead of her slowed her progress.

"Not real," she said in a whisper as a man stepped into view.

Fear tingled up her spine. Who the hell is this? What the hell is this? And what the hell is he wearing? The tunic and strange hose were filthy and his hair was long and *not* clean and those teeth. She came to a complete stop and stared at him in surprise.

Was this help? It didn't look like help. Backing up, she turned to go in the opposite direction when another face appeared around a tree ahead of her. This one was worse and he was leering at her. At least, she thought it was a leer, but it was hard to tell. He didn't appear to have many teeth either.

Without another thought she turned and ran.

Suddenly, the forest seemed full of nasty looking men giving chase. Dear God, they looked like a bunch of medieval homeless men.

If she'd had her strength, she might have been able to outrun them. But barefoot and hurt she barely managed twenty feet before they gleefully overtook her.

"Come 'er, wench, and give us a kiss," the first and ugliest one said as he grabbed her up. Hauling her around, he tried to press his lips against hers. His teeth were practically black and the stench coming from his mouth nearly made her faint. She pushed away from him in disgust as much as fear.

"Ooooh, this one's got spirit, Gill."

"She don't want none of you."

The men around her started to laugh and tease the revolting person who had hold of her now.

"Let me go, you vile man," she demanded, pushing back, now more pissed off than scared.

Surprise twisted across his ugly face.

"Oh, she's a cultured one," said a voice from behind her as he fingered her dangling earring. "She must be some rich lord's wife."

"I bet we'd get a pretty penny if we took 'er in to Lord Fenton."

"Lord Fenton don't know what to do with 'er," Gill said viciously. "But I do."

Again, all the men started to laugh.

"Looks like she cum down in dis world," a nasty voice chimed in.

Gill's hand whipped out and gave her earring a tug. It came off easily and disappeared into the pouch around his waist. Before she could react, he stepped closer and pinched her breast hard. Another started to lift up the shreds of her dress from behind.

Now she was in trouble.

Before she could think it through, she brought her knee up into Gill's groin, dropping him like a stone. Taking advantage of her freedom, she turned and fled, heading for the open meadow.

The men gave chase and a scream of desperation escaped her. There was no way she was going to be able to outrun them. Her feet were cut and bruised and her head had started bleeding again in the small scuffle.

Ignoring the pain, she ran as fast as she could, but didn't get very far before one of the younger ones caught up and tackled her in the open field. When she started to fight, he hauled her up and gave her a heavy slap that sent her head reeling.

They were all around her. One had lifted her dress up in the back. Another had his hand down the front, while someone else held a knife to her throat and whispered what he was going to do to her when it was his turn. She closed her eyes, unable to stop the tears from sliding down her cheeks.

From somewhere far away a yell penetrated her terror. She wasn't sure if it came from her or the men around her. The ground beneath her trembled. It felt like a thousand horses were bearing down on them. Suddenly the grip on her throat loosened and fell away. She opened her eyes in time to witness the man's head get severed clean off. Warm blood showered one side of her face. Startled, she turned only to encounter a huge horse with a man decked out in armor on its back, the animal's breath hot in her face. The knight, or whatever the hell he was, was slicing the men around her to pieces. For a moment the sun was blocked as the horse reared up and struck at the air. Easily, he controlled the giant beast, reining him in. Hooves hit the ground right beside her.

The man's mask was expressionless, but the eyes behind it seemed to bore into her with an unholy light. She recognized it immediately. The mask was the same one she had just seen the night before with Kate. This was the monster from her nightmares.

The devil himself had finally come to get her.

In a moment it was over, the only sound was the agitated shuffling of the massive horse. Unable to control her shaking, she took in the grizzly scene. A movement near her feet demanded her attention and she looked down. Blood emptied from the body next to her and swirled around her toes. Gasping, she tried to step back out of the sticky mess, but instead encountered another body.

Her teeth began to chatter...oh, God, she was losing it. A hand appeared next to her, and her eyes followed the length of the masculine arm up to the man on horseback. He was still holding a bloody sword in the other hand and staring at her as if she were the apparition, not him.

The fear she felt before was nothing compared to now. It paralyzed her. Her chest constricted and she couldn't seem to pull in enough air. Each breath became harder and faster than the last making her dizzy and lightheaded.

As if in slow motion, he extended his hand towards her, palm up and open as if he wanted her to take it. Shaking her head, she took a step back, her bare foot slipping on a body. The blood, the faces frozen in death...it was too much for her. Everything began to spin. The last day had drawn on her reserves and she had nothing left.

"Oh, God, let me be dead too," she murmured before the merciful blackness engulfed her once again.

CHAPTER

3

After nine years of waiting he'd finally found her, his Anna. Royce wasted no time getting her back to his camp. The few men he had left behind to prepare came out upon their return. Their faces showed disbelief at the sight of a bloodied woman in his arms. Most of his men had voiced their doubts about ever finding this woman that he had returned to England for last year.

Some, he was sure, even doubted his sanity. But Lars, his second in command, had stood by him. The men's curiosity was understandable, but he wanted no one in his tent but himself.

Anna had not opened her eyes once on the ride back and that worried him. After getting her into his tent, he gently undressed her, trying hard to keep his focus off the lovely body beneath the dress.

Wiping away all the blood, he was able to examine the extent of her injuries. Her legs and feet had multiple scrapes but nothing seemed broken. There was a cut on her wrist that he cleaned and bound. The purple bruise on her ribs gave him some concern but the worst her head.

He wasn't sure if it was the injury or the shock of what had happened that kept her asleep.

When the fever started that night, he sent his men to find the old witch of the woods. They came back quicker than expected.

Daylight was just making an appearance when he heard the sound of approaching horses. Stepping out of the tent Royce watched as the old woman rode into camp. He walked over and greeted her kindly.

"Enid. It's good to of you to come." He offered her a hand, helping her down.

"Aye, I've been waiting for your lady." The old woman barely gave him a glance. "She's hurt, aye?"

She pushed past him not waiting for a response and hurried towards the tent.

She didn't look much different than the few times he'd visited her over the past year. He'd always thought her the oldest person in the world when he was a boy and she hadn't changed much in appearance since. She was still a stubborn old goat with heavily creased skin and bony hands, but her herbs worked magic.

If it wasn't for Enid, his mother would have died that day in the meadow. Luckily, she found her and was able to nurse her back to some semblance of health.

His mother had never been the same with so many broken bones, but she had lived until last spring when he finally found his way back. So now, whenever he was in the area, he always visited her little hut by the stream.

Lars jumped down from his horse watching her go. Stealing a look around at the other men, he leaned in and whispered to Royce.

"It was as if a magic string pulled us to her hut." He shook his head. "When we approached she opened the door ready with a satchel full of herbs, and said we must be off for your lady needed her badly. The men have been so shaken they've stayed away from her the rest of the trip."

Royce glanced around at his men. They were indeed whispering behind their hands and casting suspicious glances toward his tent. Unconcerned, he slapped Lars on the back. "Thank you, my friend. You did well."

"Is she truly a witch?" Lars caught his arm as he turned to go.

"No." Royce shook his head. "But she does know a lot about the healing arts. Tell the men to rest easy and let her be so she can work."

"Your lady, is she better?"

"There's been no change. I'm glad you've returned." Royce nodded to Lars and headed back to the tent.

By the time he got there Enid had started water to boil over the fire and unrolled a long pouch full of herbs next to Anna. He sat back and quietly watched her run her hands over Anna's body assessing the damage. Without acknowledging his presence, she began asking questions.

"Did ya see her come?"

"No."

"How did she get this bump on 'er 'ead?"

"I don't know..."

"No?" She paused in her ministrations to look up at him, the firelight dancing across her wrinkled visage. "Where did ya find her then?"

"Two miles down past the falls."

"Hmph, she went over," Enid said more to herself than to him.

"Her wrist will mend as will her ribs. They're not broken, but her head...I'm not so sure," she said soberly before turning back to her work.

It had been four days since he'd brought her back to camp. If not for Enid constantly at her side, whispering soothing words and gently but firmly nursing her sore body back to health, Royce would have doubted Anna's survival.

Yesterday, she'd been so hot he'd spent the entire day bathing her in cool water. Then she had talked, sometimes so quickly, he'd had trouble following her. Even when her eyes were wide, open she wasn't seeing him. She was somewhere else entirely.

Last night her fever finally broke. Since Enid had been here she had had only one lucid moment. His hope had blossomed when she had looked directly at him and smiled, asking him where he'd been. She remembered him, he was sure of it.

But they were running out of time. They'd spent over a week in this location and it was getting dangerous. They had two to three days left at the most and then they would be forced to move.

"Go on, then." Enid nudged his boot.

"What?" He roused himself from his thoughts and stared up at Enid.

"You've barely left her side for four days. Ye need tendin' yourself." She poked at the fire. "Ye look like the devil and don't smell much better. She'll be fine. Her fever's broke and her wounds are healing nicely. She'll be up soon and I'll be giving her a bath, so out with ye'."

"You're sure?" He stood and stretched.

"Aye, I'll be getting that useless lackey of yours to help me with the water. So go, before I kick ye harder."

He grunted and left the tent suddenly feeling weak himself. Calling out to his squire to get some food ready, he grabbed a fresh change of clothes and headed for the stream. She would be up soon and he wanted to look his best. For nine years he had been waiting for this. He looked out over the water and began to undress.

Today they would meet again. What would she think of him? Would she remember? She must. She must remember. With that last thought he walked into the water and dove under.

As he surfaced, thoughts of Anna raced through his mind. Swimming to the other side of the stream that led to a quiet little inlet, he gave his mind the freedom to wander. And wander it did, back to those long legs, trim hips and small but perfect breasts. She had changed so much and yet so little in the nine years since he'd seen her last.

Physically, she'd grown in height quite a bit and her body had most definitely blossomed into a woman's form. Her face looked the same, and yet, somehow, she was even more beautiful. Those eyes, so large and luminous, the soft green of spring grass, and a perfect nose with a sprinkling of freckles that led to a mouth meant for kissing.

Her hair wasn't as long as he remembered and she had shorter pieces framing her face. It had darkened to a brownish red, shot through with gold. The color reminded him of an autumn day. He was anxious to see what it looked like clean...to run his hands through it and pull her down to kiss those red lips-

"Sir?" His squire Hayne called running into the glen interrupting his thoughts.

Turning back to the opposite shore, he struck off in long broad strokes to reach the anxious young man pacing the water's edge.

"Sir...sir, come quick, she's up." Hayne motioned with his hands.

Damn...has she spoken?" he questioned, pulling himself out of the water Royce grabbed the towel from the boy's hands, dried himself off with a fast swipe and hauled on his clothes.

"Not exactly, sir"

"What do you mean?" He demanded.

"Well, you just better come quick." Hayne gathered his sword and held it out for him. He was rocking from side to side on the balls of his feet.

"Is she alright?" he pressed.

"I don't know, but you best hurry."

Pulling on his boots, he grabbed his sword and set off at a run with Hayne following behind.

He slowed as he came into the camp. All of his men were standing in a circle with their hands out to their side as though trying to calm a wild horse. Lars was talking in a gentle voice to someone.

He pushed several men aside to see Anna standing in the middle in his tunic weaving back and forth. Her back was to him and he couldn't help but notice the long, trim legs the tunic revealed. He knew damn well she had nothing else on underneath. He glared around again at his men aware they were admiring the feminine attributes too.

Lars nodded to him, and then looked at Anna's side. Royce followed his eyes. Dear God, she held a sword in her hands. It was one of the lighter ones, but still heavy and the point of it was dragging in the dirt. She had to be weak. She had barely eaten in the four days she'd been there. He had been able to force some broth down her throat a few times but still, she had to be exhausted.

"Anna," he said quietly.

She whirled around with the sword and pointed it straight at him.

Surprised, he leaned back and put his hands out to his side. She looked fragile. Her arms didn't seem strong enough to hold that sword, but her form was excellent. The position she went into earned his instant respect. He'd never seen another woman wield a sword and he was quite sure none of his men had either.

She was staring at him with pure concentration.

"Easy...easy." He took a step back and laid down his sword not taking his eyes off of her. With his hands out at his side he gently called her name again.

"Anna."

"Who are you?" she demanded. "How do you know my name?"

"No one here is going to hurt you, Anna. Put down the sword." As he said this, one of his men moved into position behind her. He gave a terse shake of his head. He didn't want her hurting herself. Anna seeing his action glanced behind her, but instantly focused back on him.

"You didn't answer me." She took two steps forward advancing on him with quiet intensity. "Who are you?" she asked again.

"Don't you know me, my friend?" He answered in French. "Do you not remember?"

Confusion showed on her face. Out of the corner of her eye, she glanced at the man moving closer to her from behind. Starting to lose her strength, the sword slowly pointed to the ground. But when Royce made a move towards her, she whipped it back up. She was scared, weak, injured and quickly fading.

Deep down, it bothered him that she didn't recognize him right away. But he had a burst of pride surge through him watching her. She handled the sword well and if need be, no doubt, she could use it.

Now she was looking at him with something akin to anger. She was in a fighter's crouch; her green eyes were bright and her hair was blowing in the wind gently around her shoulders. To him she looked like a goddess from another world.

"No one here is going to hurt you, Anna." He dropped his hands to his side. "We just want to help. We've been taking care of you. You were injured the other day. Do you remember?"

"Yes," her voice was slight and hoarse. "You're the man who killed those...other men."

"They meant you harm," he said seriously.

"You *cut* them to pieces," she cried out. Her eyes filled and her arm started to shake. Switching positions, she grabbed the sword with both hands and began swaying back and forth.

"It was your life or theirs. Your life was not an option for me."

"What?" Her brow wrinkled and she choked out. "Why?"

"Because, my love," he said, switching to Spanish. "I have been looking for you for nine years. And I damn well wasn't going to let anything happen to you when I found you."

With a catch in her breath, she looked down and let the point of the sword drop to the ground. Leaning forward on the hilt, she bent over and took a deep breath that sounded like a sob. When she peered up at him again, tears ran unchecked down her face. Glancing around at the men, she returned her eyes back to his, confusion shining out of them.

"I don't know you," she replied in perfect Spanish. "I don't know where I am or what this place is...or what the hell I'm doing here. Please help me, sir. I'm lost," her voice cracked with emotion and she shook her head helplessly.

"No, my love," he answered, switching back to French. Then he said the first thing he had said to her when they met so many years ago. "You are found."

A look of disbelief than horror transformed her face.

"Royce?" she whispered under her breath.

And that was when he smiled at her.

"Jesus Christ..." she breathed. Her face turned deadly pale. Her sword dropped to her feet and she started to back up. Her mouth hung open as she stared at him.

"No," he said softly coming toward her, the smile leaving his face. "You had it right the first time."

"But you're...dead." She looked at him as if he were a ghost. Her voice so quiet he could barely hear her.

"Not at all, madam..." he whispered back.

"Not dead...not real." Her head began to swing back and forth slowly. "Oh God..." she muttered as her hands went up to her face and her eyes rolled back in her head. And for the second time since he'd found her, she fainted dead away.

CHAPTER 4

Anna came awake slowly. Turning to her side she studied the man sleeping soundly next to her. His dark hair was long and disheveled. His firm jaw was covered in a day's worth of stubble and his nose had a bump in the middle, like it had been broken once. He had high cheekbones most women would kill for and a dime size dimple in his chin. Along his brow line ran a razor thin scar, and he had what looked to be a bit of a shiner on his left eye.

This was a face that had been in a few fights. It wasn't quite as pretty as it could have been. Instead it looked like a man's face, from the strong heavy brows to the firm lips, and if she wasn't careful, a face she could fall in love with.

Royce. She tested the name silently and searched her memory for the recognition that had hit her yesterday. Goosebumps stole over her skin. Was it possible? Could this man really be the boy of her dreams from so long ago? Could he have changed so much?

Clipped images flickered through her mind of a boy laughing in the meadow. That had been a dream...hadn't it?

No matter how hard she tried to bring them to focus the images remained fuzzy and brief. Whatever had flashed through her head yesterday had disappeared, leaving a strange, yet comfortable sensation with this man.

Her eyes moved down his face and focused on his mouth, wide with firm lips that looked like they could smile often. Putting a finger up, she traced that mouth softly, searching for a memory of time they had shared, but nothing would come.

Royce opened his eyes. She moved her gaze up to his, keeping her finger gently on his lips. Those eyes, she should know those eyes, shouldn't she? They were beautiful, so deep and dark, ones that didn't belong on a man. They almost made him too pretty. But then again, he could never be considered pretty. Even lying here on this mat, he dominated the room. Everything about him was so...so...male.

Glancing back at his mouth, she couldn't seem to stop herself from touching him. He didn't move or say anything. He just let her study him.

"Am I dead?" she finally whispered, still not taking her hand away from his mouth.

"Not in this life," he whispered back.

"But in the other?" She moved her gaze back up to his.

"I don't know." He reached up and entwined his fingers with hers.

"Then I must be dreaming," she concluded quietly. Releasing his hand, she rolled onto her back. Gazing up at the top of the tent, her mind worked to unscramble what had happened.

Of course, this was all a dream. She glanced back at Royce's still countenance.

"You're not dreaming," he said simply.

"Oh yeah." She smiled at him. "I'm dreaming and this is a good one." She wound her arms around his neck and leaned forward, rubbing her mouth sensuously across his.

His lips were hard and firm and the stubble of dark growth scraped her chin as she moved to kiss him deeper. He was hot and the feel of his lips on hers startled her for a moment.

He sure felt real. Confused at her own response she began to pull away, but he wouldn't let her.

Instead, he slid his mouth sideways, moving forward to finish what she had started. His arms came up and crushed her to him as he rolled up on an elbow, gaining better access to her mouth. There was very little clothing between them and she was surprised at how her body was reacting to his. Her nipples hardened and blood rushed to her loins as his tongue stroked the inside of her mouth.

Never before had she felt anything like this...like him. One hand slid down her back and cupped her bottom, pulling her snug against him. He was ready in more ways than one and the hard contact made her moan when his lips left her mouth and traveled down her neck.

"A'right now, enough of that, my Lord," came an angry voice from behind her.

Royce's head came up and he glared at the person behind her.

"That's enough, I say. You're not married and 'til ye are, there will be none of that. Your mother would turn over in her grave if she saw ye molesting this girl like that. For god's sake, you'll ruin her before the morning's passed. Ye know how people talk."

Royce's eyes returned to her and she melted. She couldn't help herself. She was still curled intimately against him and she couldn't wipe away the surprise that she knew was written all over her face.

He planted a last quick kiss on her mouth before releasing her and rolled to his feet in one fluid move. Grabbing his shirt, he pulled it over his head.

"This is Enid. You can trust her. She'll help you get dressed." With a lop-sided smile, he left the tent.

If this was a dream, it was a damn good one. Whew, the body on that guy was something she didn't see every day, in fact, ever.

"Miss?"

She turned to the old woman addressing her. She was the epitome of an old hag, with crazy hair and dressed in rags wearing a heavy frown on her face.

Anna ignored her and lay back down. She stretched lazily, closing her eyes. "Oh go away and bring him back in here. I'm not ready to wake up yet."

"Not ready to wake up, eh? Well, maybe this will help."

Cold water hit her square in the face, bringing her sputtering up to a sitting position.

"Come on now. It's time to get up." The old woman reached down and grabbed her wrist calling out, "Boy, have ye got that water yet?"

Pulled up roughly by worn, gnarly fingers and ushered to the side of the tent, Anna stood disbelieving and dripping wet in stunned silence. Several men came in, depositing a tub, water and a trencher of food on the floor in the corner. They were dressed in the old-fashioned clothes similar to what Royce had on, some kind of tunic and hose combination.

They stared at her in silent curiosity making her feel acutely uncomfortable. She had little on to cover herself, just a long simple sheath of some sort, and that was wet. It took all her effort not to hide herself with her hands. Sticking out her jaw, she looked back boldly as one of the men eyed her with appreciation, gaining a wink from him.

"Oohhh, out with ye, ye bum." The old woman sprang into action, scowling at the bold fool. "The lord will have your head."

Skipping ahead of her hands, the man neatly exited the tent with a laugh.

Enid turned to face her again, intelligent eyes raking her from head to toe.

"Well, ye certainly are a mess. Now let's get that rag off of ye and clean ye up. We don't have much time."

"Excuse me? Who are you and what, aagh, let go of that. Ouch, leave my dress alone. Ow. What are you doing? There is no way I am going to fit into that bowl," she hissed at the old woman, who had stripped her naked and was trying to force her into the tiny tub.

"Get in before I push ye in and ye know I mean it."

Deciding Enid did, in fact, mean it, she stepped in and squatted down letting the old lady have her way.

Lukewarm water was poured over her head, eliciting a shriek from her, as the old woman vigorously started to wash her hair and body, scouring her raw.

"Witch is more like it" she mumbled under her breath.

"Witch, am I?" Enid cackled as she scrubbed and pulled Anna's hair. "Well, I guess you could call me that," the old woman replied and then, bending down, she whispered, "At least I'm not the white lady."

"The white lady? Who's the white lady?"

"You are, my dear. 'Tis what my lord has been searching for-you. For the last nine years he's waited for you to come. The prophecy will be fulfilled now." She paused and crouched closer, "But best keep it quiet, my dear. Ye don't want everyone to know."

The gruff voice sent chills up Anna's spine.

"What are you talking about? Know what? I'm no white lady. Besides, this is all a dream. I'm probably on some heavy medication in a hospital somewhere...or maybe I'm in a coma. Yeah...that's it...I'm in a-Owww. That hurt. What did you do that for?" She demanded rubbing the offended arm that the old lady had pinched cruelly.

"You're not dreamin, missy." Raising her eyebrows, Enid went back to washing her hair. "You're here...like it or not." She finished with a cackle.

Goosebumps rode up her arms and covered her body. She shivered despite the warmth in the tent. Settling on a fitting response, she started to reply when a bucket of cold water was poured over her head, effectively shutting her mouth.

Water was still running down her face when Enid pulled her out of the small tub.

"Alright, out with ye. Come on now. There's no time to dawdle. He's waiting for ye outside."

A towel was thrust into her hands, while another was briskly used to dry off her backside.

"Hey." She grabbed the towel. "I can dry myself off."

"Here's your shift," Enid cackled again. Turning, she pulled something out from a bag on the ground which she tossed to Anna. "'Tis the best the men could do on such short notice. You have Lars to thank for the dress. Seems he got it from one of the girls in town. It's not much, I know, but 'tis clean and will suffice for now."

Anna struggled into the shift, pulling the thin linen over her head. It went to her knees and was quickly followed by a rough dress in a shade resembling mud.

Enid handed her a large roll of some sort and a cup full of watered down red wine. Although the roll wasn't hot, it was stuffed with some kind of meat and was delicious. The wine was barely tolerable, but she was so hungry and thirsty that she finished the whole meal in minutes. She had barely wiped the crumbs from her mouth when Royce came in.

His hair was wet and pushed back from his face. He wore a simple dark tunic under chain mail that reached his thighs. Loose leggings disappeared into boots and a sword strapped to his side finished the outfit. He looked delicious.

Enid began to fuss with her hair, trying to comb out the tangles while she just stood there stupidly staring at him.

Royce returned her look.

Embarrassment washed over and a giddy laugh climbed up her throat like a shy school girl. She offered him a smile, but it only made him frown, so she frowned back.

"Are you ready?"

"Um, I think so," she stammered without meaning too. *Why on earth did she feel totally tongue tied?*

Royce nodded then looked behind her, a small smile on his face as he addressed the old woman. "Thank you Enid." Glancing back at Anna he let his eyes move over her body, "Do you think she's fit to ride?"

Enid laughed, "Och, she's a fresh one here."

Anna frowned at the old woman who winked back before replying.

"But she's ready, I think. At least she's full of spirit, and it appears her wounds do not trouble her much...right, dearie?"

Royce nodded and pulled on her elbow drawing her outside. She squinted in the light, peering at the few men who were effectively packing up the camp. Was it just yesterday she had stood out here with the sword? She had thought there were so many men surrounding her, but now there appeared to be only a few. Staring nervously, she jumped when a horse was suddenly at her elbow.

Just as quickly, the tent fell away behind her and was folded and loaded onto a cart. The camp looked nothing as it had the day before. Except for the pile of dirt covering the fire and the scorched earth around it, there was little evidence of them being there.

Within minutes the old lady had disappeared on an equally ancient mule and the rest of the men were saddled and ready to go.

Horses stamped nervously, eager to be off. All eyes were suddenly on her. Turning back to Royce, she instead encountered his stallion. She hadn't even realized he had mounted up. Her eyes followed the long line of his boots up to his face before the hand was offered. It was gloved this time and for one bizarre moment, Anna knew she had done this before with this man. A shiver danced up her spine and goose bumps decorated her arms as she stared at that gloved hand.

"Take my hand, Anna," he said.

Her eyes sought his in question, but she could get no answers from his face. He'd ceased smiling all together and instead was staring at her in a way that she didn't understand.

"Hurry, my lord, they're coming," one of his men called from the nearby trees. The others looked worriedly behind them. The barking of dogs and thunder of approaching horses echoed in the distance, giving her a start.

She looked back up at him. He hadn't moved.

She wasn't sure what to believe. But in a few minutes the choice would be taken from her.

To believe him, she would have to be mad. This might be her rescue, but then again, she'd thought that before and couldn't have been more wrong.

Making her decision, she reached and her hand was quickly caught. Within seconds, she was hauled up in front of him.

His mount danced in a nervous circle at the added weight.

"Throw your leg over," he instructed, "And thread your hands through his mane."

She did as she was told, bouncing around for a few minutes as the horse took off and began to pick up speed.

"I've got you." His arm came around her waist and he tugged her back tight, high on his thighs and snug against his belly.

"Now, bend low, over his neck and hold on, we need to move," he said. With a click of his tongue, he gave his horse full rein.

Her breath caught as the horse responded and suddenly they were flying through the forest. She was terrified and yet exhilarated. The horse and Royce moved together as one and she was melded so close to him, her body moved in sync.

It had been years since she'd had a madcap adventure and ridden like this. It was something she had done with her sister when they were kids, racing around the countryside. She'd forgotten the sense of freedom it gave her and was surprised her body seemed to know what to do.

They slowed when they came into denser forest, but didn't stop. Instead, he pressed her back hard against him as he guided the horse effortlessly down a steep ravine. Her stomach rose to her throat and she could feel her heart pounding in nervous excitement at the quick descent before they jumped across the stream bed and cantered up the other side.

She caught glimpses of his men riding beside them through the trees. They moved like raiders in the night, fast and with purpose. Here in the forest, all she could make out was a blur of movement close by. She wasn't sure how far they went until they couldn't hear the dogs anymore.

They crossed down another hill and plunged their horses into the large stream. The water splashed her feet sending a chill up her spine despite his heat and drew an elicited gasp from her. His hold tightened around her middle as he sent his horse crashing downstream. Men in front of him and behind crisscrossed through the stream and got out at the banks only to plunge back in again a few feet down.

Confused at what they were doing, she watched as again and again, a man would pull his horse out and circle back, then plunge into the stream again. They rode in the water until it widened and joined another stream, forming a large shallow river. Crossing over, they circled back around and took the opposite current, before stepping onto dry land some ways up. By now they were all soaked, but still they didn't talk. Instead, they formed a single file and headed up into the hills.

CHAPTER 5

Hours...it had been hours since they left this morning. The sun was starting to sink in the perfectly blue sky and Anna was miserable. She was hot, tired, thirsty and so hungry her stomach wouldn't quit making noise. Adding to that, her bottom was sore beyond belief.

They'd only stopped once for water and to pass around some old bread. It had been so quick, she'd barely finished relieving herself in the woods before Royce's deep voice had called to her and they were off again.

Other than a few words, nobody had spoken all day. Their silence was unnerving and the serious, intent look on Royce's face had kept her from talking.

Unfortunately, her belly didn't feel the same way.

Every few minutes it let out a growl so loud, she was sure all the men could hear it.

Shifting in the saddle once more, she tried to gain some modicum of comfort.

"Hold tight, Anna," he whispered in her ear. "We're almost there."

Ahh-Na. The way he said her name sent shivers up her spine. It rolled off his tongue like a sweet caress and momentarily left her breathless. Unconsciously, she leaned back into him, hoping for more.

"Where are we going?" She couldn't help herself from asking.

Instead of answering, he just chuckled and kicked the horse into a canter, sending her bottom high on his thighs and indecently snug against his belly. Earlier in the day it had made her uncomfortable in more ways than one, but now, she was just too tired and hungry to care.

They stopped some time later in a small glen that boasted a busy stream and a rather well put together hut. It was the first sign of civilization she'd had since her accident. As her gaze took in the bucolic scene around her, she wondered if there would be any sort of help here.

Hope flared in her chest when the door opened, but died quickly as an older couple stepped out, crossing to greet them. Although they appeared clean and simply dressed, they didn't look much better off than she was. She seriously doubted those two had a car hidden in the shrubs somewhere. In fact, she was pretty damn sure there wouldn't be a car anywhere for at least another 800 years.

As much as she wanted to get down, she was too stiff to move and became irritated when Royce just popped off the horse.

He nodded to the couple and spoke to them warmly, but stayed where he was, his arms outstretched to Anna.

"I don't think I can move," she admitted. "I'm too tired and my le-"

He reached up, interrupting her speech and pulled her into his arms. "Better?" he asked.

"Yes," she sighed, putting her head against his chest.

He walked over to the door of the tiny hut and pushed it open with his hip.

Immediately, the smell of food drifted out. All thought left her head and went directly to her stomach.

"Are we eating here?" she asked hopeful.

He nodded, easing her to her feet. "Can you walk?"

"God, yes," she said steadying herself against his chest. "You have no idea what I'll do for whatever is cooking in that pot right now."

Giving a warm smile to the older couple, she started toward the table holding onto the door frame for balance.

The hut had a fireplace on one side, a table with two benches in front of it and some kind of pallet on the floor in the corner. Two windows were open on either side of the door letting in fresh air and light making the effect rather cozy.

She closed her eyes and savored the aroma of homemade stew and freshly baked bread. Impatient, she glanced back at Royce and was glad to see him start forward.

The older couple didn't come in and Royce closed the door behind him.

Eagerly she sat down, reached for a piece of bread and popped it into her mouth.

It was pure heaven. Okay, so it wasn't as soft as she'd hoped and actually kind of scorched on one side, but it was still warm and chewy, which made up for everything else.

Her mouth full of bread, she motioned towards the door. "Where are they going? Aren't they coming in?"

Royce raised an eyebrow and shook his head.

"They're not coming in?" Anna questioned before taking her next bite.

"No, they'll be well paid for their meal and the use of their home." He reached into a bag he'd set on the floor. Taking out a very crude wine bottle, he pulled the cork out with his teeth. "Wine?" He offered.

"Yes, oh, thank you, God," she murmured holding up the metal cup he handed her. After filling it to the top, he went over to the fire and ladled stew into two wooden bowls. He placed one in front of her and took the seat across from her.

She wanted to ask about the people who lived here, but once she got a whiff of that stew, nothing else mattered and she dug in. She ate with a hearty appetite and didn't stop until she'd finished her soup and over half the loaf of bread.

Finally coming up for air, Anna sat back with a sigh, her hand resting over her belly. "That was good. It's amazing what a good meal and a cup of wine can do for a person."

Content, she watched Royce eat, surprised at his manners. A twinkle caught his eye, as if he knew what she was thinking.

"So, now what do you propose to do with me?"

His eyes took on a smoldering look and his smile grew, but he said nothing.

"Yeah," she narrowed her gaze. "Okay, that sounded bad."

His mouth curled up and once again she was mesmerized. He was so handsome. She couldn't think. Those dark orbs burned into her and she felt like, if she just leaned across the table an inch, he would eat her up.

He finished chewing his bread and retrieved his napkin to wipe his mouth.

"Damn, you're good looking."

His eyebrows shot up.

She clapped a hand over her mouth. "Did I just say that out loud?" Laughter bubbled out. "Oh, my goodness," she whispered. "I did. I'm sorry. It just flew through my head." She nibbled on her thumb nail. "When I'm nervous, I have no block."

"No block? I don't understand."

"No block. I just-just blurt stuff out."

"Blurt? Oh, my goodness? O-kay? What funny expressions you have." He cocked his head to the side.

"*I* have funny expressions?" Her hand went up to her chest.

"You do," he nodded. "I like them."

Her mouth went dry and she swallowed. Come on, keep it together girl.

"Why are you nervous?" He asked his head tilted to the side.

"Oh, I don't know," she rolled her eyes and bit her lip. Butterflies danced in her belly and she shook off the warm shiver that road up her spine. "I can't think straight around you," she admitted. Closing her eyes, she tried to concentrate. "Let's see, a few days ago, my car went over a cliff and I landed-here," she waved her hands around. "I was attacked and nearly killed by a bunch of...I don't even know what they were...miscreants? I wake up today and you're kissing me senseless, and then I spend the day on horseback riding hell bent across England. I'd say that's a pretty good reason to be a little unnerved. How's that? Is that better?"

"You kissed me this morning, madam." He pointed his finger at her and his thumb back at himself.

"I-I," she stuttered, her mouth opening and closing like a trout. Her cheeks went hot and she knew she was blushing. "I don't remember it like that."

"Have you also forgotten," he said. "That I saved your life a few days ago? At considerable risk to myself and my men, I might mention." He went on, his voice deepening to a seductive tone. "I have yet to receive proper payment, but I will accept the kiss from this morning in lieu of monetary sums."

"Really?" She couldn't stop the bark of laughter. He was flirting with her and God help her, she liked it. "Monetary sums? For a kiss? Now that is archaic..."

"Archaic?" His eyes narrowed, playfully.

"Never mind," she waved it away, trying to be serious. "Umm, where did you say we were going?"

"I didn't," he became all business. "But since you persist, we are going to Corfe castle."

"Corfe Castle?" That place was as old as the hills and miles in the other direction then she'd been traveling.

"Why there? I mean what's there, that place is in ruins and hasn't been inhabited since the sixt-" catching herself, she stopped, confused.

Closing her eyes, she shook her head a little, "Okay, Corfe Castle... and what are we going to *do* at Corfe Castle?"

"I have someone I need to see," he replied easily.

"Boy, you don't give your secrets away do you?"

"Not to anyone."

"O-kay, fine, so you don't want to talk about that. Let's talk about the other men you're with, four, right? I thought there was more this morning?"

"There were. They've gone to do something for me. We'll see them later."

"What are their names? I mean who are they to you?"

"They're my men."

"We'll, who are they? What are their names?" she asked again.

"Later..." He leaned back stretching his arms. The firelight danced off his shoulders casting his face in an array of planes and angles. Once again, she was struck with his beauty. It was unnatural to have a man be that *manly* and so good looking all in the same package.

"Aahh, more secrets." She quirked her brow, "Why don't any of you talk?"

"What's to say?" He shrugged. "They know their place."

"They know their place? What does that mean?"

"There's nothing to say. They know what's at stake and what we're doing."

"What is at stake? What are we...I mean, they...I mean you, all doing?"

He smiled, but stayed silent.

"You're not going to tell me, are you?"

Again, that secretive smile flared and it almost made her laugh. It looked awkward on his face, like he didn't smile often, but she liked it all the same.

Taking another sip of her wine, she was surprised to see that her cup was almost empty. She knew he'd refilled it once already and she couldn't believe she'd finished another cup. A warm lethargy had filled her and with the heat from the small fire, her full belly and all that wine, the long day caught up to her.

She put her elbows on the table and propped herself up with her fist, knowing full well she was grinning like a fool. When she reached for her cup again, he gently moved it away.

Leaning forward, he mirrored her posture propping both elbows up on the narrow table, bringing him precariously close to her.

"You still owe me..." he whispered.

Alarmed, she started to move back, but his hand caught her wrist gently holding her in place.

"For what?" Her heart picked up tempo, thudding heavily in her chest. She knew full well.

His other hand came up and his knuckles moved softly under her chin. Her breath faltered.

"Saving your life...again."

She widened her eyes and humor sent a twist to her mouth.

"From whom did you save my life?"

"Thieves," he said. His eyebrows jutted upward and his gaze focused on her lips.

"Thieves? Hmmm...horrible thieves?"

His mouth grew hard and flint entered his eyes. "Yes."

Before she could respond his hand moved around to the back of her neck. Leaning forward, he closed the space between them and took her mouth in a crushing kiss. His other hand came up, firmly holding her face in place as his mouth plundered hers. His tongue sought entrance and she gave it, allowing him full freedom.

He stood suddenly bringing her with him. In a second, he swept her up into his arms and stepped away from the table. She was barely aware of him moving. All she could focus on was his kiss. It was by far the best kiss she'd ever had. Her hair was standing on end and her body was responding to him the same way it had earlier with a yearning so intense, it throbbed within her.

Her arms came up of their own volition and wrapped around his neck. She ran her hands through his hair and pulled him down for a deeper kiss.

With more gentleness than she thought possible, he lowered her to the ground. Slowly, his lips left hers and burned a fiery path down her neck. His hand slid up her ribcage and cupped her breast. With a groan, he ran his finger over the taut nipple under the thin linen. Easing down her shift, he exposed her breast.

In a moment, it was in his mouth. She pulled him to her, arching into his caress. His knee came up and pressed hard between her thighs making her gasp at the wave that shuddered through her. His hands were everywhere, touching, caressing...making her body respond to him in ways she hadn't dreamed possible. It was as if they'd known each other forever...as if they'd done this a hundred times before and she had no control to stop herself or him.

Suddenly, he paused and lifted his head. Opening her eyes, she realized his face was turned towards the door and he was listening intently for something. The knock came again and she heard a familiar voice call out. The tension in Royce's shoulders left and he muttered something unintelligible under his breath before calling out that he'd be right there.

Coming back to herself slowly, she steadied her breathing as she watched him in the firelight. He looked so sexy. His hair was all over the place from her fingers running through it and his tunic was open exposing a broad expanse of chest. When did he have time to take off his armor? Oh, who cares, look at that *chest*. Her fingers itched to curl in the hair there.

He looked back down at her and frowned before his expression took on a steamy smile.

"We are interrupted again, my sweet," his voice rumbled, deep and charged.

She returned his smile with one of her own and sighed, still a little dazed.

He lowered himself for one last kiss and then popped up, straightening his tunic, before reaching down and placing a blanket over her.

"Sleep, while you can. We'll be leaving early." He walked to the door.

"Are you coming back?" She called out, hating herself for asking, let alone caring.

"Don't worry. You'll be safe," he said before closing the door behind him.

Well, he didn't really answer the question, did he?

Rolling over, she snuggled under the heavy wool blanket and patted the ground beneath her. Hey, it wasn't a bed, but at least, there were some blankets. Looking into the fire, she felt strangely at peace. Her body relaxed and she let the heat and the dancing flames lull her to sleep.

CHAPTER

6

She'd been woken up in the predawn hours by a rough shake and Royce motioning for her to follow him. She tried to sit up, but her head had burst into a post party headache and she had lain back down groaning, certain she was going to die.

Apparently, that evoked no sympathy from Royce who muttered something impolite, then promptly pulled her up forcefully into a standing position. When she had refused to move forward and stood their moaning with her head in her hands, he just picked her up, took her out and thrown her on his horse.

A pouch had been thrust into her hands as he mounted behind her and settled her into his lap. She put the pouch to her lips ready for a long drink of water and choked when strong pungent liquid instead scorched her mouth and burned its way down to her belly. She came up sputtering and coughing.

"Whiskey?" She choked out. "Why didn't you tell me it was whiskey?"

"You didn't ask."

"For God's sake, who drinks whiskey in the morning?"

"You were moaning about your head."

"So?"

"What else would it be?"

"Water."

"Water? Water won't help your head. But I have some if you want." He reached around and grabbed up another pouch on the back part of his saddle and handed it to her. The pouch was damp from being recently filled, and the water was cool and refreshing.

Taking another long drink, she looked around. They were coming out of the woods to a large meadow buried in mist. Up above, a cloudy sky hung low over the horizon, keeping much of the scenery in deep shadows. A herd of deer poked their heads up out of the fog and suddenly took flight.

It was so beautiful for a minute she was too stunned to speak. The other side of the meadow rose to a rather large imposing hill and had more heavy woodland surrounding it. Royce and him men paused before entering the meadow, each silently perusing the boundaries.

The hair on the back of Anna's neck stood up, an eerie feeling stealing over her. What were they looking for? They certainly weren't noticing the beauty of the place and they weren't interested in the deer fleeing the other side of the meadow. She kept silent, waiting as they did, for a sign of something.

Finally, Royce nodded and they started out together. The dense mist curled around them and hid all but their heads. It wasn't until they were almost upon the large rock formations that she realized where they were.

From a distance and deeply entrenched in the mist, the standing stones looked like shadows or a grouping of trees, but as they neared, she better understood the men's hesitation. They were high on the moors of Dartmoor, indeed a frightening place.

She could remember coming there as a child and crying to her father about the ghosts that inhabited this realm. Even on sunny days it was spooky, but here in the early hours of the morning with the fog lying heavy and thick, it seemed more like a living spirit. To see it in this day and age was truly amazing when time and weather hadn't decayed the massive rocks to a shadow of what they once were.

"I know this place," she whispered to Royce.

He didn't respond. A glance over her shoulder explained his silence. He was too involved with watching their surroundings. He had a heavy frown on his face as his eyes swept the boundaries.

The unease in her belly grew. She turned around facing forward, mimicking his behavior. The horses nickered softly to each other, dancing in unease, each man fighting for some control of their mount. It took longer than expected to reach the other side, but the moment they did, all seemed to let out a collective sigh of relief. She waited until they were back to single file before she spoke again.

"I know that place," she repeated.

"Yes," Royce said without question. "It's a place of danger and death. You can feel it in the air."

Confused, she looked behind her again and watched as the meadow grew more distant. It still looked creepy, and with Royce's words she imagined men rising out of the mist to follow them.

"Tis called the Valley of the Dead," Royce said. "Most know it, or at least have heard of it."

A shiver of fear ran up her spine and she straightened, not sure if she wanted to hear why.

"Tis beautiful, is it not?" he continued.

"Yes, breathtaking."

"Exactly. Tis often deep in mist and an excellent place for attack. It used to be a well-traveled path to the coast, but fifty years ago a bloody battle was fought here. Even now most steer clear. The mist is often so thick it is impossible to see your enemy, and the forest over there is said to be haunted." He pointed off to the right were a deep thatch of woods covered the area.

She remained silent, but as morning broke and the sun came out it was impossible not to enjoy the scenery. Never in her life had she seen anything so pristine and pure. There was no trash under their feet, no noise from up above and with spring emerging, even high up here on the windswept moors it was beyond beautiful.

About noon they stopped at what appeared to be the remains of a rather large building. The base of it had been stone and most of the wooden structure had burned away. Two charred, heavy doors with windows depicting the cross still remained, opening to nothing. Whatever happened here had happened long ago. Spring and Mother Nature had taken back the earth. Flowers, young trees and plants grew up in the middle of the old structure.

Royce ignored the frame and continued past it to a tiny hut that appeared to be built into the hill behind the burned-out building. Before anyone could say a word, the rickety door opened cautiously and an old, thin grungy face with a full head of crazy white hair peered out.

"Whot do ye want?" Came a strong voice, heavily accented with the Cornish coast English.

"Friar Merther?" Royce inquired.

"Ho's asken?" The wizened little elf demanded taking in Royce's appearance and the men with him.

"Does it matter?" Royce replied smoothly.

Anna watched the exchange between the two. Royce's eyes never left the old man's face. He kept his voice even, soft and yet commanding- just like he did with her.

The man seemed to ponder this before his shoulders shrugged, the door pulled back and he emerged. He was dressed in a long brown robe that had seen better days. It was well worn, torn in a few places and filthy. As he walked forward, his odor preceded him and Anna covered her nose and turned her head. He smelled like he slept with pigs.

"Depen's on wat ye want..." he said walking past Royce. He seemed not to care one way or another about the group.

"I need the Friar to perform a service for me. Are you Friar Merther?" Royce asked again, pausing for a moment before adding, "I've got coin."

The man stopped walking and turned back. His eyes grew small and greedy. He glanced at each man again as if he was taking stock of them, his eyes barely resting on Anna before speaking.

"Whot kind of service?" he asked suspiciously.

"The marrying kind," Royce replied so simply and smoothly, she jumped in her seat.

"Married?" Turning around, her eyes wide, she glared at him, "I'll not marry you."

The old man laughed and said, "I'll do it."

Royce dismounted and held his arms up to Anna who was staring at him with eyes of the devil and a look of fury on her face.

Before she could say anything else, he reached up and pulled her out of the saddle. He slid her to her feet slowly, holding her body tight along the length of him. She needed to know who was in charge, but as his manhood pressed into the juncture between her thighs, he feared he was closer to losing control than she was. She fit perfectly and it took all his strength not to keep her there.

"Let me go," she demanded, pushing against him in obvious embarrassment. Hot color flooded her face as the little priest laughed lustily beside them.

He reigned in his temper, reminding himself to be gentle. This would be a surprise to her. Struggling against his arms again, she pushed back and he released her. He tried warning her with a look to keep quiet, but with little avail.

"I'm not going to marry you," she said again much louder.

He flexed his jaw and stared back at her while the old cleric laughed harder beside them. The rest of his men had dismounted and were standing quietly, exchanging glances.

Anna turned to march away and that he couldn't allow. He grabbed her arm and pulled her farther from the group. While his grip was strong and struggle as she might he didn't want to hurt her.

After they had entered the woods and were out of sight of the prying eyes, he turned and faced her. Putting his fists on his hips, he looked her straight in the eyes.

"I didn't ask, Anna. It's not a choice. We must marry."

"Like hell we do. Dream or not this has all gotten way too crazy," she sputtered back her posture matching his.

He narrowed his gaze and tilted his head trying to look stern but couldn't keep the smile from his face. She looked so charming. Her hair was wild, all curled about her face in windblown abandon. Her skin was pink from the sun and the green of her eyes shined brightly back at him. God, she was beautiful. His Anna. Always so head strong and determined. How he had missed her these past years.

Of course, she would say no. She always had at first. But now was not the time for argument. He hardened his jaw and wiped the smile from his face.

"We're getting married," he said, steel in his voice.

"You can't make me marry you," she said stubbornly. "And don't give me that stone faced look. That might work on everyone else buddy, but not on me."

She was right. That never had worked on her. He chuckled and humor entered his voice.

"I can," he grinned. switching tactics, he went on gently, "I don't need your approval."

"To marry me?" Her voice came out in a disbelieving squeak and her hand hit her chest in question.

"Right." Again, he kept his words soft. "I don't need for you to say yes...but I want you to."

"Don't look at me like that?"

"Like what?"

"Like you want to have me for dinner," she glared back at him.

"But I very much do want to have you for dinner," he chuckled and put his arms around her.

"Stop *that*. You're doing it again," she pushed at his arms.

"Doing what?" he pretended not to know.

"You *know*. Doing *that*. Making me go all weak inside and I'm still mad. I can't think straight when you look at me like that. And I am not going to marry you. I don't even know you." She continued struggling halfheartedly from the circle of his arms.

"You do know me," he said into her hair, pulling her tighter.

"No-I don't," she exclaimed pushing him away this time.

He sighed and looked at her, his head tilted.

"And don't look at me like that either."

"Like what?"

"Like, you don't know what to do with me."

He tried to stop the twist of his lips but couldn't.

"Oh, I know what to do with you." He reached for her again, but she held him off with a hand to his chest.

"Oh, please." She glared at him with righteous indignation and began to list her reasons on her fingers.

"First of all, I'm a mess. I mean look at my hair. It's in such a tangle, I'll never be able to get a comb through it, besides the fact that I haven't showered in, well-I don't know how long, but suffice it to say a long time."

"What's a shower?"

Instead of answering, her mouth flattened and she glared back at him with the same look of steel he'd given her a moment before.

"You look fine to me."

"I know I do to you," she huffed. "Somehow I think having had a bath within two weeks is considered clean here."

"Are you saying, you think we are all dirty?" he quirked his eyebrow at her.

She crossed her arms over her chest and made an exaggerated motion with her head towards the clearing where the Friar was still standing with his men.

He smiled a little and agreed, "Oh, yes, well to him a bath a year would be too much. Come now, Anna." He gently took her arm and turned her back towards the others. "They are waiting."

"What?" she pulled her arm back and stood ram rod straight, her hands fisted at her sides. "You can't be serious. I mean, why do you want to marry me?"

"Why not?" He asked frustrated.

"Well, because..." she started and then hesitated.

He could tell she was searching for a reason and he crossed his arms over his chest, enjoying the emotions that were dancing across her face.

"I'm not a virgin," she finally threw out as if that would change his mind.

"I know." He smiled.

"You know?" Her brows drew together and she gave him a funny look. Shaking it off, she continued, "Fine, whatever...Okay, second-oh, God, this isn't real. You're not real. God-why can't I just wake up?"

"Well if this isn't real, why does it matter whether you marry me?"

"I don't know. It just does." Tears gathered in her eyes. "I'm not supposed to get married like this."

"I don't understand."

"I'm supposed to get married to somebody I love in a beautiful dress, in a beautiful church with my family and friends around. Not in some dirt colored piece of linen, next to a burned out old church with a nasty Friar to somebody I don't know."

He hesitated and when Anna looked back at him he clenched his jaw. Could he be wrong? After all this time, maybe there was somebody else. He had to know.

"Is there another?" He demanded.

"No." Her answer was quick and sure.

Relief filled him. Not that another man would matter now. Anna was his-and always would be.

"Then what?" He asked, frustrated.

"I don't know you. Let alone love-."

He decided not to address her other hesitation. She loved him. She always had and soon enough she would remember.

For her, he'd learned patience.

For her, he'd wait.

"You said my name on the day I found you," he reminded her gently. "How can you say you don't know me?"

"You told me your name."

"No. I did not." He cocked his brow and stared intently into her eyes.

"You didn't?" She searched his face, uncertainty showing clearly in her expression. Taking a deep breath, she looked away before shaking her head and going back to her original point.

"Okay, well I admit that is weird, but...that doesn't mean anything. I don't know why I said that. Maybe it's because I was being attacked by a bunch of crazy men, or maybe it's because I was just in a terrible accident and had a bump on my head...or maybe I heard someone call your name," she said as though she was trying to convince herself as much as him.

He watched her with narrowed eyes. Finally exhaling deeply, he reached for her hands. "You know me Anna. In your heart you do and if you can't see that yet, you will. Trust me. You have to trust me."

"Oh God, your being charming again...why can't you be charming a little bit more?"

"But I'm always charming," he said in feigned surprise.

She laughed and once she started, she couldn't stop and soon he joined her.

A few minutes later with tears running down her face, holding her belly, Anna was gasping for breath when they were interrupted by one of his men.

Her time was up.

"Sir, he's becoming a bit cranky."

They both looked towards the scrawny little friar who was getting vocal with the men trying to hold him back from coming to where they stood.

"Think of it as an adventure," Royce winked. Grabbing her hand, he began pulling her back through the trees.

"What did you say?" She asked, her eyes growing large.

He looked back and smiled.

"You heard me."

He changed directions when they cleared the woods and headed towards a walled off area behind the old burned out church. The friar was complaining and being pulled along by Royce's men, but she didn't pay much attention. Instead she was focused on a stunning array of pink, white and purple that met her eyes. Like a secret garden unfolding before her, flowers and herbs stretched waving faces upwards dancing towards the sun. Honeysuckle and lilac bordered the inner sanctuary and grew in wild abandon up the walls giving off a heady scent. Vegetables sprouted in neat lined rows at the front and grapevines shaded the back but there in the center was a tiny orchard of fruit trees all in bloom. She was enchanted. All her life she'd had a thing for flowering trees in the spring. Until her sister had died nine years ago, it had been her favorite time of year. Since then she'd always hidden when the blossoms had come out, ensconced inside, busy till June. Her father had known what she'd been doing, but most of her friends had not understood her aversion for missing the glories of spring.

Now here she was with this man, the one who claimed to be from her past, a past she didn't want to remember, let alone acknowledge.

Her old defenses kicked in and the natural aversion she had purposefully developed caught up with her.

She pulled hard on his hand.

"Why are we here?"

"Because you always said you wanted to get married under a cherry tree in the spring." He looked back at her with that twinkle in his eye again.

Stunned, she stared at him and before she could stop herself she asked in a choked whisper, "How could you know that?"

Her head was spinning and a tiny crack formed in the memory wall she'd put up years ago...a young man laughing, a toothy white smile, dark eyes dancing with mischief...a cherry tree...

"Anna, say your name for the friar," Royce's deep voice rang out catching her attention.

Pulling her focus back, she found herself standing before him. Her hands were held fast by his and the small, distasteful friar was begrudgingly saying the words that would bind them together for life.

Goosebumps tingled up her spine.

"Anna Harrington," she responded as if in a trance.

"Your full name," Royce said meaningfully.

Her eyes snapped back to his.

"Annaysis Whitney Harrington," she said finally.

The friar paused in his reading and his eyes shifted between the two of them. A small frown gathered on his face until Royce growled for him to continue.

The friar started up again, but his words fell deafly on her ears in

Latin until it was Royce's turn to speak. The heavy timber of his voice reverberated through her and she realized for the first time, she didn't know his whole name.

"Royce Barrett De'Mark Sutton," he said clearly.

After that it went quickly, a few more words and the friar finished. As soon as the last words were spoken, he turned to Royce and held out his hand for payment.

Royce reached into a pouch by his hip and withdrew a few coins placing them in the grimy outstretched hand. Turning away from Anna, he caught the man's wrist before he could count his coins.

"You did not see us. You do not know me. You understand?" Placing his other hand on the hilt of his sword he met the man's eyes, the threat unmistakable.

The friar blanched and looked around at the other men, none of whom had spoken but who all now had their hands on their swords.

Nodding his head with a jerk, he tugged at his hand and then pulled harder until Royce released it. With a few backward glances, he ran up the hill and disappeared behind the church.

Royce had become all business again and began barking out orders to his men. Anna thought about the last few moments. It was done. They were married. And not even a kiss to seal the deal.

Never in her life had she imagined she would get married like this. If this was a dream it was the longest one she'd ever had and had just taken another turn in bizarre town.

Taking a deep breath, she looked up.

Royce was staring at her.

"What?" she asked.

He didn't speak. Instead, he put his hand on her waist and gently drew her forward. Keeping her gaze until their mouths met, he leaned down and kissed her. His lips were firm and before she could stop herself, her arms curled around his neck.

There, under the cherry tree, she welcomed his kiss as the blossoms floated down around them. For a moment, it was perfect. He was perfect and in some bizarre way he was the man she'd been waiting for all these years.

CHAPTER
7

The day passed quickly. Anna was hoisted up behind Royce and they took off at a good pace, riding around a few more scattered huts and down through a wind-swept valley. Anna kept her silence, letting the scenery slip by.

Once again, her mind touched on the accident, and then the first time she'd seen him. She had called him by his name, but that had been more in surprise, not because she recognized him...right?

How long ago was that? Two days? Three? A week?

Lying next to him on the mat yesterday, she'd searched his face and then later his manner for some remembrance of him and her and the past. But her mind seemed to block all of that out letting only brief flashes float out now and then. Still, she was hesitant to open that Pandora's Box and allow herself to dig deeper.

She'd spent the last nine years burying everything and refusing the memories, but why? Had it been that bad? What happened that made her do that? Why was she so afraid of her past?

Yes, her sister's death had been devastating, the funeral, and then that horrible fight between her grandparents and her father. After that, he had packed them up and they had left England for good. In one fell swoop, she had lost her whole life.

Since then, there had been numerous disappointments throughout high school, college, and that horrible break up with Brian, her ex-fiancé, but none had been so bad that she refused to commit them to memory.

She remembered having vivid dreams when she was a child, dreams that she insisted were real. Her family had teased her often about them. There had been a boy in them, yes, she remembered that. But the rest wouldn't come. It wasn't so much a memory, more of a feeling...one of warmth, happiness and comfort.

She'd always thought once her sister had died, that's when those feelings disappeared. There were black spots in her mind, dark days so devastating that she hadn't been able to function.

Thinking about it now brought it all back in a rush and she felt like she was spiraling down that hole again.

Her breath caught in a sob and tears gathered in her eyes. She pressed her forehead into Royce's back.

Don't go back there. She tightened her hold on Royce.

As if he knew what she was thinking, his arm came back embracing her, holding her close to him.

"Don't think about it." He glanced over his shoulder. "It's over...it's in the past."

Instead of questioning how he knew what was running through her mind, she just accepted it. Drawing comfort from his comment, she let his self-assurance wash over her. Her thoughts dissipated like the fog with the sun and she felt herself come back to the present.

Dream or not, this was her reality now, for however long it will be and he was her husband. There were so many mysteries about him that it scared her. Who was he? What was he really? And what the hell where they doing riding hell bent through the country?

Whatever it was, she had to let it go, which was hard for her. To trust in this man now was something that was not in her nature. And yet, holding onto Royce felt right. It felt right, right now, but what about tomorrow? And what would happen when she woke up? Would she remember him? Remember this? Did she want to remember this? Sighing deeply, she laid her head against his back and gripped him harder around his waist.

Yes. She did want to remember. Please remember...please.

Opening her eyes, she tried to take note of her surroundings. Here she was, sitting behind this incredible man on the back of a huge horse, cantering easily down a lush valley. The sun continued to play peek-a-boo with the clouds and warm wind caressed her legs as they rode.

If there was such a thing as bliss, this might be it.

It was late afternoon when Royce stopped again. The sun was still warm, promising a pleasant evening. Anna was ready for a break, but not too thrilled with where they stopped.

"Why are we stopping here?" she asked.

Royce jumped down and swung her off. They had barely spoken since their wedding vows and the spell of their earlier intimacy was broken. He was back to giving her as little information as possible.

"This is where we'll stay for the night," he replied.

"This? But what is it? There's no place to sleep?"

He turned and faced her, but she couldn't see his expression with the afternoon sun in her eyes. "There's water over there," he answered in a clipped tone, then pointed behind her. "And we'll sleep in there."

Anna turned and saw the building. Disappointment flushed through her. It was another burned out shell of something with no roof.

"What is that? It's half there." Turning in a full circle, she shielded her eyes from the late sun trying to find some form of civilization. "Where are we?"

"We're near the coast, a few miles north," He removed the saddle and led his horse down to the stream for a drink.

"Well, are we near a town?" she asked hopeful as she followed behind. "Can't we sleep in a bed? I mean, why do we have to sleep out here?"

"No, we're not near a town, at least a few miles out. Besides we don't want to go to town."

"We don't? Why not?"

"Because I don't want to be seen."

His answer frustrated her. He said it as though that was enough of an explanation and then walked past her up to where his men had already set up camp near the burned-out building.

Fine. She needed a minute anyway. Feeling dirty and parched, she made her way to the stream and took a deep drink. The water was cool and refreshing.

It was a wide stream, moving swiftly in the center but had several pools off to the side that looked deep enough to bathe in.

Looking behind her, she accounted for all of the men.

"Screw it," she said under her breath. "I betcha he'd really like that expression." The thought made her laugh. Walking out of sight, she quickly pulled off the two slips. Putting them near the edge of the stream, she slipped into the clear water. Without another thought, she dipped her head under and swam to the other side.

"Who gave you permission to bathe?" Royce called out from the shady bank behind her as she surfaced.

"I did," she said, feeling bold. She wasn't surprised he was there. He always seemed to be close by.

"Should I come in and join you?" he reached down to remove his tunic.

"No," she yelled, splashing water his way.

He chuckled and moved into the light. He was wearing that crooked smile she found so charming. In his hands he held a piece of cloth and a chunk of something.

"Here's some soap and something to dry off with." He put it down at the edge of the bank before taking a seat in the shade against a nearby tree.

"You can't stay there," she said when he didn't move.

"Why not?" He returned her words from earlier.

"I'm naked," she stated the obvious. *Why did he make her so flustered?* "And besides, I need some privacy."

"But what if you drown? I would never forgive myself if I wasn't here to save you."

"I'm not going to drown. It's four feet of water."

"One never knows..." He picked a piece of grass, stuck it in his mouth and began chewing on it.

"Oh, fine," she said. Inching over to the side, she reached up to take the soap. Of course, he'd placed it just out of range and she would have to stand to get it. Hunkering down in the water, she asked him sweetly, "Could you please bring the soap closer?"

He grinned at her wolfishly.

Just as she suspected, he'd done it deliberately.

Two could play at that game. She carefully placed her arm over her breast and came up out of the water. Once out, she could feel his gaze and modesty stole over her. Uncomfortable, she snatched the soap and sank back under, swimming to the other side.

Ignoring him, she quickly brought the thick bar to lather, soaping her hair and body, before dunking under to rinse.

When she looked back, he still hadn't moved. She bathed leisurely, paddling around the small inlet before the coolness of the water started to make her shiver. It was time to get out, whether he was watching or not.

As she drew closer to his side, he looked to be asleep. He had one leg propped up with an arm hanging casually over it, his head was back and his eyes were closed.

Maybe she could do this without him seeing. Dunking under one last time, she ran her fingers through her hair to release as much of the tangles as possible before getting out. She scooted around to where he had placed the towel and peeked back towards the tree. From here she couldn't see him.

Keeping an eye out for any movement, her hand patted the ground, searching for the towel. All of a sudden it was caught in a strong grip.

He hauled her out of the water in one quick move and held her wrist fast.

She shrank from him in surprise. The smile was gone from his face. In its place was a look of such naked hunger that it frightened her. Pulling away from him, she was shaking, but not from the cold. His stare devoured her from head to toe and back up again. The whole thing couldn't have taken less than a few seconds, but it felt like forever.

She started to say something.

"Silent," he hissed.

Abruptly, he flung the towel around her, covering her body and pulled her back hard against him. In one fluid move, he removed his sword from his scabbard just as somebody came towards them.

They were not the sounds of somebody that wanted to be heard. They were measured steps, steps of stealth and deceit.

Within seconds, she was shoved to the ground. Royce swung his sword back, ready to strike just as a man jumped out of the brush with sword held high.

In a tangle of sheets, she tried to scoot back and without meaning to, let loose a scream.

Locked in combat, neither man noticed. She had never seen a battle to the death before and didn't want to look but couldn't help it. The clash of steel against steel filled the air. The other man was smaller than Royce and, in a moment, it was over.

Others came running, crashing through the brush. Royce's men burst onto the scene with swords drawn, but the man was already dead.

"Where there's one, there are others," he said. "Go find them and bring them back to me. He wears the clothes of a knight but fought like a peasant. Find out who sent him."

Four of them turned and disappeared into the woods in silence. But the youngest who rode with them, stayed waiting for Royce's order. Without looking at him, Royce bent to clean his sword on the dead man's clothes. "Saddle up our horses," he ordered. "We can't stay here tonight."

Anna remained still, unsure what to do.

Her gaze flicked over the dead man. Blood seeped into the ground around him and his eyes were open, his face frozen in a scream. Bile rose in her throat and she clapped a hand over her mouth before it escaped.

Royce was studying the man's face. Satisfied, he stood with a grunt, turning towards her and held out his hand.

"Are you hurt?" he asked with a frown.

"I don't think so," she stammered, letting him pull her up.

Nodding, he looked like he wanted to say something else, but instead, pushed her towards her clothes.

"Get dressed and quickly. We have no time to waste."

"Did you know him?" she asked, pulling the dirty dress over her head.

"No, but I recognize the clothing."

"What do you mean?" She came out from behind the brush, trying to ring out her hair. "Do you mean you know who sent him?"

"Maybe." He had his hands on his hips and he was watching the other side of the stream as though he expected somebody to come charging out. "Come, we must go," he grabbed up her hand and pulled her along.

"Why would somebody want to kill you?" she asked, holding up her skirts and struggling along behind him.

He didn't respond.

"I mean, what are you? Some kind of bad guy?" she asked. "Some kind of thief?"

"No," he said tersely.

"Well, what then?" Hurrying to keep up with his long strides she went on. "I mean, why would somebody try to kill you?"

"It is not for you to question."

"Excuse me? Somebody just tried to kill you and maybe me. I think I have a right to know what I'm dealing with here."

Reaching the horses, he threw her up in one motion and mounted behind her without answering.

She turned her head to continue her questions.

"Hush woman," he gritted out. "You'll alert the whole countryside of our presence if you don't cease your chatter."

Thoroughly insulted, she snapped her mouth shut and turned forward. The rest of the men had saddled up and were waiting nearby. Embarrassed at Royce's rebuke, she bit her lip, her face going hot. She wouldn't meet any of the men's eyes, choosing instead to stare forward and focus on nothing.

It freaked her out how quiet these men were. It felt like they were always sneaking up on her.

This world was so different and silent. She needed to pay more attention to what was going on around her. Obviously, there were people that wanted Royce dead and she would be better served if he stayed alive. At least, that was the argument she used to justify her worrying about him and the attack on his life.

One of the men nudged his horse forward, "There's evidence of another, but he's long gone."

Nodding, Royce didn't say anything. He just kicked his horse forward, knocking her back into his arms. Sighing, she closed her eyes. When would this day end? Her bottom was sore. She was hungry and right now she wanted nothing more than to be off this horse. She was pretty sure the horse felt the same way.

With the late afternoon warmth quickly dissipating, her bath now seemed like a distant memory and a bad choice. She was freezing and try as she might she couldn't stop her teeth from chattering.

Royce muttered something under his breath. Pulling a thick blanket out from behind him, he sent it swirling around her, tucking in the sides.

The heat of his body and the gait of the horse made her drowsy and her eyes closed against her will, but before she fell asleep, she couldn't help but add one last comment.

"You smell" she muttered, snuggling into his arms and was rewarded with a deep chuckle.

CHAPTER

8

Voices called out waking Anna. She looked up to see somebody high atop a castle wall holding a torch peering down at them.

"Lord Sutton," Royce's deep timber answered back.

For a moment nothing moved and then the sounds of a drawbridge being lowered clanked nearby. Turning their horses towards the noise, the men waited patiently.

"Hold your tongue tonight, Anna," Royce whispered in her ear.

Sitting up straight, she looked back at him. He was watching the men above her.

"What? Why? What do you mean?" she asked confused.

"Keep silent about your delivery from the river. None are to know but mine. Where you came from is for my ears alone," he said meeting her eyes.

"But what if someone asks?"

"Follow my lead...you still speak Spanish?" He prompted her a little with a shake and then asked in Spanish, "fluently?"

Answering in kind, she replied, "Yes you dirty dog, as fluent as if I was born there, but my French is better".

Chuckling, he replied in French. "Oiu Madam, your French is beautiful, but the accent is not correct. Tonight, we need your Spanish. I will tell them we met when I was returning from the crusades. Found you in Madrid and couldn't leave you. Can you do that?"

"But of course," she answered perfectly in Spanish.

"In case someone does ask, say your father is descended from-."

"Robert de Halverson of Flemby," she said without thinking.

Surprise showed on his face. "How do you know of Lord Halverson?"

Shrugging, Anna paused. "I don't know why I said that. I just remember my grandfather mentioning him a lot and being descended from a long line of Halverson's...our ancestors from Flemby."

"Perfect," Royce smiled. "Yes, say that. But only if they ask," he added sternly before turning his attention back to the wall opening before them.

The heavy drawbridge crashed down the last few feet. The men did not hesitate, the horse's hooves rang out hollow as they crossed. Anna dared not look down at the narrow bridge. On the other side they entered a dark tunnel and came out in a small bailey. As the last man came off the bridge Anna could hear the chains begin to move, drawing the bridge back up and the door closing with a heavy thud.

"Where are we?"

"Restormel," he answered quietly.

A few guards came out to meet them. Most of the buildings in the bailey were dark and looked uninhabited. It was unnerving. Shadows shifted with the moonlight around them. The stone structure was at least four stories high. Lights flickered back and forth in open windows above but there seemed to be little movement inside.

Royce dismounted and helped her off before going forward to greet one of the men.

"William, it's good to see you," Royce said easily.

"By the Gods-Royce? Is it really you? I thought you were dead and buried on the continent." The man hugged Royce to him. He was older with a full beard, long shaggy hair and a slight limp.

"I just returned. I apologize for the late hour, but we came to beg a night's stay from you my friend."

"No matter," he waved his hand dismissively. "I don't sleep much anyway. Of course, you can stay. It's not much, but we've got a hot meal for you and a warm fire. Come, Come..." he ushered them forward. His glance touched on Anna, but when Royce offered no explanation he continued on inside.

They entered through a bottom door and went up the stairs to a large interior room. A few servants lay sleeping on the floor nearby. For the most part it was empty and dark except for a fire burning in a large pit on the opposite wall with a few chairs surrounding it. Long tables and benches had been scooted back and lined the walls. Rushes covered the floors and the whole place smelled fresh, like a barn in spring.

"Pull out the tables," William yelled, kicking a man asleep on the floor. "We've got company. Wake the cook and tell him to put the stew on and bring out some bread. Light, we need light. Light those torches and hurry with some ale."

Royce's men moved a couple tables and benches out from the walls towards the warmth of the fire, setting up one for Royce and Anna before taking their own seats.

A series of satisfied grunts could be heard when they sat. Her smile grew; for once she was glad to see that they were human.

When she turned back she gave a start, both Royce and the older man were waiting patiently for her attention.

Royce held out his hand and pulled her forward, "Lord Cardingham, I would like to introduce you to my wife, Lady Anna Harrington."

Lord Cardingham's bushy eyebrows disappeared under the frizzled white hair. His smile grew. She began to offer a hand and then quickly pulled it back and dropped into an awkward curtsy.

"Lord Cardingham," she nodded politely.

"Married?" His voice full of disbelief. "You?" He chuckled and slapped Royce on the back. "Why I never thought to see you married. She's a beauty. You've done well." Turning back to Anna his voice boomed, "Call me William. I've known Royce from way back and I'm happy to see him home again, too many years on unfriendly shores. These old eyes never thought to see you again, Royce, let alone a bride.

Welcome." He turned and called out to someone behind him. "Gem, come over here."

A young lad hurried forward, dropping his eyes as he neared.

"Would you like to change, my lady? Freshen up? Gem, get her bag from the stables."

"She has no other clothes," Royce interrupted. "We ran into some trouble on the way here. Tis the reasons we arrived so late at your door."

"Trouble?" Robert frowned. "Not again. This country hasn't been safe since..." he paused looking at Anna then changed the subject. "No matter. Gem take her upstairs to Mabel's rooms. My daughter keeps a trunk of dresses there and you are welcome to have any one of them. I'm sorry to say I don't have any maids to help you my dear. They've all gone back to the village for the night. Ever since my beautiful daughter left, I've had no reason to keep a young maid here," he chuckled. "Too many men around for her own good and I can't protect them all."

Anna glanced at Royce. He nodded and said, "We'll wait for you down here, be quick."

Gem led her up two flights of stairs that hugged the inner wall and curved around the building. On the second flight, Gem turned and entered a room just off the main hall.

It was simply furnished, a fireplace on one wall and a bed across from it. A large trunk stood at the end of the bed. Gem went over and opened it for her, putting the candle on the table next to it. Bowing low to her he said, "I'll be up with some water for you my lady. Is there anything else?"

Glancing around, Anna asked for the one thing she didn't see. In Spanish she asked, "Do you have a comb for my hair?" When he didn't reply, she asked again in English. "Comb?"

The boy nodded and was gone.

After the door closed, Anna explored. The bed was a heavy pallet made of straw covered with blankets. It was lumpy and smelled like the hall. She couldn't wait to lie down on it. But a knock on the door brought her to attention and she called out for him to enter.

Gem came in with a large bucket of water which he poured into a bowl on the table and a small crude comb, placing it next to the bowl.

"Lord Sutton has gone to get cleaned up. He bid you to come in the half hour. They will be holding supper till then. Do you want me to come back up for you?"

She nodded acceptance.

This time when he left, she hurried over to the trunk and peered inside. Pulling out one of the dresses, Anna frowned. Good ol' William didn't seem to notice that his daughter was a bit smaller than she was. These clothes would be a tight fit indeed.

Thirty minutes later Anna opened the door at the knock and second guessed her decision when she heard Gem's indrawn breath.

She knew the dress was tight but had no idea whether it was appropriate or not. She'd put it on without anything underneath and the bodice was so low it felt like her breasts were falling out. No matter how hard she tugged the damn dress wouldn't budge, so she'd forced her breasts in as low as possible and decided she wouldn't breath much tonight. But now with Gem's gasp, she was worried again.

"Is this not satisfactory?" she asked backing into the room.

"No, no," he put up his hands to halt her. "My Lady looks quite satisfactory."

Anna blushed still unsure.

"I apologize," he stammered. "It's been awhile since we have been graced with such beauty."

She ran her hands down attempting to straighten the sides of the skirt again. She shrugged and gave him a smile, "It was the best I could do. So, lead on, I'm famished."

The boy's head tilted in question before turning to lead her out. Anna straightened, reminding herself to be less familiar.

As she drew close to the fire, all the men turned to stare. At once Royce's men pushed back their bench and stood with big eyes and then bowed to her as she walked by.

Royce had changed too. He was wearing a simple tunic open at the throat over leggings, his dark hair was still damp and his top clung to his chest as though he'd bathed in a hurry.

When she glanced at Royce his look of surprise quickly transformed to a dark frown with a heavy brow. She stopped, certain now she had worn the wrong dress. The deep green color of the velvet was beautiful, but much too hot for a night like this. Unfortunately, it was the only one that fit...sort of.

The dress was not only too tight in the bust but too short in the length by a good four inches showing off her ankles and bare feet. She put a nervous hand up to her windswept tangles. The comb had been useless. She could only guess at what it looked like, but without a mirror or any sort of pins there was not much else she could do.

When Gem's knock had come she had been desperately working on her hair, but neither comb nor fingers would get the job done and with her stomach complaining she had given up. Now standing here, she knew she'd made a mistake. All the men were staring at her like she had two heads. Only Lord William moved forward, eagerly taking her hand and welcoming her to the table.

Supper was a short affair. She wondered why she'd even tried to take such care with her appearance when Royce did nothing but put his head down and eat. The dark frown never left his face while Lord William couldn't have been more charming.

He regaled her with stories about Royce as a youth and had her laughing so hard her belly hurt. Talking all the while, he leaned forward offering her the tastiest cuts of meat, more bread and filled her cup twice until Royce put his hand over it, saying she'd had enough.

Those had been the only words he'd said in her general direction all night and even though Anna knew he was right, the ale was definitely going to her head, it was enough to annoy her.

"I would love some more ale, sir," she smiled throwing off Royce's hand. "Thank you for offering."

Lord Robert's head fell back and he gave a shout of laughter.

Royce growled.

"This is grand, Royce. A woman with spirit. She's the one for you. None of those milk sop London beauties. Oh, my friend goes out and finds himself an English rose deep in Spain with spirit and looks."

Anna giggled because Lord William's amusement was so infectious and good hearted. But Royce growled again and pushed back his chair drawing Anna up with him.

Anna started to protest saying, "but I'm not finished-."

"Yes, you are," Royce replied tersely.

Turning to Lord William, he bowed and thanked him for the use of his home for the night, assuring him they would be gone on the morrow. Lord William waved him away, bidding them both a good night. His chuckle could still be heard as they mounted the stairs.

"Let me go." Anna hissed under her breath as Royce continued to pull her up the stairs.

Finally, Royce had enough and swept her into his arms taking the stairs two at a time. His mouth was grim when he pushed open the door to her room. He didn't release her until he'd kicked the door shut. Immediately, she fled to the other side of the room.

The fire had been started and there was a stack of wood next to it. The pallet had been changed and the bed turned down. Candlelight flickered through the room casting them both in a soft glow. The room smelled sweet, the atmosphere was romantic and inviting, but it barely registered with her.

Both of them stood there, staring at each other with hands on hips and fire in their eyes. Anna wasn't even sure why he was mad, but his response to her and man-handling today was enough.

"What is your problem?" she said.

"My problem, Madam? I'll tell you what my problem is...my wife comes down dressed like a wanton, flirting with all to see. I told you to hold your tongue tonight madam, not flaunt it." Dropping his arms, his hands curled into fists and stepping towards her, he asked in Spanish, "Do you not remember your Spanish?"

She colored, he had asked her to mind her tongue and speak Spanish, but she'd forgotten. Taking the defensive, she said, "I'm sorry, you did ask me to but Gem didn't understand me and when I got downstairs I... I forgot," she stammered. "But the dress wasn't my fault," she continued her anger returning as she tried to explain. "I had no help and that woman is at least two sizes smaller than me. This was the only dress that kind of fit." She waved him off. "But that still doesn't give you the right to manhandle me like that."

Taking another step towards her, his voice was low and charged. "It does give me the right. After all, you are my wife."

"In name only mister," she bit out.

His mouth twisted in a half smile and his eyes glittered. She should have retreated, but she was so irritated now she couldn't stop. "You have no right to order me around like that and—wait-what are you doing?"

Royce was walking towards her slowly like he was stalking a frightened animal. His attitude had changed from an angry man to a man on the hunt. He backed her across the room and Anna felt herself retreating. Lifting her eyes up to his face, her jaw went slack. It was the face of desire, the one she'd seen earlier today by the river.

"Not in name only," he purred.

"What? No-stop it Royce." She swallowed hard and pushed against his chest trying to halt his advance.

He captured her wrist easily and drew her towards him. Again, she noticed the glint in his eyes, but the smile had disappeared from his face. In all seriousness that brooked no argument he said, "Anna, I have waited for nine years. Nine years to make you my wife in name and now you shall be mine, fully. We will finish what we started."

Chills tingled up her spine. "What the hell is that supposed to mean?" she snapped, snatching her wrist back as if his touch burned and taking a step away from him.

Royce's mouth hardened but he didn't hesitate. "You know what it means. Now, come here."

"Why, because you know about the cherry tree, and that decrepit little old man said a few words in Latin and pronounced us man and wife. Like hell I will. I don't just do any man's bidding—ever. I don't care what you say."

"You lost your maidenhead to me that day."

Her intake of breath betrayed her surprise, "Excuse me?" Indignant, she stuck her chin out and put her hands on her hips. "You don't know what you're talking about."

"Nine years ago, that day under the cherry tree."

Anna felt the blood drain from her face and then the heat rise. She knew her cheeks were bright red.

"I did not," she interrupted infuriated. "*We did not*. And don't call it that." She said as angry as she could, but the moisture was already leaving her mouth. Once again, another crack appeared in her memory. Laughter...dark eyes, warm kisses, a pinprick of pain...and the heady scent of cherry blossoms floating down around her...

"You did-we did. We pledged our love to each other." He moved closer. His voice lowered to a deep timber that sent her heart racing.

"That was a dream-just like all of this." She shook her head and backed up. "I-I don't really remember any of that..." But her confidence was undone. She turned her back on him and tried to walk away.

"The hell you don't." Anger laced his voice and it seemed he had lost all patience. She knew she had tugged on the tiger's tail once too often today but couldn't seem to stop herself. He pulled her around to face him, his dark eyes glittering dangerously.

"I remember full well what happened that day and every other that I spent with you," he said thickly. "I have searched for you for the last year, waiting for God to send you to me. That was not a dream. This is not a dream. You are here whether you like it or not and tonight I will fully make you mine." He paused before adding with narrowed eyes and a twist to his mouth. "That was virgin's blood on my cock—yours."

Before she could stop herself, her hand whipped out and smacked him hard across the face. "How dare you," she hissed.

He didn't flinch. Instead he grabbed up her other arm and pressed her back against the wall. Holding her arms above her head he spoke with clenched teeth, "I dare more." Bending down, he hesitated as if trying to garner control, his lips just brushing hers before giving in and devouring her mouth with his own. Effortlessly he held her, her arms suspended above her head attacking her mouth with his passion. He let go of her wrists and let his hands roam free down her body.

She was overpowered by the sheer size and strength of him. His touch was tender yet demanding, moving over her body in a way that her breath caught and she began to lose her senses again.

Anna whimpered, spurring him on.

"Remember me, Anna," he breathed into her mouth.

Shaking her head, she looked at him through tear laden eyes. "You're a dream—not..."

"No." He grimly shook her shoulders against the wall, before bending down and plundering her mouth once again.

"Remember me, Anna." His voice was seductive and filled with years of yearning. He brought his hand up her leg under her skirt and caressed the skin softly. The blood pounded in her head and she felt her body answering him.

His arms came around her and he hitched her up on his thigh, pressing into her intimately. His lips left her mouth and burned their way down her throat.

She felt the bodice go slack and pull away from her as he untied the strings at the back. In a moment the gown fell forward giving him full access to her chest. Gently his mouth sought her breast, first one and then the other, where he teased the nipple, sucking and pulling it taut.

A moan escaped her throat. It had been so long since anyone had touched her like this. Lifting his head, he said against her throat, "Remember me, Anna".

"No," she choked out in a whisper.

"Remember me, Anna," he said more forcefully. His hand stroked up her thigh and found her soul. A finger dipped in causing her to arch against him.

She gasped, her eyes opened to meet his. He was staring at her hard and it took a moment for her to realize he was waiting for an answer.

Breathing through her nose, her head nodded and a tear slipped down her cheek.

"Royce-."

His gaze searched her face for a moment, before lowering to her mouth. "Say it," he whispered against her lips. "Say the truth-say you remember me".

"Yes," she whispered, nodding her head.

"Louder," he demanded. "Say it louder."

"Yes, I remember you," she said thickly.

For a moment he just stared at her, his eyes hot and heavy with lust.

Finally, bending down, he captured her mouth again in a hungry kiss. Once those words were spoken, they were his. She knew it. She was his and he would hold her to it.

His mouth and hands were everywhere caressing, touching, taunting her in ways she thought impossible. She could feel him, hard, pressing into her and she echoed his moves. He held her there against the wall, moving into her until she thought she would die.

Leaning back from her for a moment, he removed his tunic and hose in one quick move, her dress soon followed and puddled at her feet. Naked before her, she couldn't help but stare at him. He was magnificent, all hard and sinewy with a trail of dark hair leading a path to his groin. Her heart fluttered in her breast and she knew she wanted this as much as he did.

He picked her up and turned with her in his arms to the bed. Laying her down softly, he moved on top of her parting her thighs with his knees.

"I can't wait any longer. Give way, Anna… Give way..." he groaned against her throat.

She ran her hands up his back and reveled in the feel of him. When he sought entrance, she gave it, tipping her head back and opening herself fully to him. He paused on her threshold, teasing them both before plunging forward and sinking himself deep inside her.

Gathering a breath, he lifted himself up, cradling her gently between his arms and began to move slowly. She gasped at the sensations dominating her body. She had no more control than a runaway train. Faster, he went and she matched him move for move, hurtling forward until both cried out in ecstasy.

For a moment neither moved, both stayed locked tight letting the spasms rock over them until they subsided. Royce's breath was heavy on her throat and she was curled tight hugging him to her.

Finally breaking away from her he rolled to his side bringing her with him and snuggled her close. Their bodies were wet with sweat and the smell of sex permeated the air. Royce let a chuckle escape him and said with assurance, "You remember me".

Anna's strangled laugh joined his. She blushed, playfully hitting him in the shoulder.

Turning to her again, he rolled up and said wickedly, "I'll not let you forget again." His hair a mess hanging in his face. Gently she pushed it away and looked into his eyes.

"Again?" she asked, arching a brow playfully up.

"Again." He smiled wolfishly at her before bending down to take her mouth in another kiss.

CHAPTER 9

Anna awoke slowly, not wanting to shake the pleasant laziness that hugged her body. The first thing she became aware of was the soreness between her legs and the heaviness of her breasts. Warmth spread through her body and settled in her belly. A sense of shyness washed over her at the things they'd done last night.

Her hand slid forward, feeling for Royce and came upon empty linens instead. She squinted into the late morning light that danced on the wall. A thick smile spread over her face and she closed her eyes, letting the night play out again in her mind.

Amazing...the man had done things to her she didn't realize could be done, sinful and delicious at the same time. He hadn't let her question. He wouldn't let her think. He had just done, and oh dear God, it had felt so good.

Pressing her thighs together, she slid her hands down her body, reliving how he had touched her here or kissed her there. A sigh escaped her as she cupped herself, letting the mad heat resurface and swirl through her until a noise from behind caught her attention. Turning over, she pulled the bedding to her chin and stared at the young girl moving familiarly about the room setting things to right.

The girl tisked as she picked the green velvet off the floor, shaking it out and folding it proper before placing it in the trunk again.

Anna watched her for a moment before the little maid noticed she was awake.

"Oh good, you's awake," the girl said, her accent so thick Anna could barely understand it.

Remembering Royce's earlier words, she nodded but kept silent.

It didn't seem to matter. The maid just kept right on talking. Dusting her hands off on her apron she poured water from a jug into the wash basin.

"I've set out a different dress for you, one that will fit."

The girl looked over her shoulder with eyebrows raised as if assessing Anna's body. "The velvet's no' right, much too hot for this time of year. Besides it's one of my mistress's favorites and she'll be right upset to see it gone."

Coming over to the bed, she motioned for Anna to get out. "'Tis time to go. No more sleeping. You'll sleep half the day away. Out with you, and quick wash up. The chamber pots behind there…well, go on now," she said with authority, pushing her behind the curtain.

For one so young, she sure was bossy. For a moment Anna was embarrassed, sure that the night's activity showed on her form, but the girl took no notice.

Instead, she handed her a towel and told her where to wash and then when she thought Anna wasn't doing it fast enough, she pulled the towel out of her hands and began vigorously scrubbing her body with the wash cloth, not leaving a place untouched.

Anna gritted her teeth and refrained from saying something rude. But when the girl got to her privates she yanked the towel out of the smaller hands and turned away to wash herself there as gently as possible.

The dress that the little maid slipped over her head did fit better. It was much more comfortable and allowed for easier movement with her arms.

Once again, it was two dresses with a light slip underneath. The first was a cream linen underskirt split up the sides at the bottom, nothing fancy, but very soft that went down to her feet. The second piece was like a long sleeve dress with bell arms that fastened at the wrist and was an inch or so longer and fuller at the bottom in a soft green color. The last one was a heavier material, sleeveless, that tied at the bodice and had a full split skirt in a darker shade of green.

It was quite pretty and she was glad to have this girl here to help her get dressed. She wasn't sure if she would have worn all this if left on her own. But the best part was what she did with her hair.

A knock on the door and a clipped, "Come in" from the little maid brought Gem with a tray of food, a simple meat pasty and a cup of foaming ale. While Anna ate, the girl fussed with her hair, talking to herself all the while.

"Oooh, why'd you have to cut it? So pretty. Don't do that again..." On and on she went never stopping for an answer.

Somehow, she managed to work out the tangles and braid it all back into a tight bun. Then she covered it with a simple piece of linen held in place by half a dozen pins.

"Go on, clean your teeth," she handed Anna a small twig newly cut.

When she hesitated, the maid stepped forward and started to take the twig from her hand to do it herself, but Anna frowned and moved her arm away.

"Clean," she motioned with her hands in an exaggerated motion as one would a toothbrush. "Go on now-hurry."

Putting the twig in her mouth, she was surprised at how fresh it tasted, like newly cut mint. The soft twig did indeed do its job like a toothbrush. She worked at her mouth with a vengeance until the girl handed her a cup of water and told her to rinse and spit.

"All done," the maid said standing back to admire her work. But as she stood up the maid noticed her feet and exclaimed, "Oooh the slippers. I forgot." Going over to the door, she withdrew a couple of long pieces of cloth from a basket she'd brought. "Don't know if they'll fit, but we'll try. You're so much bigger than our fair Mabel. Good thing

Lord Cardingham let you use his lady's things," she tisked again and bent to the task.

"Do you mean Lord William's wife?" she asked curiously.

Looking up, the young maid seemed surprised that she spoke, but continued talking as she slipped on the stockings and tied them at Anna's knees. "Oh yes, 'is third wife, Lady Elanor. She died winter last. Not a healthy one that, two stillborn babes and such a big boned lady too. You'd think she would be a good birther, but no..." she shook her head.

"There, all done now," she repeated, standing back again. Reaching into her basket, she pulled out a small, shiny piece of metal.

Anna looked at her distorted reflection, turning her face from side to side. It was like staring into a fun house mirror, but she got the general idea. She felt pretty, free floating without all the constraints of modern day clothing. Smiling with satisfaction, she thanked the girl and let her lead her out of the room and down the stairs.

The main hall was empty and the girl continued on outside into the bright sunshine and over to the stable where Royce waited with his men and Lord William. In the light of day, the bailey looked so different with men and women working all around.

"Aah, the young lady is ready," Lord William held out his hand in welcome.

Royce was standing next to him with his hands on his hips, wearing his perpetual frown. He nodded curtly to her, before turning back to his men.

She ignored him, which seemed to cause Lord William a great deal of mirth.

"Thank you for the dress," she held out her skirts and smiled generously at Lord William. "It really is beautiful."

"It was my sweet Eleanor's. She's gone now and best to use it, eh? This seems to fit better, not that I didn't enjoy the dress last night," he finished with a wink and a chuckle.

"Thank you again, William, for the horse." Royce cleared his throat nosily beside them. "We appreciate your generous hospitality."

"Horse?" she asked, turning to look.

"Lord William has generously offered to sell us one of his daughter's horses," Royce motioned to the pretty palfrey, saddled and ready to go.

It was half the size as Royce's horse which was flattening its ears and showing its teeth at the little mare, but at least Anna would have her own mount.

"Oh, thank you. She's beautiful." She walked over to pet the velvet nose. "What's her name?"

"Something pretty," Lord William waved it away. "I can't remember. Name her what you like. She needs the exercise-going to rot here."

Royce motioned her up. With a quick hitch she mounted easily, but she couldn't stop the small grunt she made as her body met the bony back of the horse. Swallowing hard, color stole up her face betraying her embarrassment. She peeked up under her lashes and met Royce's eyes. They glittered, dark with desire. A smile played around his lips and he laid a gentle hand on her knee and gave it a squeeze before turning away. Warmth spread through her again at that gentle touch and all discomfort fled.

She waved goodbye to Lord Cardingham and clicked her horse to follow the others out the gate and across the moat.

She hadn't been able to see the moat last night, but it was larger than she had first thought. At least a ten-foot drop to the water and with the narrowness of the bridge, she said a prayer as her horse crossed it. The wall itself was all wood and well built. At one point they had started to build with stone, but the project looked abandoned now.

There were a number of small huts huddled around the entrance, intermingled with animal pens and beyond that quite a few fields were being worked by the peasants. For the most part, it looked well-constructed and profitable.

The villagers stopped and stared, eying them with interest as they rode by. But Royce and his men never took notice. Instead, they rode right through town, scattering the crowd like a flock of chickens.

They followed the River Fowey until they came to the little coastal town that bore the river's name. It was late afternoon and the town was doing busy trade along its shores.

Shopkeepers hawked their produce, calling out in booming voices to lure people to their booths. The town itself was not as neat as Restormel. Here the people lived off the sea and the pungent smell of fish hung heavy in the air. Birds circled noisily above as a fisherman's boat pulled into dock to unload its catch. Men and women eagerly moved forward anxious to get the freshest fish for their evening meal.

Royce stopped at a small tavern and dismounted, handing his reins to one of the men, bidding them to wait outside for a moment. Anna sat comfortably on her horse enjoying the sights around her.

They had taken their time today, clearly not in the rush they had been. It was that or Royce had taken pity on her and let the horses amble.

Either way, she was enjoying it, both the gentle mare and the interested looks Royce cast her way.

Royce came out and offered his arms up to her. "We will sup here." Then to his men he added, "He isn't here yet."

"Who?" she asked, letting him lead her inside.

"Lars. One of my men, a blond fellow, you might remember him from the other day when he tried to sweet talk you out of your sword."

"Oh, yes," she laughed. "I do remember him."

The inside of the tavern was dark and musty, smelling of ale and fish. Only a few people were seated, busily chatting in their heavy Cornish accent. Royce took a seat at the farthest table, his back to the wall with her on one side and his men on the other. In minutes, hot piping rye bread was placed before them followed by a fish stew and thick frothy ale that tasted wonderful.

No sooner had they started eating when two men came in and Royce and his men stood, greeting them with murmured voices.

The first man she definitely recognized, the blond fellow Royce had mentioned. He was richly dressed in a bright blue tunic; a cape was thrown over one shoulder and a black hat sat rakishly on his head. Vivid blue eyes accompanied an impudent smile which he flashed her way when he saw her. Her first impression was of a strutting, preening peacock.

She didn't remember him looking quite like this.

"I understand congratulations are in order." He clapped hands with Royce, but his eyes were on her. "You look quite different my lady...better," he added quickly when he saw Royce raise his eyebrows. Clearing his throat, he dipped his head and bowed, "Pardon my lady, I mean to say, you look well."

He pushed a few men aside and took the seat across from her and put one arm on the table. With a glint in his eye he asked her gravely. "Are you feeling well, my lady?"

By no means immune to his charm, and after having no conversation with any of Royce's other men, she was happy to respond. "Yes, thank you I am doing...well." She paused on the word just as he did.

"Good, good," he clapped his hands together. His eyebrows rose in appreciation and he reached across the table to slap Royce on the back again causing easy laughter among their group.

Royce scowled back pretending to ignore them all. Breaking off a piece of bread and dipping it into the remainder of his stew he asked under his breath, "Were you able to meet?"

The peacock's eyes flicked back to him and changed for a moment. He reached for the bread. "He's due in today. Problems in Wales. Word reached the coast about a challenge to the throne."

"But the crown is secure..."

"So they say. Still there are people who do not want change," the peacock said. Popping a piece in his mouth, he added, "There's a price on your head again."

Royce snorted.

"It's been raised. You're not safe here. We should get you out."

"Go where? Back to France? I have nothing to go back to."

The two of them were talking so quietly Anna could barely hear them. They talked as they ate, hardly looking or acknowledging each other. It appeared like they were just joining in conversation with the other men around them.

"Just a castle and title," Lars said his tone sarcastic.

"No," Royce shook his head. "England is my home. Okehampton is mine by right of birth. I've been gone too long. It's time to go home."

"I heard Hugh destroyed it."

"Not all of it. With the king's permission I can rebuild."

"Not if Louvain can help it," the peacock muttered. Noticing Anna's interest, he dusted off his hands before waving them around. "My lady," he addressed her in a booming voice. The other men in the room stopped to listen. "Have you met all the men?"

Anna started at his sudden inclusion. "No," she shook her head.

"I thought as much. They are a quiet, self-serving bunch of rotter's," he joked merrily, pounding his fists on the table. Suddenly, he was the strutting peacock again.

"Let me ask you," he leaned forward, put an elbow on the table and held his chin, his face serious. "Did he tell you I was one of his men?"

"Yes, he did," she mimicked his posture.

"I knew it," he pounded on the table, and then pointed a finger at Royce. "He always does that, but I'm not. I'm not one of his men."

"Well, who are you then?"

Calling out for more food and ale, Lars laughed again. "I'm higher in rank then him, that's for sure. Well into the king's favor."

At that comment Royce made a grunt.

"You think not, my friend?" Lars kept on, "I am, wait and see. One day I'll be lord of the realm." He raised his arms dramatically. "Bar keep, food and ale," he called out again to the man who was wiping his hands on his apron at the door to the kitchen.

The man nodded and ducked back inside, emerging a few minutes later, his arms laden with food.

"I don't know a more disreputable lout I've ever come across," Lars went on pointing to Royce and winking at her. "No matter the favors you've done or your years on crusade. Our good king's own servant he is."

Royce's mouth twisted, but he remained silent letting Lars go on.

"First of all, let me introduce myself," he said seriously, with hand on chest. "Lord James Northwood of Ashford at your service my lady, he said and then leaned down to whisper in her ear, "But you may call me Lars." Giving her a wink and a nod, he went on, "None of that lord nonsense."

The men around him chuckled.

"To my left," Lars put his arm around the older man who had come in with him, "a more notorious scoundrel you will never have seen, John Barry of Sussex. Overtook a whole army of infidels, he did. He doesn't say much but he's good to have around."

The older man watched Lars with a queer look to his eye, before turning to Anna and giving her a mocking smile.

Lars leaned forward and pointed to the large red-haired man, addressing him as such, "The red headed fellow to John's left is Keefe O'Brien. He's from Ireland. A truer savage, I have yet to meet."

Keefe bowed his head to her, his large smile revealing a few missing teeth. He said hello in a heavy Irish accent that made a few of the men exchange laughs.

"This...this here is Denny." Turning to his right he put his hand on the young man with light brown hair and soft hazel eyes. "Royce's squire, a yearling, but has the heart of a poet and the soul of a fighter."

The teen blushed scarlet and squirmed under Lars' hand, ducking his head and keeping quiet.

By now, the men seemed to be enjoying Lars' antics and waited for what he would say next. The patrons at the other table had stopped talking and were openly listening now, and the owner of the establishment had come out from the back again to assess the commotion.

"Beside him is the ugly one of the group, Phillip De St. Armand, a chevalier who's come down in this world, the French spat him out and left him for us pour English to deal with." Lars turned and spit on the floor with dramatic flair.

"I'm the pretty one, my lady," Phillip said with a rich French accent, causing the other men to laugh.

Pretty was a good way to describe him. He had rich brown hair and light eyes in a delicate face. He was a bit smaller in stature than the other men, but she'd noticed was quick on his feet.

"And last, but not least, is Jerold Adams from Somerset, a dangerous man, well on his way to winning the hearts of all the maids from here to London," Lars said, pointing to the man who sat at Royce's left. All the men laughed at Lars' description.

He did indeed look dangerous, but not in the way Lars had described him. He had lots of black hair but his teeth were crooked and, somehow, the smile never seemed to meet his eyes.

He nodded to her but kept quiet. She'd noticed he was more watchful than the rest and she'd been uncomfortable around him from the start.

"Now you have met us all, my lady, a merrier band you will not see, I assure you," Lars finished with a small bow.

"It's a pleasure," she said politely, looking around at all their faces. The men just grunted and went on eating their meal. She glanced at Lars and raised her eyebrow as though to question him. "Oh yes, they are very merry indeed."

"The merriest." Lars smiled with a slow wink and a nod.

After the meal Royce took Anna upstairs, showing her to their room for the night. It was horribly small, with barely enough space for the bed and a single chair.

"We won't fit on that." Going over to the bed, she tested its firmness and found the lumpy mattress sorely lacking.

"We won't be sleeping here," he said, coming into the room.

"We won't?"

"No, I have things to attend," he stated, shutting the door behind him and taking her in his arms."

"What? You're going out?" she leaned back to look at him.

"I have business," he nuzzled her neck.

"Business? At night?" she asked. "What kind of business?"

"Business, an errand...not something for you to question."

"Not like another lady?" She couldn't stop herself for asking.

He leaned back taking in her cold demeanor and his head tilted, one eyebrow shooting up. "Jealous?"

"No, I didn't mean that," she pulled away from him and went over to the small window. Peering out for a moment she tried to choose her words carefully before continuing. "I just thought you would be here."

His smile reappeared. He came to her gathering her in his arms again, his dark eyes glittered. "I want to be here," he replied lustily, "but

I have something I need to do. You have nothing to worry about. One of my men will be outside all night. You'll be safe."

"Which man?"

"Does it matter?"

"No, but I... I don't think I like that Jerold Adams much."

"Who?" Royce asked.

"Jerold Adams, one of your men. You know, the dark-haired fellow."

Royce smiled. "Aah, yes, Jerold," he said with a chuckle.

"Why couldn't you have introduced them to me? Don't you even know your own men?"

"Not by those names." Royce laughed again.

"What?" she widened her eyes, "Those aren't their names? Any of them?"

"No, but you can call them by those names if it helps. I can't promise they'll answer." He gave her a crooked smile.

"Even Lars?"

"Well now, that's not really his name, but it's what we call him. As for the rest, I'll introduce you soon enough."

"I don't understand? Why all the deception? Why all the intrigue?" she asked, walking away again before rounding on him. "Wait a minute, what about you? Is Royce really your name? What was it, Royce Barrett Sutton did you say?"

"That is my name," he walked over to stand before her. "Royce Barrett De'Mark Sutton..." He paused with his hands out, palms up. "I could not get married under someone else's name, now could I?"

"But people know you here, that man last night knew you, told stories about you when you were a boy?"

"Yes," he said carefully, his eyes narrowed. "I knew him well when I was a boy. I haven't seen him in years. He's one of the few people I trust or trusted, I should say. Here, nobody knows me, I haven't given my name to any and except for the few times you or Lars said my name, none have heard it. My name doesn't matter any longer, but the others..." He shrugged his shoulders. "There are other people involved," he said simply before a knock at the door interrupted them.

Lars came in, all smiles and showmanship gone, his face serious. He nodded to Royce. "Robert's here."

"Where?"

"Downstairs."

"I'll be right down," Royce said.

Lars nodded at her and turned to leave. It took her a moment to believe that was the same jovial fellow who had greeted her earlier. Now he looked like an actor dressed for a play in those ridiculous clothes.

"It's just for a few hours." Royce kissed her on the forehead and started for the door. "I'll be back to get you soon. Rest if you can."

"Wait...what was all that down there with Lars-the price on your head?"

Royce paused, the playfulness of the moment before gone. In its place stood the hard-cold stranger, and as if weighing his words, he said slowly, "It means I have to be careful."

"Careful? Careful of what? Of whom? The men you were running from the other day?"

"Yes, careful of them. They took something that was mine and I'm here to get it back." His voice was brittle.

Her mouth went dry as she looked at him. Another crack in her memory appeared. A tremor stole up her body and, suddenly, she remembered.

"The castle...Okehampton? Your uncle..." she said slowly as if seeing him with new eyes.

The muscle in his jaw twitched. "Yes-you remember."

Dread tingled up her spine sending chills throughout her body. "Fire...I remember fire..." she whispered. "And men...and death...from a dream so long ago." Visions rose up as she spoke. Her body went stiff, every hair standing up on end.

"It wasn't a dream," he bit out. His face full of anguish, he turned and left, closing the door after him.

Putting her hands up to cover her eyes, Anna sank on the bed trying to block out the images that threatened to overtake her.

She did remember.

Voices played over in her head, screams of pain and terror. He was right. This was no dream. This was a memory and there was no escaping it.

CHAPTER 10

A boy...the meadow...spring flowers brushing her fingertips. High wispy clouds drift in a bright blue sky. The wind was just right, bringing a cooling breeze up from the river.

He was late today.

He was never late, but Anna wasn't worried.

She sat down, lying back in the tall grass and cupped a daffodil bouncing near her face. She let herself remember. Was that just yesterday? She closed her eyes. She could still see the canopy of pink and white above her, still smell the intoxicating perfume of lilac, orange blossoms and sweet alyssum.

Gentle hands.

Insistent kisses.

Eager bodies entwined in innocent exploration.

Her finger ran over her lips and continued down tracing the path his mouth had taken. He said he loved her, wanted to marry her one day.

A distant rumble disturbed the pleasant hum of the nearby bees. A yell. Shouts. A scream and then another as a shadow moved in and blocked the warmth of the sun. She opened her eyes to a great cloud of billowing smoke. More screams filtered up from the small village below.

Alarmed she sat up and immediately regretted it. Her nostrils quivered with the foul stench. She shrank back covering her nose. The putrid odor of burning flesh seared her senses and made her gag. Beneath her the ground began to tremble. Like a match catching spark fear radiated up her spine.

Unsure what to do, she kept still as a rabbit, her eyes desperately searching the meadow. Where was he? Should she hide? But were to go and what of Royce?

"Ah-naa." The piercing cry came from the road below.

Standing slowly, she waited poised for flight when he called again. "Ah-naa."

She saw him then, running up from the village sword in hand. He was filthy. Dirt and pitch covered most of his face and clothes. His tunic was ripped and torn, soaked in blood.

"*Run, Anna,*" he screamed.

Frozen in place, horror filled her as she watched men on horseback riding up the hill behind him. Patiently they stalked him, bloody swords in hand, waiting to attack.

Suddenly, everything slowed. She could hear Royce yelling her name as if from far away. The loud thud of her heart competed with the drumming of the horse's hooves. She was rooted to the spot like a trapped animal awaiting her fate. Royce was running towards her so slowly, she thought, surely, they'll run him over before he could reach her.

And then he was there, in front of her, yelling with all the desperation in his voice and the agony of the day in his eyes. He grabbed her shoulders, it was as if an electric shock pulsed through her body.

"*Run, Anna,*" he turned and pushed her on. "*Run!*"

But it was too late...too late for both of them.

She lurched upward the scream lodged in her throat, gasping for breath, her heart wild, reaching for Royce but the image was gone. Looking around the small room, she tried to get her bearings. The sun had set leaving the room in near darkness.

She was safe.

Breathing hard, she tried to focus and let herself remember.

What had happened after that? Oh God, that had been a bad one, a bad dream. Okay, not a dream...not a dream, but a memory. Shivering, she laid back down drawing a blanket up over herself. Exhausted, she let the tears come. Covering her mouth, she fought the desperation that had returned with the dream...no, not a dream, a memory...a horrible memory.

Oh God, what happened back then? What had happened to Royce? No wonder she didn't want to remember.

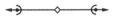

After that Anna had been sure sleep was the last thing she'd be able to do. But the last few days had drained her and she'd fallen into a heavy slumber only to be woken sometime later by Royce.

He got her up and out of there with the stealth of a practiced thief. Before leaving, he covered her clothes with a long dark cloak similar to the one he was wearing, removing the pretty piece of linen that she still wore in her hair and pulling the hood up to hide her face.

A few men were waiting behind the back barn, the horses saddled and ready. She couldn't tell who they were because they were all wearing long cloaks with the hoods up hiding their faces.

She had no idea what time it was, but the moon hung low in the sky and the stars where still magnificent. The wind had picked up and she shivered glad for her cloak as they started off.

Once they were well away from town and out of sight of the last crofters hut, they turned south. The travel was slow along a line of ragged cliffs. It didn't appear to be a far drop, but with the lengthening shadows from the moon it was a scary ride. She wanted to ask Royce where they were going but knew better. So far nobody had said anything and she was reluctant to speak.

They came to an inlet and Royce stopped, helping her down. Taking her hand, he began walking to the beach below.

She grabbed his arm when she saw the steep slope, but he turned and put his mouth next to her ear.

"Come, Anna, we have no time to delay."

The descent seemed to take forever and she was hot and sweaty from the exertion by the time they reached the beach. Only one of Royce's men had followed them, the other two stayed at the top with the horses.

They were greeted by Lars and a new man who was introduced as Robert. He was tall and well dressed with a light beard. His gaze was piercing. Instantly, he stepped forward and grasped her hand raising it to his lips. "My lady."

Uncomfortable, she pulled away and sidled around Royce. He pushed her under a small overhang to avoid being seen.

"Wait here with Denny just in case," Royce whispered.

Denny eased his cloak aside enough to give her a nod. She felt better with him beside her. Her eyes adjusted. It was funny how well she could see on the beach under the guise of the moon. The light danced and reflected off the white sandy beaches.

Lars uncovered a small lantern and waved it back and forth towards the ocean. A returning light answered and within minutes she could see a small skiff with two people bob its way towards the beach.

The minute they got close enough, Royce pulled her out onto the beach following the other men and ran towards the water. Lars, Robert, Royce and Denny, waded out and caught the boat as it came close to shore then turned to help her in. Once she was seated all four men turned the boat and jumped in, each taking up an oar and rowing furiously out to sea.

She could just make out the large shape with high masts rocking gently on the waves and men moving around its deck. It took all six men another good half hour to reach the ship. The sea was rougher than it looked from shore and they were rowing against tide and wind. Pulling alongside the vessel, Royce was at her elbow.

"Can you climb?" he motioned to the rope ladder hanging off the side.

"Yes, but I'm soaked and the cloak is so heavy."

"You must wear it. Your dress is too light and could be seen from shore. Besides you'll be thankful for it later," he said pushing on her bottom as she started to climb.

A man from above reached down grabbing her wrists and suddenly she was up and over the side.

Somebody else covered her with another dark blanket and led her to a sheltered spot out of the wind. Pushing her down, he bid her in a rough voice to stay put.

She was fascinated as she watched the crew work. Without words, everyone seemed to know exactly what to do. In minutes dark sails were raised. They billowed out; catching the wind and the ship was off.

It was exhilarating. She wanted to get up and help or, at least, look over the sides. This was a much larger vessel than she had imagined and once it got moving it literally glided through the water.

She looked for Royce on the deck and found him working the sails with some of the other men. Counting Royce there were fourteen men that she could see.

Once they were out of sight from land and the ship was moving at a good clip Royce came over to stand in front of her.

"Your teeth are chattering," he frowned.

"I'm fine. This is amazing," she said, not even realizing how cold she was.

"Have you sailed before?" He took a seat next to her. His shirt sleeves were rolled up and his hair blowing around his face. His face was an amazing jumble of angles and shadows.

"No, not like this. I didn't realize how fast these ships go."

He put his hand up to her face. "You're frozen clear through, your skin is like ice," he stated accusingly.

"Well, there was not much I could do about it," she teased.

"Come." He took her hand as he stood.

"I don't want to go. It's so beautiful out here with the stars, sailing at night. I've never seen anything like this," she said stopping him and tugged on his hand to sit. "Look there's Orion's Belt, there's the Big Dipper and, that's the Little Dipper."

Royce sat back down. Grabbing up his wool cloak and another blanket, he tossed off her wet cloak and the soggy blanket on her lap.

Covering her with his cloak, he added the fresh blanket and wrapped her up tight. Pulling her into his lap, he ran his hands up and down her arms trying to warm her up.

"Dipper? There's a dipper in the sky? And who's Orion? Are you talking about the Gods in the stars?"

"Sort of...see over there, the three stars, that makes up Orion's Belt. That's the North Star, there I think, oh that feels good. I didn't realize how cold I was," she wiggled in his lap.

"Saints alive, woman, quit your moving. You tempt me beyond my will." He wrapped his arms around her firmly to keep her still.

"I'm sorry," she chuckled. And then gave her bottom a saucy wiggle.

"That'll do, madam." He gave her another squeeze before leaning back with her nestled in his arms. Heads aligned together, they gazed up at the stars remaining quiet for a moment.

"Do you believe in destiny?" He asked.

Turning her head to look at him, she took in his rough beard, the straight shape of his nose and the firm chin, leaning her forehead onto his. "Tonight, I do..."

"Yes, tonight I do too, for never have I seen such a beautiful sight," he said his eyes meeting hers.

"Such a flirt," her smile grew.

"And you, madam, are a tease." Clearing his throat, he repositioned her. Tucking the blanket tighter around her before returning her to his lap he said, "Now tell me about your Orion."

By noon the next day they had rounded the western tip of England and started north up the coast. They spent four days on the ship, and it was the longest four days of Anna's life. The charm of the first night wore off quickly once they had left the calm waters of the channel and headed north where the water became choppy.

She awoke to crude curses and shouting from men landing beside her as they jumped down from the rigging. She'd fallen asleep curled in Royce's arms the night before looking up at the stars and believing in destiny and handsome rescuers and came awake in a cold corner unbuffered by the wind on the hard-wooden deck.

The reality of her present situation sank in when she tried to move. Her body was stiff and sore and the crick in her neck seemed to go all the way to her feet. Her mouth had the gritty taste of old socks. Rubbing the nape of her neck to ease the pain, she glanced about.

Half a dozen pairs of eyes stared back at her with open lust. Perhaps this might not be the charmed life she'd been imagining last night. Most of the sailors were so sunburned their skin had the look of well-tanned leather and their hygiene left much to be desired. Rotted teeth, raised scars and facial hair besides, these men stunk. Even with the wind blowing away from her, she could smell them.

To make matters worse, just on the opposite side from where she sat was where they used the latrine. They just popped over the rail and squatted off a little platform rolling with the waves. And they didn't care who saw.

In fact, they were quick to take down their pants, slow to bring them up and happy to display what they carried between their legs if she happened to glimpse their way.

Trying not to panic she glanced around in search of Royce, instead she saw Lars. Getting to her feet, she stumbled over to him, working to keep herself up right with the bucking of the ship and the stiffness of her joints.

"Lars," she yelled, trying to be heard over the wind.

"Good morning my lady." He turned to her and gave her his lopsided grin.

"Where's Royce?" she shouted.

He pointed up and her eyes followed the long line of the mast. Tangled in the rigging above Royce was fiddling with one of the sails. Her heart caught in her throat watching as he scrambled around like a monkey. He had his shirt sleeves rolled up and his hair was blowing wild around his face.

She hadn't even realized she'd screamed until Lars took her arm and dragged her into the small cabin in the back.

Closing the door behind him, he looked at her thunderously. "You cannot show your fear here."

"What? What did I do?"

"Listen Mistress, these men are a very superstitious lot. As is, they wanted nothing to do with a woman on board. Even now they think you are bad luck. In the blink of an eye, they will throw you overboard if they think you could bring down this ship." He calmed and pondered her.

"Maybe it would be best if you stay out of sight. These are the captain's quarters, but I'm sure we can talk him into giving them up to you for the duration of the journey."

Swallowing, she braced herself against the wall and tried to understand what he was saying. All the while her stomach began to churn, flip flopping with every roll of the ship.

"I'm sorry. I didn't realize I made a sound. Yes, it would be good to stay in here," she said. At least she was protected from the prying eyes and the elements outside.

It certainly wasn't glamorous. As spare as any she had ever seen with only a rope bed hung in the corner, a chamber pot in the other attached to the floor and the small desk bolted to the side.

"Here, lay down, before you fall down." Lars helped her to the swaying cot. "You've gone white as a sheet. I'll get Royce. It's not safe for you outside, so stay put."

Moaning when the ship hit a particularly big wave, she suddenly felt sicker than she ever had in her life and was happy for the help to the cot. But the cot ended up being worse than standing. She swayed back and forth continually, and within the confines of the cabin the air seemed thick and fettered. That was how Royce found her, curled up tightly, holding her stomach.

The first few days she tried to eat only to have it come up later, so the last two days she refused most food and liquid taking only the occasional wine and biscuit. Not that she was missing anything. By the second day most of the food was hard as a rock and just as unpleasant to eat. Royce came in and tried to coerce some food down her throat at first, but when he witnessed its return moments later, he just lay beside her and held her trying to ease her shaking body.

She felt too awful to be embarrassed and clung to him whenever he came in to rest. He would scoop her up and hold her, his voice singing soft ballads until she fell asleep.

When she awoke on the fifth morning the ship was blessedly still and the calling voices announced they'd reached a port. Thankfully, Royce came in, bundled her up and carried her off to some waiting horses. She was too weak to even walk. He'd passed her to Lars and mounted up before reaching down for her.

They didn't ride half a mile before he stopped at a boarding house. Gathering her up again in his arms he went in calling for food, wine and a hot bath to be sent upstairs. A few hours later she was clean, full and asleep on a bed that didn't rock. It took two days for her to regain her strength.

"You're up," Royce called from the doorway.

Anna turned to face him hesitant, knowing all he had done for her in the last week. "Thank you for the dress. The other one was surely ruined."

"Quite. We had to burn it," he said making her choke back a laugh at his ungentlemanly joke. Coming forward, he fingered the material taking in her appearance.

"It is not as fine, but it will do for now."

It was light brown and very plain. Serviceable was what she would call it. Putting his hands to her shoulders, he turned her around. "You've lost a bit of weight this past week. It doesn't fit as it should. We'll have to see about another dress."

He was right. The fit was a little too big on top. She'd definitely lost weight. Her body felt rubbery and frail, even now after two days of good food and sleep. Before Royce had come in she'd nervously fidgeted with her appearance, trying to see her reflection in the knife she used to cut her food. But the pale woman with runaway hair looking back at her seemed a stranger.

He was all business again, not the gentle man who had held her shaking body and nursed her back to health. He was looking at her as one might a horse he was interested in purchasing. Even though they'd spent the nights together, he had yet to touch her intimately since that time at Restormel.

Not that she could blame him. She wouldn't have wanted to touch her either this past week.

"Are you sure you should be up?" He looked her over with his perpetual frown. "You look like a fawn too scrawny to flee," he said his hands on his hips, eyeing her up and down.

She made a face at his comment. "Yes, I feel fine." But when he cocked his brow at her, she rolled her eyes and said, "Much better. I feel much better."

"You were very sick. I was worried," he stated his eyes narrowing.

"Yes, well, I've never been on a ship in that kind of weather before."

"It was a bit of a gale, but we had a good headwind and made good time. It's easier on deck when you can see the horizon."

"Yes, I'll remember that for next time," she said sarcastically, turning to walk away, before thinking to ask, "There's not going to be a next time, is there?"

He chuckled but didn't reply.

Wanting to change the subject she went over to the small window and glanced into the busy street below. "Where are we?"

"Barri." He turned to his satchel on the floor and filled it with the few belongings he had brought with them. "I've acquired horses. We can wait one more day if you need it," he said over his shoulder.

"No, I'm good. At least, I think I'm good. My legs are a little shaky, but other than that I feel fine," she assured him, walking around as if to prove it.

Taking up his bag, he nodded again and held out his hand. "Good. Come then. The other men have arrived. We'll break our fast downstairs with them."

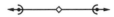

Reaching the bottom of the stairs, Royce led her into the busy common room. Lars sat at the back with some men. She recognized young Denny at a table, Jerold and Phillip sat across from them with the man she'd met on the beach, Robert something, but the other two standing next to Lars were new.

Royce pulled up short when he saw the newcomers with Lars. He cursed under his breath, his grip on Anna's arm changed. He hesitated and began to withdraw from the room before they were seen, but it was too late. Both men turned at their entrance and headed straight for Royce.

While Royce and his men were dressed simply with the padded tunics over the mail coat, these men wore clothes heavily decorated with stitching and jewels.

The short one with graying hair and a mean face took no notice of her at all, but the dark-haired man with the pale blue eyes gave her a start. When he turned to face her a shock of recognition jolted through her and she pulled back instinctively, nausea filling her stomach.

"I didn't know you were back, Sutton. I thought you were still over killing Saracens," said the man with the light eyes.

"What are you doing here?" Royce asked in distaste.

The man paused, the cold smile leaving his face as he looked at Royce, before painting it on again and saying with false cheer, "Why, our ship had trouble. We're on our way south."

"Don't let us keep you then." Royce pushed past them and continued toward the back, but the two men followed taking a seat across from them at the table.

"You forgot to introduce us to your charming companion, Sutton."

"No, I didn't," he said. Ignoring the two men, he took a chunk of bread, broke it in half and passed a piece to her.

The blue-eyed man laughed at Royce's rudeness. Taking up her hand, he kissed her wrist intimately flicking his tongue over her pulse point. "Let me introduce myself, my lady. I am Alan Mortimer and this here is-."

Before he could finish, Royce's knife was under the man's chin.

His false smile still in place, Alan released her hand and leaned back from the table.

"Just thought you might want to share," he leered at her.

"No," Royce said his voice clipped and stern. "I do not."

"You don't like to share anymore? What a pity. Ahhh, does Therese know?"

Royce didn't flinch.

"His lady love in Jerusalem," the man gave her a sly look. "Didn't he tell you about her?"

She wanted to smack that smug smile right off of his face and it took all the control she had, not to. She had met people like him before, people who live to make others miserable. They were no different now than they were in her time. He was trying to cause trouble and as much as she didn't want to let it bother her, she couldn't help but wonder about this other woman.

She bit her tongue instead and returned his smirk with a glare of her own.

Alan just chuckled. "She's got spirit this one. I like her. How much for her? I could use a new whore."

At her gasp and Royce's fist pounding on the table, Phillip and Jerold immediately stood. Coming over to their table, they took a seat on either side of the two men crowding them together.

"She's not a whore. She's my wife. Do not dishonor her again or you will have seen your last sunrise."

"Wife? You? Her?" Alan asked in mock disbelief. He looked her over again as though to see her worth. "I don't believe it. You gave up all that for this? Hmph, but if you say so..." Glancing next to him, he paused pretending to have just noticed Royce's men. "Ah, your reinforcements are here...But where's the red-headed fellow? The traitorous one, you know, the bastard son of King Da-."

Once again swords hissed being drawn and, suddenly, there was an eruption. Anna was thrown back while all the men jumped up and began shouting at each other. She backed to the corner, drawing her feet up, trying to make herself as small and inconspicuous as possible.

This was the second time that she'd been in the middle of a fray and it scared the hell out of her. The men were pushing each other and pointing, exclaiming back and forth, throwing out words like bastard and traitor.

Jerold quickly held Alan while Phillip fought to contain the other man. Alan and his friend were obviously outnumbered and didn't really seem to want to fight. Instead, they were taunting Royce, and Lars was trying to push him back.

Finally, Alan pulled free of Phillip and spat at Royce's feet, calling him something in a mangled version of Arabic that Anna didn't understand. Royce obviously did and he fired off his own round, answering Alan in the same tongue. Alan wiped at some blood coming out of his nose, only managing to smear it across his face. His eyes burned with intensity and hatred. Finishing his speech, he picked up his hat and walked out of the room.

Everyone was silent for a moment snatching glances at the men who had caused such a commotion. Lars released Royce, hissing at him to stop in French. Righting the benches, he called behind him in a normal voice for more food.

"That wasn't smart," Lars snarled. "Why do you let him get to you like that?"

"Whoreson." Royce was still staring at the door where the men had exited. "You remember what he did in Lisbon...thirty people...innocent women and children." He spit on the floor before continuing, "The man's a bastard. I should have finished him when I had the chance in Jerusalem."

"He's protected. You know that, as well as I do." Turning, Lars looked at her still form hiding behind a fallen chair and motioned for her to stand. "Anna, come out its safe."

Royce immediately turned following Lars' stare and walked over to her. "Are you alright?"

"Yes, I'm not hurt. What was that all about?"

"Nothing," Lars said quickly, glancing back at Royce before he could say anything. "A man from our past it seems we can't get rid of, an albatross around our neck. Come, eat. We don't have much time now," he finished as Royce pulled her up.

She looked between the two men and their set jaws and narrowed eyes. Whatever was left unsaid she wouldn't find out about now.

The owner of the establishment came over to see what was broken and demanded they leave at once. Lars jingled a purse in front of the man's eyes before pulling out several coins and laying them into the owner's hand. He claimed it was an old feud between two men who fought for the king in the Holy Land. How easily Lars passed the whole thing off. Perhaps, indeed that was all it was. It was amazing how many coats the man wore. He seemed to always be playing a character and she wondered at his true self.

They ate fast, practically shoveling the food in their mouths, all anxious to be off. Denny was waiting for them outside with the horses saddled and ready. She was happy to see she didn't have a horse and would be riding with Royce again. Hopefully that would give him a chance to explain.

CHAPTER 11

"So who's Therese?" Anna tried to keep her voice causal.

Royce made a grunt that sounded more like a laugh.

"It certainly took you long enough, I've been wondering when you would ask."

"I've been working up the courage," she peered back at him over her shoulder. "So now I'm asking, who's Therese?"

"A woman I know."

"That's it? That's all I get? A woman you know in Jerusalem?"

"She was not in Jerusalem, she was my betrothed and I left her in France."

"You're betrothed?" Jealousy flooded her system. Before she could gain control of it, she heard herself squeak out, "You mean a 'to marry' kind of betrothed?"

"Is there another kind?" he asked, raising his brow.

Her mouth dropped open. That hurt.

His eyes narrowed. "It's not what you think."

"I don't think you want to know what I'm thinking," she said, irritation rising up in her.

Turning back to watch the road ahead of them, he cleared his throat. "It was my grandfather's choice, not mine...I never agreed to it. It was done without my knowledge or consent."

His simple reply diffused some of her anger. She digested this information before asking a question she wasn't sure she wanted answered. "Is she really waiting for you?"

"No, you don't need to worry about her."

"Why not?"

"Because it was always you I was going to marry. I came for you," he said intently, his eyes staring at her in a way that made her heart jump.

Heat stole up her face. A shy smile began and grew. His answer surprised her. It was not the answer she had expected, but it was enough, and it pleased her more than she would ever admit. She let the matter drop.

Facing forward again, away from his regard, she tamped down the butterflies that had invaded her stomach. She pretended to study the landscape and tried to get control of the feelings those simple words had induced.

The men had spread out a little. Two were riding behind and the other three were up front somewhere. They were passing through a rather large glen with heavy forest on each side and snuggled in his arms, she was suddenly curious about him in a way she hadn't been before. This man with his few words and gruff countenance made her feel special and more than anything she wanted to know him now.

Once her face cooled, she turned back to him, her wits gathered. "Have you really been in Jerusalem all this time?"

"No, just the last few years," he said, keeping his eyes straight ahead.

"What were you doing there? Fighting for the Crusades?"

"In a manner of speaking."

"Why did you go? I mean, I heard that's where men went to make their fortune. Is that why you went there?"

His eyes came back to her and he studied her face. "It was not a choice."

"You mean you were forced?"

"That's what a vassal does for king and country," he said with a grim smile.

"You know in my time, they are still fighting there. Peace is something they cannot achieve."

"It is a futile war," he agreed.

"But what about before that?" She treaded carefully, not fully wanting to go back to the last time she'd seen him.

But he wouldn't let her avoid it. "You mean after the meadow?"

"Yes." She swallowed hard, her words a whisper, "After the meadow."

Looking back to the road, Royce's eyes swept the area ahead of him, his jaw hardened before answering. "I was taken prisoner, ransomed off to my grandfather. A truer French bastard you have never met," he said with no humor. "When my grandfather got called to support the king, he brought me with him and I finally got my freedom."

"How did you do that...get your freedom, I mean?"

"When we left for Damascus, my grandfather and I got separated on the ships. He went with one army and I with another, not his idea, I imagine. It was the last time I saw him and a better day I'd never imagined in three years."

Clearing his throat, he paused a moment. "A storm blew us off course and we missed the battle completely. Instead, we helped capture Lisbon. I found out months later my grandfather had died in Damascus.

"When I finally returned to France, I discovered he had betrothed me to a spoiled woman well used. I was to have his title, her land and would be granted rights of Okehampton upon our marriage, which is mine by birth anyway.

"I wanted nothing to do with her or her land, titled or not, told her and her father so and left. That's when I came to find you," he finished, looking down at her.

"That is the short story," Anna said slowly. "Somehow I think that's not all of it though."

He smiled. "But it's enough, yes?"

"Yes," she smiled back. "It's enough."

She took a deep breath. They'd left the forest and had come out to a high moor where grazing sheep dotted the landscape. She bit her lip then looked back at him.

"Are you at all curious about me and what's happened to me these last years and where I come from?"

"I know what happened to you and where you come from," he said without pause.

"You do? How could you know?"

"For the first nine years you were a part of my world. For the last nine I've been a part of yours."

"Are you kidding?" Shocked, she stared at him. "What does that mean? What are you talking about?"

"I've seen...I've watched. You were in my dreams. I know you better than you think." His voice rolled out with quiet intensity.

Shivers crept down her spine. "How is that possible?"

"You hid from the world at first." He went on, as if he didn't hear her, his gaze staring straight ahead. "No spring. You hate spring." Sliding his eyes her way again he asked, "Do you remember now why you hate spring?"

She tensed, the quickening beat of her heart pounding in her ears. Closing her eyes, facing forward and gritted her teeth, "I don't want to talk about that again."

"What of Brian?" He pressed, surprising her. "He was a mistake."

She turned around so quickly, she nearly lost her seat. "How do you know about Brian?" she whispered, shocked. "How could you possibly know about Brian," she said shaking her head slowly.

He had been her first serious boyfriend. They had met in college in fencing class. After years of staying away from swords, suddenly she had wanted to try one again and signed up for a class her freshman year, figuring it would be easy credit. Brian had been one of the teaching assistants and recognized her talent immediately.

After two years of chasing her, he had finally talked her into dating as well as going out for the Olympic fencing team her junior year. For some reason she had left practice early one day and discovered him in bed with another woman. After the initial hurt of being betrayed, she had felt relief and been happy to move on.

"Why do you think you went back early that day from practice? You were not tired," he stated, his eyes holding hers in a penetrating stare.

She couldn't breathe. Her chest was so tight it hurt. "Oh my God... are you telling me...how could you know?" she croaked out, tears filling her eyes. "How could you know about that?"

His eyes slid to her face again and his mouth was hard. "You know what I'm saying and you know it's true. If you think on it, you'll remember."

"How...I don't underst—how is that possible." She stuttered. Suddenly feeling panicked, she turned forward, her mind buzzing with his words. But her quick movements and awkward position made the horse shy and Royce had to turn his attention away from her. She grabbed onto the mane as the horse began to dance around bucking her from her position on his withers.

"Put your leg over him and sit still," Royce yelled, rearranging her in front of him. "You're making him nervous."

Still the horse fought, so Royce kicked him forward sending him into an uneven gait across the ridge. She held on, her mind trying to focus on what Royce had said.

Impossible. It was impossible what he was saying and yet, as she thought about it, shivers were running up and down her spine. Every hair on her body was standing on end. Hadn't she told Kate that she felt like she was being watched, like someone was waiting for her?

"Oh God, you have been, haven't you?" she said, realizing it was true.

Royce leaned forward and whispered in her ear, "Just as you've seen me this last year."

"That was you?" Her head swiveled back. "All those deaths. The killings?" she gasped with tears in her eyes.

He held her gaze for a moment, his jaw working and a mask closed over his face. It was like seeing him for the first time.

"More than you know," he gritted out, his voice flat and emotionless, his eyes as closed and dead as she'd ever seen them.

No, she'd seen those eyes before many times...the eyes of the damned...devil eyes...eyes that had haunted her every move. Yes, she knew those eyes very well. Tearing her gaze away, she turned forward and choked back the tears, trying to move herself away from him but he wouldn't allow it.

He kicked his horse harder sending her back into him and held her there tightly. He had to know she was struggling to get away and for the first time since she came here, she felt the familiar terror of her dreams rise up.

What in the world had she happened into? Maybe she was in hell and he was the devil, charming her one moment at a time, drawing her in further and further until it was too late.

A few of the men had ridden ahead and set up camp by a small stream well away from any village. By the time Royce and Anna joined them dinner was already caught and roasting on a spit, the smell hung in the air making her stomach queasy.

They had not said a word to each other the rest of the day. Anna had used up all her strength trying to keep herself upright and away from him so that she wouldn't have to endure his touch. She didn't know if she was more troubled by the thought of him somehow watching her all these years or the fact that it was him haunting her dreams since her father died.

Those nightmares had practically destroyed her. As much as she didn't want it to be him, she couldn't deny it...it was him, all of the dreams...him.

They had to be.

The boy that she'd grown up loving had turned into a monster she had come to hate.

The evening passed quietly, few words were spoken. Even Lars seemed to have nothing to say. She sat as far away from Royce as possible without being obvious.

His face was a careful mask, but his eyes were another matter. They followed her every move and the few times their gazes had caught, something deeper had shone in his, something she hadn't seen before, the troubled look of someone who had suffered great pain and loss. It was a look she knew well, a look she had worn herself these past years. And try as she might, it couldn't help but affect her. One way or another, this wasn't over between them.

When the meal was done, he stood and put his hand out for her, motioning for her to come. When she didn't move, he blew out heavily and came at her with determination. She scooted away from him and started off in a different direction. Without pause, he grabbed her by the arm and pulled her away from the light of the campfire and far enough from the men so they couldn't hear.

"Obviously this conversation isn't done yet." He released her and put his hands on his hips.

She rubbed at her arm and turned to face the other way.

"Anna...talk to me."

"I can't right now."

"Why?" The one word was hard and clipped and demanded an answer.

"Because of what you are, because of what you said and because of what you did..."

"What did I do that offends you so?" he asked harshly.

"You are a murderer." Disbelief that he could even ask that filled her voice as she rounded on him. "You are a thief. You have practically ruined my life this last year. I don't know how you did it and I don't think I want to, but I can't look at you, let alone be with you...now or ever."

"I offended you? By what? Staying alive?" His voice was as angry as hers. "Look at me Anna," he pleaded. "Look at me."

Raising her eyes to his face, she stared at him bitterly, trying not to let her warring emotions show in her expression. He was standing there with his hands on his hips, his form stiff, and yet even in the dying light she could see the strain on his face.

"When they took me that day, I wanted to die, but I didn't. The only thing..." His voice cracked with emotion. "The *only* thing that kept me alive these last years was your image I had when I laid down at night to sleep." He paused and his words become choked. "I couldn't talk to you...I couldn't touch you...but I could see you and sometimes, you seemed to know my thoughts.

"I don't know how. I can't explain it, any more than I can explain any of this. But that was all I had and that was enough...it had to be... and as for killing? Yes, I've done murder...more than you could ever imagine and you have no idea what that does to a man's soul." His eyes were bright with unshed tears. Swallowing hard, he began to shake his head. "You are my salvation...Everything I did...I did to get back to you."

For a heartbeat they stared at each other, the echo of his words washing over her. Their meaning soaked in and penetrated the numb haze she'd used to protect herself these last years.

Tears filled her eyes and she took a step towards him wanting to believe and start over, but a voice called out in warning and the sudden sounds of fighting nearby caught them both off guard.

Instantly, Royce became the soldier automatically reaching for his sword. The mood was broken and the moment forgotten, they turned and began running back to the campsite. He grabbed her hand and pulled her along behind him, ducking behind the trees until he got a better view.

"Stay here," he whispered. Pushing her down behind some boulders, he ran off into the darkness.

All around her the sounds of battle raged. It seemed as if, suddenly they were surrounded by an army. Off to her right a man came close and paused spotting her.

She turned and started to run but was quickly caught. A hand clapped over her mouth. "It's Jerold, my lady," he whispered in her ear. "Shhh, we must get you away,"

"But what of Royce?"

"He'll meet up with us." Jerold took her by the elbow. "You must come," he gave her arm a tug. "Hurry...to the horses."

Skirting just outside the light of the fire she caught a glimpse of

Royce and Lars fighting. Philippe lay off to the side and by the angle of his body, no doubt he was dead. There was no sign of Robert or Denny anywhere. Royce and Lars were outnumbered two to one. Reaching the agitated horses, Jerold let go of her arm long enough to release the reins of one. Again, she was grabbed from behind and the shriek she let out alerted Jerold, who came around with his sword and severed a man's hand clean off.

The man fell back screaming under the nervous mare's rear hooves. The animal fought the bridle as Jerold pulled Anna forward.

Out of the corner of her eye she saw Robert running towards them. Jerold had to of seen him too, but he didn't stop. He threw her up and handed her the reins.

"Ride as hard and fast as you can, my lady." He shouted up to her.

Stepping back, he released the bridle to give the horse a smack, but Robert had come in front of them blocking her escape.

When Jerold turned, Robert plunged his sword deep into Jerold's belly and grabbed hold of the reins, ripping them from her hands.

Jerold fell to his knees. Instinctively, she jumped down trying to help Jerold but Robert took hold of her arm before she could and jerked her out of the way.

Robert put one foot on Jerold's chest and shoved him back releasing the sword from his body. Blood poured forth soaking his tunic and began pooling on the ground.

"Jerold," she cried out in disbelief.

Briefly his eyes flicked to her. "Jerold was my father's name," he choked out. "I'm sorry, my lady, for not protecting you better." Returning his gaze to Robert, blood bubbled from his mouth as he spoke, "I knew you couldn't be trusted."

Without warning Robert's sword swung out in an arc, neatly opening the man's neck. Jerold fell back, arms wide, eyes unseeing as the blood soaked her feet.

She didn't even realize she was screaming until Robert shook her hard.

"Shut your mouth," he yelled, pulling her forward and holding her in front of him so Royce could see them. "That's enough," he roared, putting the blood-soaked sword up to her neck. "Put down your weapon or I swear on your mother's grave I'll finish her just as I did your uncle."

Royce stopped in his tracks, his chest heaving with effort. In a haze, she watched Robert as he held her at arm's length, the edge of his sword thrust up under her chin. She knew she was cut. She could feel the welling drops of blood trailing down her neck to her bodice, but she didn't care.

All she could concentrate on was the man's face holding her. With the hood of his chain mail up and his hair swept off his face the resemblance between him and Royce was uncanny.

He was an older version of Royce and she was surprised she hadn't noticed it before. The difference was the cruelty that lined his mouth and the way his dark eyes glittered with malice.

Royce took a step towards them, his face a mask of disbelief.

"Don't do it," Robert yelled and then shook her, opening a larger cut on her neck. She gasped in pain bringing Royce to a stop. He stared between the two of them as if unable to believe he'd been conned by a man he had trusted. Fury like she had never seen before filled his face and for the first time she recognized true rage.

"What the hell are you doing, Robert?" Lars yelled from the other side. Anger written clearly in his profile, he walked towards Robert before another man hit him on the back of the head and his body crumpled to the ground.

Royce made a move to help him but Robert pressed the sword deeper into her skin.

"I'll kill her. I'll cut her pretty little neck if you take one more step."

Hate blazed from his eyes as Royce let his sword fall to the ground. Instantly, the men waiting behind jumped him, kicking and hitting him until Robert finally gave the signal to stop.

Her vision was fading, she grew cold all over and wasn't sure if it was from shock or the loss of blood. All the men's words began to sound far away and she couldn't understand what all the shouting was about.

When Robert shook her one more time and she felt the sword cut even deeper into her neck she thought for sure this was it. It became painful to breathe, light burst in her head and then everything faded to black.

CHAPTER

12

Sunlight filtered through the trees above. Anna blinked and tried to sit up. Pain shot through her neck. She was on a horse being held uncomfortably by the man behind her. With a clumsy hand she fingered the heavy bandage covering her wound.

"Welcome back, my lady," said next to her.

"Robert?" she asked, her voice a coarse whisper.

He was riding next to her, still in his blood-soaked tunic. So last night had happened... She hadn't been sure. He looked foggy and sounded as though he was talking to her through a long tunnel. Her body felt thick and rubbery. She strained to focus on him.

"You remember. It's the first time I think you've said my name."

"Where's Royce?" she managed.

"You sound terrible, didn't you sleep well? Didn't my good man take tender care of your sleeping form or was he too rough?" Robert mocked before answering her question. "Don't worry. He's back there. In worse shape than you, I imagine."

"Why?" she couldn't stop herself from asking.

"Why what? Why is he in worse shape than you, or why would

I do this?" But instead of waiting on her reply, he just smiled and continued in his sarcastic voice. "Quite the charming little conversation you seemed to be having last night. Too bad you were interrupted, but it couldn't be helped. It looks like you were about to make up."

He tilted his head and sneered, "Such a shame we had to disturb that lovely, heartfelt scene."

She was fading in and out and everything seemed surreal. When the horses' hooves echoed on wooden planks she opened her eyes. Stone walls reared above her blocking out the sun. A large metal and wooden gate came into view and then the sun again. She tried to speak but her throat hurt too badly and every time she did it sounded like a croak.

They came into a large courtyard where a man in a heavy red robe was waiting for them. Blackness crept around the edges of her vision. She put her head back trying to stop the dizzy waves that were making it hard to concentrate.

"Ah, ah, ah, Princess, no more sleeping. It's time for you to wake up," Robert said beside her.

The man holding her shifted sending shock waves of pain down her neck. She jerked upward trying to cover her wound and protect herself. The horse had stopped and she was passed down into Robert's arms. He gave her a shake setting her teeth on edge. She opened her eyes and gave him her best glare.

"That's better. I wouldn't want you to sleep through this," Robert gloated.

Somebody came forward and tied her hands in front of her and then loosely put a gag in her mouth. Not that she would have needed it. She was in too much pain to talk.

"We don't want you spoiling the moment, now do we?" Robert threatened in her ear. He greeted the man waiting near the door.

"My lord, I have brought you a gift." Robert bowed his head respectfully.

"A gift? Fun. I do love a good gift." The red robed man came forward and waved a hand disdainfully in front of her. "Not just her, I hope."

"No, my lord, I have Lord Sutton and Sir Thomas Carrick of Hampshire."

"What of Ramsey? I asked you to bring him to me. He's the one I need. These others are just pawns."

"My lord," Robert bowed his head. "He escaped in Fowey. I had hoped he would meet up with them in Barri, but he didn't show. I have men working on it."

"Who?" the man barked sharply.

"Mortimer and Fitzborn, sir. They've gone north to secure the other ports. He won't escape again."

The man in the heavy red robe hesitated. "Good, bring him to me when you find him. He's important. Without him none of this will work. Sutton will do for now to appease the king, and maybe Thomas too. We'll have to see what we can make on the grounds of treason."

Anna perked up as he walked to the back.

"Greetings, Lord Sutton," he addressed Royce. "Always such a pleasure to see you. I'm sorry it is under these circumstances. I did warn you, however, about coming back to these shores, didn't I? That is unless you had, of course, married that French bitch. Then we could have allowed it. But with all this," he waved his hands around. "These... treasonous acts, against your liege king? You know, you really are a horrible, little thief. Trying again to take my land and title right out from under me."

"It's not your land," Royce said. "You stole it from my uncle. It's my land and I'm here to get it back."

"Really, all this about a silly little piece in Cornwall. Not that I need it you see, but still, I can't have it...all this discord...First your uncle and now you. Well, that's quite impossible now. The Duke of Anjou will never govern here. We'll see to that."

"King Stephen has already declared it. He has promised him the crown," Royce ground out. "There is truce between them."

"You know as well as I do that will never happen. What with Scotland and the resurrection, broken promises...tsk, tsk, tsk, that bastard son of his out to save his brother's crown-working against us. You men don't know when to stop, do you?"

"You are one man against many. Prince Henry will rule England and with King David you will be outnumbered."

"On the contrary, that will never happen because little Gordy won't reach his father and brother in time and you, my dear man, will be tried in London by the end of the month."

"For what?"

"For crimes against the crown, of course. You know we found numerous letters in your possession, implicating you and your merry band." Snapping his fingers, a man stepped forward and handed him a dozen or so letters tied together. Louvain shook them in front of Royce's face. "Tsk, tsk, tsk. The king will be *so* disappointed in you, conspiring not only against him, but Prince Henry too, and all for your own gain. Here he thought to trust you with such important information."

"You bloody bastard," Royce growled. "They'll never believe it."

"But they will. Such a pity you turned. What did they say...like a brother to the prince, saving his life and all? Is that how you earned your spurs? On the field of honor? How very dramatic. Your grandfather certainly would never have let you have them.

"That was a mistake to let you live. If I'd known those fools were going to sell you back to France, I would have slit your throat myself. But see, isn't it funny how life works out. In letting you live, your tiny, little, insignificant life will now have a purpose."

Laughing at his own words he continued, "You, the simple son of a knight, nephew to a Baron in Somerset, the middle of bloody nowhere, Cornwall...and here you have risen to title. Amazing, isn't it, what a man can become in today's age? Hard to keep the peasants out, don't you think, Robert?

"But what strikes me as funny is we would all be bowing to you if you had married that French bitch."

Coming to stand in front of Royce again, Anna could see the back of Louvain gesturing towards her.

"Which brings me back to the rest of my present...I heard you married, Sutton."

Royce's eyes flicked forward to her frame and she made a small noise hopping to let him know that she was alright.

"Leave her alone," Royce gritted out, moving towards her. He barely got two steps before one of the guards came up from behind and hit him in the back of his head with the flat of the sword. Royce dropped to his knees.

She struggled in Robert's arms trying to get down, but he simply squeezed her tighter and gave her a shake sending little stars dancing behind her eyes. Already exhausted, by the time he was done she was near to fainting again.

An amused smile crossed Louvain's face. He frowned at her trussed-up form. "Looks like we will need some lessons in manners, eh, my lady?"

Turning back to Royce he said with false cheer, "What was I saying? Oh, yes, now what kind of host would I be if I left her all alone? I'm sure she is scared and needs...comfort."

He paused in his words and studied her. "In fact, I think I was mistaken. She looks like quite a beauty under all that dirt." Louvain smiled slyly. "We shall have to get her washed up and take a better look at her, hadn't we, Robert."

Robert chuckled.

He stepped closer and pushed her hair out of the way. He fingered the bloody bandage around her neck. "What happened, my dear? You look injured." Glancing at Robert, Louvain asked sternly, "Did you injure my present?"

"My lord," Robert replied nervously. "It was necessary to get Sutton to stop,"

"Well, how badly did you injure her?" Louvain continued. "She looks awfully pale."

He snapped his fingers in her face, bringing her focus from Royce.

"Don't look at him, my dear." Louvain held her gaze. "He's a dead man."

With a flick of his robe and an evil smile Louvain turned away, calling to the rest of his men before going inside. "Lock them up and bring her upstairs. See to her needs before we lose her."

Panic flooded her veins as she watched Royce being dragged away. Just before she lost view of him the reality of the situation hit her and she began fighting in earnest. Ignoring the pain in her neck, she spit out the gag, calling to Royce.

The thought of not seeing him again made her crazy. She needed to tell him that she was wrong last night, she hadn't meant it.

She had felt like she had stopped breathing when Robert and Louvain had started talking. The thickness in her brain had evaporated and all her focus had been on them and trying to hear what was being said. In the back of her mind, she kept trying to control the whole situation as one would in the middle of a nightmare, hoping it would somehow, magically, end without trouble.

A last burst of energy surged through her. She pushed out of Robert's arms to go to Royce. She barely got three steps before she was grabbed, but still she fought kicking and biting any who came in range. With satisfaction she noted that one guard had caught a kick to the groin and doubled over in agony. The man who she was biting started to howl when she drew blood. Still, she didn't let go and the salty taste fueled her anger more until something hit her on the back of the head making her knees give way and the ground come up to meet her.

Coming too, Anna tried to move and winced. Stars burst behind her eyes. She put her hand up to her head, gingerly feeling the wet sticky bump on the back of her skull.

The day's events replayed in her mind. It took a moment to identify the metallic taste in her mouth—blood…probably from that soldier she had bitten. She needed water. She tried to sit up but cool firm hands pushed her back down.

"Royce," she murmured.

"Easy…easy, my lady. We'll not 'urt you."

"Where am I?" She opened her eyes and let her vision clear. Dread set her heart to racing as she looked around her. "This room…what is this room?"

"Don't worries about that now dear," the gentle voice continued talking to somebody else. "Take 'er dress off. Och, where's the blood coming from?"

"I think it's 'er head, but it could be 'er neck. I'm not sure..."

"Those brutes. They don't know when to stop, do they? Practically killed 'er."

"Better for 'er, if that be the case...better for us too."

"Not for us to decide. Besides he said to fix 'er and we 'ave no choice. Quick like, get the basket."

"What do you want in it?"

"We'll start with bathing 'er body. Bring some cool water. She's 'otter than blazes and let's get some salve on these cuts quick like and then...och, there she goes...it's better dear, sleep."

Anna slept, blessed sleep. She drifted in and out, waking only when forced by one of the two women taking care of her.

Snippets of conversation intruded on her consciousness, altering the path of her dreams. Sometimes she felt like she was floating above the room looking down on her inert body and watching people enter and leave.

Her dreams were hard to distinguish between what really happened in her life and what happened with Royce. Vivid dreams, snapshots of her family in happier times, her sister, her grandparents and Royce. Happy moments interspersed with her nightmares and deluged her mind. Faces became clear, puzzles connected and questions got answered while her body healed. The longer she slept the quicker they came, one memory after another, but it was the last dream that finally woke her.

It began with Audrey telling her who she was going to marry before blending with talking to their father. And then Royce...everything Royce-his life, his love, his battles...all overlapping, all coming together, all preparing her for what lay ahead.

"Do you see the boy?" Audrey asked, pushing her long blond hair behind her ears.

"What boy?" She stood, abandoning the little creek that wound its way through the edge of the meadow.

"Over there." Audrey pointed, "At the edge of the woods."

"I don't see anybody." She went to stand next to her sister, wiping her dirty hands on her smock. "Where are you looking?"

"Right there...he's right there." Then calling out to the invisible child, Audrey offered an invitation. "Do you want to come and play?"

Anna got up on her tiptoes and looked. Her big sister must be right. She never lied to her.

"Okay," Audrey called out and waved as if she was talking to someone. Then she turned back to her and took her hand to lead her home. "You're filthy. Grandmother will be angry. She told you not to get this smock dirty."

"But the frogs are out, baby ones and I want one."

"Forget about the frogs. We must go. Grandmother will worry."

"What of the boy?" She stopped to look back.

"Oh, he's gone. He had to go. He swore he's going to marry you one day," Audrey replied as she faded away, her voice still ringing in Anna's ears. "He's going to marry you one day..."

The scene changed and she was back in the meadow on one of her many walks she used to take with her father. "Trust your instincts, Anna," he told her and it echoed in her mind when she became a teen sitting in the movie theater with friends.

A moment later, she was a little girl again romping through her field all alone until she heard someone coming. She crouched in the tall grass and waited to be discovered. Skinny arms and bare knees topped off with an unruly mop of black hair the boy came towards her swinging a stick like a sword. He froze dead in his tracks when he saw her.

"Who are you?" he asked, more curious than alarmed.

"Anna," she replied." She picked a yellow wildflower and spun it under her chin. "Who are you?"

"I'm Royce." His face screwed up in question. "How old are you?"

"I'm four. How old are you?"

"I'm seven, well, I will be soon." He puffed out his thin chest and squinted. Dark serious eyes studied the landscape. "Where do you live?"

"Over there somewhere." She stood and dusted off her hands on her white nightdress. "I'm not sure really. We just moved here and it looks the same, but it's different. I went to sleep and woke up here." Shrugging her shoulders dramatically, she threw out her hands and giggled. "I guess I'm lost."

He regarded her with a puzzled expression before breaking into a wide smile. Suddenly he reached out and tagged her yelling. "No, Anna, you are found," then sprinted away watching over his shoulder as she followed.

Their laughter floated up to the clouds only to come down again to a few years later to when they would sit and talk, exchanging lessons in French and Spanish. Each more determined to show up the other with their knowledge and range of the different languages.

His voice deepened again. He changed into a tall, gangly teenager smiling down at her as she lay back on a blanket of cherry blossoms.

"You are found, Anna," he whispered.

He bent to kiss her and his face aged into the man she knew now and he was holding out his hand to her.

"You are found, Anna," he kept repeating. "You are found."

She put her hand in his and he was gone, and she was falling. Her heart dropped into her stomach, his voice echoing in her head.

"Now you must wake. It's time to wake."

Anna's eyes popped open. She sat up straight gasping for air. She put her hands to her head, breathing deeply at the realty of her dreams and tried to calm her racing pulse. There had been so many of them. Holding herself upright, she waited for her eyes to focus, letting the last of the dream fade from her mind.

It had all been so real.

As her vision adjusted she gazed around the room and her heart plummeted. She remembered where she was and how she got here. Lying back down, she closed her eyes and then snapped them back open seeing the chains swaying above her head.

There were four of them, moving slowly back and forth in the breeze.

Are those handcuffs? Squinting in the soft, early morning light she stared in disbelief. The chain over to the left ended in a pair of manacles and made soft clinking noises from the wind that blew in through the open window.

Her hands gripped the bed coverings instantly noting their softness. She hadn't felt anything like this in months. It felt like silk. She took a better look. It was silk, red silk in fact, with heavy tassels and beading. Thick roping was attached to both the head and the footboard.

Her gaze fell to the side and the pillows lumped up next to her on the large bed. It was definitely the biggest bed she'd seen yet in this time and the most extravagant, covered with silk pillows and velvet hangings, all in different shades of red. There was a thick rug on the floor in front of the fireplace and a few chairs were spaced around the room with large pillows grouped on the floor. At the other end was a huge dresser. Its doors were opened wide to show off all manner of gowns in a dazzling array of color. On a long table there was an ewer and a basin with a comb next to it. What looked to be a hand mirror and little pots and jars were scattered around.

She had never seen anything like it and it sent a chill down her spine. This was a room of passion.

Her jaw set. Instead of fear, she got mad. Anger settled in her gut when she figured out why she had been put in this room. This was not a lady's room in any sense of the word. No, this was where one kept a prisoner...a sexual prisoner.

"Shit," she muttered. "How are you going to get yourself out of this one, Anna?"

CHAPTER 13

Anna spent the morning testing her body and exploring the room. She felt better than she had in weeks. The bump on the back of her head was still there and sensitive, but the cut on her neck didn't hurt anymore.

Her dreams were once again with her, but now she felt a better understanding of what had happened and why she was here. She was able to identify many of the faces that had been blurry before.

Since coming back to Royce, she would look at a person and images of their life would flash through her mind. She hadn't understood or paid much attention, most of her focus still being on Royce. Now the images together made up the puzzle she was trying to solve. She was surprised at how clearheaded and strong she felt.

A few hours later, the lock turned and she hurried back to bed, drawing the covers up to her chin. Two women came in and when they saw her up, the older one sent the younger out.

"Tell his lordship she has awoken."

Coming over the old woman looked at her with a keen eye. "So you're up. It's about time. If it twern't for your color I would have given up sooner, but his lordship's entranced. Wanted to make sure you lived. Don't think that's a good thing though, probably better if you died."

Ignoring that comment, she cleared her throat to speak.

"Wha-what of my husband?" She croaked. "Do you have word of my husband?"

The old woman went to the door and peered out before closing it. She put her finger to her mouth and whispered, "You best not talk of him. He's soon to hang. My lady the queen is here and she wants him sent to London for a hanging. Lord Louvain isn't ready to give him up yet." Shaking her head, she mumbled to herself as she walked away. "Better to hang, than what he has in store. Say your prayers for him, madam. The man's a monster."

"Who? Who is a monster?"

The women's head swiveled back and wise old eyes regarded her with pity. "Lord Louvain, Mistress, better to hang." Then pointing at Anna, she went on, "Better you didn't recover."

They contemplated each other for a few minutes before the women took another big sigh and got to business. "But you're up. Knew yesterday you were going to survive. Ye quit your babbling and your fever broke in the night...ate quite a bit. Do you remember?"

"No," she shook her head. "Not really."

"Hmph, well you did seem foggy. Your eyes were all glazed. Sometimes that happens..." The old woman hesitated before asking, "Ye had the dreams, didn't ye?"

Startled, Anna gave her a sharp look. "What dreams?"

"Ye know what I'm talking about."

Her face grew warm but she refused to admit anything.

The old woman nodded and said assuredly, "Ye had the dreams. That's good. They'll tell you the answer's if'un you pay attention." Holding up her finger she shook it at Anna, her gaze intense. "But you must pay attention. Did you pay attention?"

Compelled to answer, she nodded.

The woman stared at her a little longer then turned away. Shaking her head, she mumbled about giving her too much of something for it to work. Grabbing up the little hand mirror, she came back to the bed.

"Too late now anyway. I did the best that I could for ye. Now there's no going back. Your color's good and the cut on your neck weren't near as bad as I thought. The bump on your head bled a bit and some scrapes here and there, but my potions worked and took care of them," she declared moving forward to check Anna over. Removing the bandage on her neck, she handed her the mirror.

The long thin red scar was ugly, but the skin had knitted together quite nicely and looked to be healing well.

"I feel so much better...clearheaded."

The old woman studied her for a moment. "Hmph," she mumbled. "Yes..." her voice was drawn out. "Sorry about that."

"About what?"

Shrugging thin shoulders, the woman looked down at whatever she was mixing in a cup and then handed it to her, motioning for her to drink. "I gave you something, to help you heal quick, but it makes the mind clear."

Anna stopped drinking to stare over the earthenware rim at her, but the woman gently pushed the cup up, forcing her to swallow the remains. The taste was sweet, but now she was worried about what was in it, and before the woman took it away, she looked at the dark remains in the bottom.

The old woman laughed at her expression. "That weren't nothen but tea and honey. Thickens the blood and helps your strength." Then she sobered again, turning away. "But as I was saying, the lord was afraid of losing you. Told me you weren't to die or it'd be me with my neck in a noose. So I gave you something...not the best thing for a young girl in your situation."

"What was it?" she asked, getting out of bed.

"Can't tell you that, dearie. It's a secret." The old woman cackled, holding a finger up against her lips, and then directed her to the curtain. "But you best get behind those curtains and through the door to the tub while the water is still hot. We have much to do and little time. Quick like...so we can get ye dressed before he comes. Don't' want to encourage him too soon now do we, mistress."

An hour later Anna was standing in the middle of the room trying to pull up the dress she had on.

"This doesn't feel right. It's too tight and way too low. My God, my nipples are showing."

The woman left her hair and came around the front to examine her. "Yes, they are, but that's the way he likes his women," she said simply.

"His women? Christ, I look like a whore. Is that what I'm supposed to be?"

"Now, I'm not religious like some of the folk around here, but you keep talking with that mouth and you'll get yourself burned as a heretic...not that it would be worse than what he has in store for you," she muttered under her breath before finishing in a normal tone. "I'll not tell, but I wouldn't say something like that again."

"Fine." Her mouth flattened into a hard line. "But answer the question. What exactly am I here for?"

The woman looked at her with pity, "You already know that, dearie."

A small scratch at the door sent the old hag into a flurry. Quickly, she finished, pinning up Anna's hair and called out for them to enter. When she saw that it was only one of the lads who came in to remove the bath water she scolded him mercilessly.

"You's supposed to call out. I'm trying to get his lady ready and you made me muss up her hair. Next time I'll tell him you're the problem. I'll not get whipped for your insolence."

The boy kept his head down, pulling on a lock of hair respectfully as he went by. But on his way out the door he peaked up at Anna, throwing her off guard completely. She could do nothing but stare. He winked at her and then looked at the old woman's back before tucking his face down into his collar again and shutting the door.

It was Denny.

Anna didn't have long to wait. The woman had just finished putting the room to rights when the door opened and Robert came in. He was clean shaven and well dressed in a muted tunic with a simple shirt underneath and dark leggings. He was a handsome man and once again the similarities between him and Royce amazed her. How could she not have noticed before?

The old woman looked up surprised and went to stand in front of Anna protectively.

"You may go," Robert stated. He stood beside the door staring at her with his hands on his hips.

"But, my lord. Lord Louvain is to come. He said-."

"He's busy with the queen. He'll come later tonight. I want to talk to her first."

The old woman stammered and hesitated.

"Out," he snarled and started over to the poor woman, raising his hand to strike her.

She hunched down and ran from the room, throwing back a look of caution at Anna.

Following her, he shut the door with a slam and then turned slowly, leaning back against the wall. His eyes were hot with lust as he took in her appearance.

"Hello Princess." His voice was quiet, his smile sardonic. He chuckled to himself as he pushed off the door and began walking towards her, "It's just that right now you don't look too much like a princess."

With her chin up, she faced him.

"I know what I look like."

"Do you now?" Stopping in front of her, he ran a fingertip along her jaw. "Tell me then...what do you look like?" he said in a low whisper.

"Like a whore," she responded, a challenge in her eyes.

"Yes." He laughed. "You do...like a whore. It looks like your neck has healed." His finger tipped up her chin and he pulled down the piece of lace the old woman had tied there.

"Get your filthy hands off me, you lying scum." She smacked his hand away.

Surprised, he stepped back before laughter lifted his face again. "You are a fresh piece. I envy Louvain tonight. Are you sure you don't want to have a go with me? I could get you ready for him." He stepped forward, sure of himself.

But she didn't back down. "I know who you are."

"Of course, you do," he answered, still amused at her show of bravery.

"No. I know *who* you are and *what* you did."

"What did I do?" he asked his cold eyes revealing little.

"You were the one who betrayed Royce's uncle. It was your idea to sell Royce to his grandfather and your idea to send Royce to Damascus. But your little plan didn't work, did it? His grandfather grew to respect him, even providing for him in his will."

The smirk froze on his face.

"By the time you caught up to him again he was a favorite of the Duke's and untouchable. How many times did your sword almost find its mark? Two? Three? All the while calling yourself friend...you didn't save his life. You tried to end it. As his brother, don't you think you should have a care?"

He blew out of his nose, as a calculating look came into his eyes. "Now how would you know that? Hmmm? Royce didn't tell you, did he? Our names are not the same. We didn't grow up together. We never even met 'til the Crusades...we just discovered it months ago. In fact, nobody else knows."

"You knew. You've known all along."

He smiled again, his eyes narrowing, searching her face. "Yes, I've always known, but the question is, how could you, my lady? How could you have possibly known?"

"You look exactly alike."

"Not really. Actually, not at all except for maybe our size." He took one step at a time advancing on her, his hands behind his back. "One man looks much like the other, don't you think?"

"No. Your faces are similar. Your eyes, even your manner."

"Our face? Not at all. As for our manner, well, I shall have to work on that, but you only just discovered, eh? And as for our eyes, hmm... that is interesting. Now I think we look nothing alike, his eyes are brown mine are blue."

"They're not blue. They're a muddy hazel and have none of the true beauty of Royce's."

"Try again, my lady." Laughing, Robert shook his head. "Or should I call you...white lady." He paused, letting his comment sink in before continuing. Shaking his finger at her he said, "I know you too, my white lady." He smiled at her surprise. "Oh, yes, I recognized you at once. So the prophecy is true. You've come to help the rightful monarch assume the throne. I could barely believe my luck that night you came down to the beach. Finally, the woman in the flesh."

When she didn't speak he advanced again.

"I saw you, you know. A myth, they said, surrounding my brother. If we were to win you would appear calling to my brother. Do you have any idea what you did for the men my...white...lady? Once you were spotted running among the people the men would go into a frenzy."

He paused before emphasizing his next words, "A *killing* frenzy. After a while, it didn't matter whether you appeared or not. The men felt lucky just to be led by Royce...can you imagine that?" He shook his head. "No matter how hard I tried, I could never get to you first."

His face turned dark and threatening. "You were supposed to be *my* white lady...*my* talisman. But, instead, you came to my brother, my *half*-brother...the one who's gotten everything, including our father's love, while I was swept under the carpet and left to rot with the happy title of bastard painted on my back." His voice lowered again and the smile reappeared. "I got tired of waiting. Now you're going to help me."

Here she thought her news would surprise him, but instead he had surprised her...again.

"You're wrong. I can't help you." She continued backing up. "I'm not who you think I am."

"Oh, but you are, my lady...my...white...lady." He came up to her as her back hit the wall. "Trapped, my dear? Are you comfortable?" His hands moved up to either side of her head, blocking her escape. "We're going to get very comfortable, you and me. But Louvain, unfortunately, has you first. You know when you make a deal with the devil..." He smiled again, all charm, his eyes on her lips. "But then I'll get my turn. Hopefully, he won't use you too badly."

"I'm not afraid of you," she bit out, using the last of her bravado.

Once again, he smiled and his eyelids lowered. Leaning into her, he pressed her back against the wall. His mouth found her ear and blew into it before whispering, "You should be."

CHAPTER 14

"Are ye sure yer alright?"

The old woman had stolen in again minutes after Robert left. Casting an eye up and down her form, she checked her wounds. "At least you're not bleeding again. I've sent for Louvain and he wouldn't like that."

Throwing an evil look over her shoulder, she went on, "That Lord is troublesome." Shaking her head, she glared at the door, tsking under her breath. "Already beaten two of the downstairs maids, not as bad as Lo-." She frowned and would not meet Anna's eyes. With a grimace she finished, "Well, just not as bad."

Another maid brought in food and drink and the old woman ushered Anna over to the table urging her to eat.

"Best to keep up your strength."

She knew the woman was right. She did need to eat. She choked down the soup and was half finished with the bread when Louvain came in.

She narrowed her eyes and swallowed the piece of bread in her mouth lest she choke on it. Trying as hard as she could, she kept her expression as neutral as possible. Her gut told her this man fed off fear and that might be an advantage she could use later.

With a nod of his head, the old woman picked up the tray and scurried out, bowing low, leaving Anna alone with him. As much as she didn't want it to, her heart fluttered in her breast and her mouth went dry as he approached.

"Ahhh, my dear," he said pleasantly. "They told me you had awoken from your nap." Giving her a thin smile exposing his brown, crooked teeth, he stopped right in front of her.

Time had taken its toll on the man. He was tall, a few inches taller than she was, with thin brown hair, a bulbous nose and an unpleasant smile. He wore a long blue robe trimmed in gold with a simple jeweled belt. The robe almost hit the floor and swirled around his shod feet as he walked.

She stiffened on her seat, trying to ignore his beady eyes. They traveled over her, taking in everything about her appearance. He waited, just staring down at her until she got up the nerve and finally looked back. His hands were folded in front of him, long fingernails almost like a woman's, graced lily-white hands.

Seeing her glance, he smiled again and brought his hands up to her face for her to examine, slowly turning them over, back and forth.

"Aren't they perfect? The perfect instruments to give pleasure...and pain." His smile turned evil.

Her heart plummeted. This guy was crazy.

He walked over to the bed and began to pull on the roping attached to the headboards. He gave each a savage tug before he turned and looked back at her, snaking one hand down to rub against his rising evidence of excitement.

Reaching down under the bed, he pulled out a long, dirty chain that looked to be stained with blood. On one end of it was a collar. Large and cumbersome, it was fitted with a lock and had two smaller manacles attached to it.

"Am I going to have to use this? Oh, I do hope so," he continued with that same foul smile.

Her mouth fell open and all warmth drained from her face, causing him to laugh in delight.

"Mmmmm, you are going to be fun. I can feel it," he said with satisfaction.

She started to shake. She couldn't help it. He scared the hell out of her.

"But not too soon," he laughed at her expression. "I wouldn't want to ruin my entertainment. Of course, I had you examined, when they brought you here. It really would have been so much better if you had been awake, you know. I love that moment when women realize what is about to happen to them," he looked up with a faraway smile and an expression of excitement lit his face.

Shaking himself out of his memory, he turned back to her. "It was so impolite of you to fight like that, before the fun even began. It's much better once they get you in here and my doctor examines you." Clapping his hands together, he continued, "Oh, the struggles, hips pumping as my men hold you down and the doctor pulls up your skirt. I was excited for that.

"But you went and ruined it. My men had to knock you out. Now was that really necessary? Hmmm?" He shook his head at her and waved a finger in her face as a parent would to a naughty child.

Putting his hands on his hips, he moved towards her. The smile left his face and was replaced with a deep frown. "Don't do it again." His voice deepened and rang with a seriousness that made her blood run cold.

Grabbing her chin in his hands, he forced her to stand. She wanted to look anywhere but into his watery blue eyes, but his hold on her chin tightened and kept her focus on him.

"Every time you struggle against me or my men, Royce suffers for it. I can be kind, even in my cruelty. What you and Royce receive from me will all depend on your actions. Do you understand?"

He raised his eyebrows at her and she nodded yes. Seeming satisfied, the evil smirk came over his face again. "Let's test it, then," he whispered as his other hand reached up and yanked her bodice down.

She cried out as the material gave way, ripping clear to her waist, exposing one breast. Her natural reaction was to cower and try and hide herself, which only delighted him more.

Tears stung her eyes as he continued holding her chin cruelly in his grip. His face grew rapt watching her. Slowly, his gaze drifted down to her exposed chest. His other hand came up and cupped her breast, squeezing it tightly. Still holding her chin up, he bent and fastened his mouth on her nipple. She arched towards him in pain when he bit down. Her hands came up to his shoulders to push him away, but he pulled his mouth back just enough to speak.

"Ah, ah, ah, no struggling or I'll start with cutting off his fingers."

Gasping, she stopped immediately and let her hands drop to her sides, biting her lip to hold back the cry. Her tears fell freely, running down onto his hand holding her chin. Pulling back suddenly, he straightened as if surprised.

"Such a waste, my dear," he said releasing her breast. He ran one finger up her face to gather her tears. "Pleasure and pain, almost the same thing, you know."

Putting his wet finger in his mouth, he leaned forward and whispered in her ear, "I like your tears. They taste as good as I know the rest of you will."

She cringed and closed her eyes, fear practically disabling her.

Releasing her chin, he turned and walked towards the door. Stopping just shy of it, he faced her again. "Tonight, I will come to you. The maid will bring in clothes for you to wear for my pleasure. You will put those on and be ready for me or suffer the consequences." With a swirl of his robes he turned and left, the door closing loudly behind him.

Her hands came up to cover herself and she backed up until she came to the wall. Sliding down to the floor, she tried to catch her breath, tears rolling unchecked down her face.

What in the hell was she going to do? If it was like this for her, then what of Royce? Her head fell forward onto her arms and she let the tears come. Not a few tears...no, a long, hard wail, punctuated with sobs.

That man was obviously crazy-both of them were. How was she going to get herself out of this? She didn't know who to trust. The one man she'd been afraid of was the man who gave his life to save her.

Robert, the man she had taken little notice of, barely talked to and seen even less of the last week was the traitor and Denny, well she had no idea what to think about Denny.

And now this psycho.

Thinking back on her dreams, a conversation she'd had with her father years ago came to mind. It had been a habit of theirs to take a walk late in the afternoon after the sheep were fed and homework done. Often times Audrey would join them if she was home, but this time her sister had been out with her friends.

"You're awfully quiet tonight, Anna."

She smiled, feeling the heat rising to her face at the memory of Royce and what they had done the night before. Just over there, in the middle of the orchard.

"You've been really quiet lately. I'm sorry I've been too busy for our evening walks."

"It's okay." She dismissed his concern with a wave and chose her next words carefully. "You loved mom, right?"

"Of course, I loved your mother."

"Well, how did you know?"

"Know what?"

"She was the one?"

He stopped walking and turned towards her. "Do you have a beau?"

"Sort of...I don't know, maybe..."

"Someone at school? You've get a crush? Who is he?"

She hesitated, sticking her hands in the back pockets of her jeans. "I'm not ready to talk about that yet."

"Alright." He quirked his brow. He'd always been a little on the uncomfortable side talking about feelings, which is one of the reasons he had been more than happy to move in with her grandparents after Anna's and Audrey's mother had died. Raising two little emotional girls had been, at times, over his head. "Then what do you want to talk about."

"How did you know mom was the one?"

A sad smile stole over his face. He never liked to talk about her. "I just knew." He gave a shrug. "All I can tell you, Anna, is you have to trust your instincts. And you, my dear," he took hold of her shoulders to rock her back and forth. "You, my dear, have great ones. I think I trust your instincts over everyone else's."

"Even Audrey's?"

"Even Audrey's. Your sister is bright and gifted, of that there is no doubt, but she lacks the street smarts that you've always seemed to have."

"But you say I'm always getting myself into trouble."

"True. You do have a tendency to test your limits, but you don't let it stop you. You don't do anything to hurt anybody that's for sure. Yeah, you make some mistakes, but we all do and are you really listening to what that little voice is saying in your head when you do something stupid?" He leaned down to tap her on the forehead. "Don't forget how much power you actually have. Never let someone take that away from you, and most of all, trust your instincts. Listen to your gut. The right guy's out there for you."

The image faded from her mind. Her gut was telling her she had to get the hell out of here, but how? And she wasn't going anywhere without Royce.

Wiping the last tears from her face, she got up and searched the wardrobe for a new dress. Pulling out the most modest one she could find, she quickly took off the torn gown and threw it on the floor. She laced up the new one as tightly as she could. This one wasn't coming off without a fight.

Going to the window, she stared down into the courtyard, looking for any avenue of escape. A few people were coming and going. Despair threatened to swamp her. How was she possibly going to get away? How could she possibly save Royce let alone herself?

Once again, a few tears crested. She had just pulled the stool near the window to lean her head back against the wall when a scratching came at the door. Tensing, she waited.

The lock turned and Denny slipped in. Her heart gave another lurch and hope surfaced. Dressed in the same servant's clothes as before, he was hunched over and his face wary as he approached her.

"My lady, are you alright?"

"Denny? Oh God, is it really you?" Coming to her feet, she wiped her face. *Please let him be a friend.* "Do you know where Royce is?" she asked hopefully. "Is he here? Is he alright?"

"He's in the dungeon my lady. Are you well? I saw both Lord Robert and Lord Louvain leave. Did they do anything to hurt you?"

Choking a little, she gave a bitter laugh. "No, but they both want to." Still wiping at her face and the fresh batch of tears that threatened to well, she went up to him. "Forget about them. Have you seen Royce? Is he hurt?"

"I haven't been able too yet, but I heard he's...alive." He looked at her anxiously.

Worrying her hands, she began to pace, "Denny, we must-."

"It's Hayne, my lady."

"What?" She stopped and turned around.

"My name is Hayne, my lady," he began, "My father was a knight killed in the Crusades. My mother died two years ago and Royce took me in. I'm sorry for the deception, but my mother...my mother is...or was a Plantagenet. Not that I have any connections to the crown, or any direct connections...but it's best if no one else knows my name, at least for now...especially Robert...or Louvain." He nervously twisted the ragged hat he had pulled from his head.

"Why are you telling me this?" Confused she stared at him. Why now when all their lives were on the line?

The young man in front of her straightened, standing tall and sober, he went from child to adult in the flash of an eye. With shoulders back, he squared his jaw and determination filled his young face. "Because if Lord Sutton and Lord Carrick die all is lost and my life is over. I wanted you to know. Just in case...otherwise, none will understand the risks we took to bring Prince Henry to crown."

Pausing, his face flashed again, the slight lilt of his French accent coming through in his anger. "There is word of an assassination attempt. We don't know where or who as of yet, but you can be sure Louvain has his thumb in it somewhere. We do know it will be blamed on King David and his allies. All will be lost."

Shaking his head, he looked down for a second. "Louvain means to put his own on the throne and betray the truce between the two. If that happens, he will continue raping and pillaging the land and the people with the rest of the lawless Barons that are of his mettle, as they have done for the last ten years...all behind the back of King Stephen." Taking a breath, Hayne began to pace in front of her, his face a mask of concentration.

She blinked at his transformation. For the last few weeks she had barely noticed him working on the fringe of their small group. But watching him now, she realized she had sorely underestimated him, just as she had the others, and she began to wonder how much else she had missed.

"Robert already knows I escaped. He just doesn't know I'm right under his nose. We don't have much time. They leave with Royce in two days."

"Where are they taking him?"

"To London, to be tried for treason."

"A trial?" she asked optimistically.

"A mockery, to appease the people. And then he will be drawn and quartered and hung for entertainment."

The blood drained from her face and she sickened and swayed.

"My lady." Grabbing her arm to keep her upright, Hayne led her back to the stool. With urgency in his voice he spoke, "As we speak the queen is riding out and Louvain will come for you tonight. It must be tonight..."

"What must be tonight?" She met his gaze.

"You must take care of Louvain."

"Take care of him?" she repeated, and then fire entered her eyes. "Oh, I'll take care of him. I'll kick his bony ass from here till Tuesday." She stood angrily. "Dress me up like a tart...dirty s.o.b. You don't know who you're messin' with. I've been taking kickboxing for years. Let's just see what you get, cause it ain't gonna be pretty."

Hayne seemed shocked at her words but watching her punch an imaginary foe made a smile spread across his face and he chuckled soundlessly.

"Royce never told us," he said, his young voice cracking.

"Told you what?"

"How much spirit you have, my lady."

"Why is everyone so surprised? And why do they keep telling me I have spirit?"

Hayne motioned for her to stay quiet as footsteps passed by her door. Both waited as someone paused just outside, the voices of two people engaged in chatter floated in.

After he was sure they were gone Hayne bent his head to hers and whispered, "This is what we're going to do."

CHAPTER

15

The two maids had been in hours before bringing supper and a new gown of a light gold. The sheer material of the dress was once again so low it barely contained her breasts. Anna was sorry to lose the one she had laced so tightly. She had felt odd comfort from the constrictions of the dress, like it was a barrier between her and her fate.

When it was stripped away and the new garment put on, she felt completely exposed. Her hair had been let loose and brushed until it shone and fragrant perfume rubbed over her arms and legs. It was everything she could do to keep silent and not lash out at the women who had set about their tasks. After they left she had nothing to do but wait.

It was well past dark when the lock clicked and Louvain came in. She swallowed hard, hoping and praying Hayne would keep his word.

Her skin immediately began to tingle at the thought of what she had to do, but her mind was clear and she curbed her fear. Her hands itched to do damage. For some reason tonight, he represented all the struggles she had suffered through the last nine years. She had never hated and yet feared somebody so much in her life.

He was dressed richly in another deep blue and red robe. It was obvious he'd been drinking; his cheeks where flushed, his eyes were glassy and his bulbous nose a beacon of bright red.

A servant followed him into the room, setting down a tray of food and wine on the table before lighting the fireplace. On his exit out, he gave her a pitying look that didn't help her nerves.

She looked back at Louvain. They both eyed each other as the door clicked shut and the lock slid into place. Even though she was expecting it, her heart plummeted and no doubt it showed on her face.

His smile grew as he approached her. Putting his hand in her hair, he let it run through his fingers lightly.

"You have really amazing hair...light and dark at the same time. Rich brown mixed with red and gold, it's all the colors of a fall day." Taking a long sniff, he breathed out and sighed. "I do so love clean hair."

His touch was almost gentle. But she wasn't fooled for a minute.

"They did well with you. Hmph, not that it would be that hard. They had a lot to work with." He smiled again as though to charm her. "I don't think I've ever had the pleasure of a woman like you. If you behave, I might have to rethink your fate." He walked around her in quiet appreciation.

Coming up behind her, he whispered in her ear, "I've already told Robert to find his own entertainment for tonight. I want you all to myself, and I have a feeling we're both going to enjoy it." To show he meant it he pulled her hips back hard into the evidence of his arousal.

That was all she needed to hear and before she could stop herself, her body reacted. Without conscience thought, her elbow came back, catching him in the abdomen. A soft oof blew by her ear.

Before he could catch his breath, her right foot with the slight wooden heel on the slipper came down on the instep of his foot. She turned in one motion and forced the palm of her right hand up into his nose. The satisfactory crunch spurred her on. Her knee came up hard connecting into his groin. As he doubled over in silent agony she added another move, putting her elbow to his face. The whole thing couldn't have been more than ten seconds and Louvain was flat on the floor.

She was panting hard and couldn't believe what she had done, but instead of stopping to think about it, she grabbed the chain under the bed and attached the collar around his neck and began rolling him and wrapping the rest of the chain around his body.

Blood was pouring from his nose and mouth. He began to rouse but she kept wrapping. When he realized what she was doing, he started to struggle, and managed to reach out and grab her hair with one hand.

"Bitch," he muttered through his bloody mouth.

But instead of stopping, she reached for the hair combs she'd found on the table and stabbed at his hand savagely, until he started to howl and let go. The minute she had her freedom, she stuffed a rag in his mouth and brought her elbow down again on the side of his face then continued tying him up.

Hayne had cut through all the silk ties on the bed. She grabbed one and tied Louvain's hands behind his back with his feet trussed up like a turkey.

He was staring at her in disbelief. Apparently, nobody had ever gotten the best of him, let alone a slight girl. She began talking as though they were having a nice conversation just in case somebody was listening on the other side of the door.

"Thank you for your compliment on my hair. I think your robes look very nice. What do you want me to do now? Like that?" she said as though scared. "Oh no, I can't do that, but I will if you want me to."

The expression on his face was almost comical, sheer hatred combined with incredulity, but it didn't stop her.

Leaning down into his face, she changed her tone for his ears alone. "You sick, sadistic, bastard. You messed with the wrong girl."

Straightening, she looked into his eyes so he could see the determination written in her face. "I'm taking my life back and it starts now." Pulling her fist back, she punched him right in the nose.

Giving the ropes a final tug to insure their tightness, she stood and delivered a hard kick to his mid-section and then brought a vase down on his head to knock him out completely.

At that moment she didn't really care if she killed him. She had never wanted to kill anything, let alone anybody in her life. Right now, she so badly wanted to run him through with the small knife Hayne had left, but something inside her wouldn't let her. She just rolled his body out of the way under the bed.

Going over to the wardrobe, she pulled out the hidden clothes Hayne had brought. Stripping off the horrible gold dress Louvain had chosen, she threw it under the bed next to him and quickly pulled on the simple dress and half boots. The dress was a little small and the shoes too big, but she didn't care.

She went to the door and called out for the guard. Within minutes, the door clicked open and a guard peered in. Instantly, she pulled him forward by his hair and hit him hard on the back of the head with one of the bowls. The pottery shattered and he dropped like a stone, out cold.

Just as she was trying to drag him from around the door, footsteps sounded in the hall. She froze as the door pushed open again to reveal Hayne.

"Bloody hell. That was fast," he exclaimed in a whisper. Handing her a cloak, he ordered, "Watch the door." Grabbing the guard's feet, he quickly pulled him out of the way.

She returned to the entry, happy to give Hayne the duty of tying up the guard.

"How did you do that?" he whispered after spying Louvain's still form under the bed.

"Years of self-defense classes and more fear than you can imagine. Now, hurry up."

He extinguished all the candles and came to stand next to her. She swirled the cloak he brought over her shoulders and peeked into the hall. It was empty. Hayne motioned for her to put her hood up to hide her hair, and then turned for one last glance around the room. Steeped in shadows it looked deserted. Louvain's still form could not be seen stuffed under the bed and the guard was ensconced behind the curtain.

"Let's go," he whispered. "Stay behind me."

Taking one last deep breath, she followed Hayne out and locked the door behind her, pocketing the key. Now all they had to do was find Royce.

The halls were deserted. Hayne walked ahead of her carrying a chamber pot he'd grabbed from the room to look purposeful in case they were discovered. A few times he'd stop and Anna knew to flatten herself against the wall. Muffled voices could be heard over the banister at the end of the hall from the great room below. Hayne said most of the guards where gathered there. They didn't pass anyone.

It was eerie, the whole castle seemed quiet. The maids probably kept to themselves at night in case they crossed paths with one of these horrible guards. She doubted there would be much care about what lady they found roaming the halls in the dark.

It felt like they had been walking forever before Hayne finally motioned to the door of the dungeon. She went first while Hayne waited at the top. Creeping down the dark stairs, she knew they were in the right place by the smell alone. It reeked of death and rotting waste.

She covered her mouth with her cape to stop from gagging and slowly eased her way down, keeping her back against the stones and feeling her way with her feet.

The clink of chains and two voices that she didn't recognize gave her pause as she neared the bottom. Light from a torch fell over two guards huddled at a table in the corner playing some kind of dice game. There were a few empty wine bottles on the floor near their feet.

Her eyes searched the room. Two closed doors. That had to be where they were keeping Royce and Lars. Her heart increased its tempo as she thought about what she had to do. The longer she waited, the faster it went.

Draw them out, he said. Distract them so I can get into position. Easy for Hayne to say, he wasn't the one doing it.

Giving herself a mental shake, she closed her eyes for a minute. *Come on, girl. You can do this.* Taking a deep breath, she pushed back her cloak and started forward, her hands at her waist, rolling her hips.

"'ello?' she called out. "Ed? Is you down 'ere?"

Both guards turned at her voice, startled.

"Who is it?" one asked, standing and putting his hand on his sword.

"It's me, Bridge. Ye damn fool. Where the 'ell have you been? I've been waiting for ye."

Both guards looked at each other. The rattle of chains and muttered curses came from one of the rooms.

Sliding the cape off one shoulder, she sauntered closer into the light with her tongue caressing her top lip.

"Mary told me I was to come 'ere for Ed. Is you 'im, big fella?" she eyed one of the guards suggestively.

"Or is you Ed? It don't matter to me. I's just want me money...if ye know what I mean." Taking one hand, she ran it up to her breast and cupped it intimately.

"I'm Ed." One of the guards stepped forward.

"The 'ell you are. I'm Ed," the other said, pushing the first away and walking towards her.

"'Old up 'ere, I can take ye both, ye just 'ave to be patient ye see." She walked closer to them.

"Me first."

"No, me first. I'm in charge down 'ere."

"Gent'lmen, first things first. Let's see your money."

Both men dug into their coat pockets and produced a couple of small coins.

At a growl and some whispering from the cell she pretended to be startled.

"'ho is that?" she began to turn and walk away.

One of the guards grabbed her arm and said, "Nothing, there's nobody, that's just a couple of prisoners."

"I don't want no trouble."

"No, no," both men said in unison. One of them walked over and hit the door. "Shut up in there." Strutting back to her, he said, "Don't worry. They're chained up and I gots the only key 'ere." He shook a couple of keys on his belt.

"Alright, then...let's get to it. 'ho's first?"

"Me."

"No, me."

"You'll do." She grabbed the smaller one's arm and led him away. "Where can we go?"

"Over 'ere." He eagerly pulled her into a dark back corner.

"Oww! That 'urt! What is that?"

"My sword...'ere let me take it off."

"Ooh, that's better. Now lie down on the floor, close your eyes, an I'll make all your dreams come true," she kept her voice deep and seductive.

"Jemmy? What's going on back there?" the other guard called.

"Wait your turn, ye blimey idiot. Ee's almost done."

The other guard was peering into the dark corner when she sauntered forward. The top of her bodice was ripped open and one of her breasts was showing. The guard's eyes fastened on that display and he never saw Hayne coming.

"Is he out?" Anna asked breathlessly as she ran up to him rearranging her top.

"Yeah," Hayne whispered. Smiling at her he added, "Nice job, my lady. Even I believed you. Here's the keys. I'll take care of these two. You get Royce and Lars out."

"Royce?" she called running over to the cell.

"God dammit, that better not be you, Anna. And if that little weasel is with you and put you in danger, I'm gonna-."

Ignoring his outburst, she pulled open the door and rushed in, just happy to hear his voice.

Both Royce and Lars were on their feet. In the darkness she couldn't tell how badly either was hurt. Running to Royce, she threw herself against him.

"Thank God," she said against his chest.

"What the hell do you think you're doing?" he started angrily.

"*Shut up*, Royce." Lars yelled from the other end of the cell. "Anna, Hayne, get us the hell out of here before someone else comes."

Fumbling with the keys, she was suddenly shaking so badly she couldn't open the locks. "I've got them...I just...my hands aren't..."

"I'll do it, my lady." Hayne came up behind her and gently took the keys from her hands to open Royce's manacles. "My lord, are you hurt?" Hayne asked before going to Lars.

"No, I'll be fine," he answered crushing her to him in a quick hug.

"I'm sorry," she started to talk, started to apologize. "I shouldn't have-."

He silenced her with a quick kiss.

"Later, my love, we'll talk later," he said turning to business. "Get the other guard. Drag them in here. Lars, put on his tunic." He grabbed up the one who was starting to come to.

It took a few minutes and a couple of well placed, well deserved hits for the men to be locked up just like Royce and Lars, with rags stuffed in their mouths. Hopefully, if anybody came looking, they would think Lars and Royce were still stuck in their cell and the guards had gone off for pleasure.

Lars delivered a couple extra kicks and muttered some choice words to one guard before leaving the cell. Seeing Anna's wide-eyed look as he passed her, he said gruffly, "He had it coming."

Royce pulled the dirty tunic over his head and looked at Hayne. "How much time do we have?"

"A few minutes, maybe more, Louvain's taken care of, but I couldn't find Robert."

At Louvain's name, Royce's jaw hardened but he didn't say anything.

"How do we get out of here?"

"We take the north wall. It's the farthest but will take us right to the edge of the forest, unless that gets cut off, then we have to go by river." Hayne handed the two swords he'd taken from the guards to Royce and Lars.

"Lead the way," Royce motioned, pulling Anna close for a quick kiss then keeping hold of her hand. They started up the stairs with Hayne in front.

"How are we going to get out of here?" She whispered in a shaky voice, all the nervousness she'd been keeping in check started to flood her system.

"I don't know. Just keep to the sides. Follow me and don't speak." Royce gave her hand a squeeze before turning forward again.

Lars took up a protective stance behind her as they left the dungeon. So far, so good. The castle was still quiet for the most part.

They had just rounded the top of the stairs past the dungeon when they surprised their first guard. He was ahead of another man obviously on their way to replace the others for the night. Hayne killed the first, but the second got in a good yell before going down.

"Dammit," Lars swore from behind.

"Come on," Royce growled, grabbing her arm and pulling her back in the stairwell.

Two more guards appeared on the landing above them and the hue and cry was on.

Silent no more, Royce, Lars and Hayne fought protectively around her as men started coming from above and below.

One man got around Lars and was going for Royce's back. Anna picked up a fallen sword and stepped in front of him, thrusting it deep into the man's neck.

The shock of seeing somebody's blood run down the sword made her stop. She yanked on the weapon trying to dislodge it from his neck, but it wouldn't move. Suddenly, his body crumpled and her sword slid out like it had been stuck in warm butter.

She froze, stammering, "I think I killed him."

Lars turned, hearing the hysteria in her voice. Raising his sword, he neatly sliced open the man's neck. "No, I did."

By then Royce had finished off the men at the top of the stairs and reached down yanking her up by her arm.

"Come on," he roared, taking the stairs two at a time. "We can make it to the top."

"Then what?" Lars yelled, following with Hayne picking up the rear.

"I don't know."

CHAPTER 16

"Which way to the upper ramparts?" Royce hissed to Hayne once they reached the main hallway.

"This way," Hayne motioned, taking the lead.

Stunned, Anna allowed Royce to pull her along. Below guards were yelling instructions. The castle was coming awake and if they didn't get out soon there would be no escape.

"The river." Royce yelled to Hayne. "Get us to the river."

"Hell and damnation, not the river," Lars cursed.

Turning down one of the corridors, Hayne found what they were looking for and both he and Royce kicked open one of the doors to the upper ramparts on the south side of the castle. Royce pulled her through and yelled for Lars to "Bolt the door." They needed every moment they could get.

The darkness in the stairwell was alleviated by a half moon shining through the windows. A movement to the left made Royce flatten her to the wall as someone bore down on them. He released her hand to engage the guard. One downward swipe of his sword and warm blood showered her face making her scream.

"My lord, to your left," Hayne called out. Lars stepped forward blocking a sword meant for Royce's neck and took care of two more guards, as she stood paralyzed against the wall.

The fighting was so fast she was having a hard time reacting. The whole thing seemed like a horror movie that she had gotten caught up in. She still couldn't believe she had killed a man. She'd had no choice, but still...How many had she killed tonight? Louvain? His guard?

Suddenly, Royce reached back, grabbed her hand and hauled her forward again, pulling her over the dead men.

"Anna, focus," he yelled, snapping her back into the present.

Taking the stairs two at a time he opened a door that led to the outside ramparts. Anna had never been up this high and fear seized her as they stepped outside onto the thin ribbon of stone in the dark night. The wind tore at their clothes and the uneven stones made her stumble as they ran down the path in the darkness.

Thunder rolled through the sky and clouds moved across the moon obscuring its light. At the other end of the ramparts somewhere there was a set of stairs. She looked back at Lars and Hayne following close behind.

She could hear men pounding at the door Lars had barred, trying to gain access. They only had a few minutes before they would make it through.

Light flared at the other end of the ramparts. Men were coming up the stairs and through the doors. Muttering a curse, Royce stopped and looked over the edge. She stepped up beside him and gasped. It was at least a thirty-foot drop to the river below.

Royce turned and grabbed her by the shoulders.

"We have to jump," he yelled, his voice breaching the wind and the roar of the river.

"Jump down there? Are you crazy?" she yelled back, dumbfounded. Staring into the blackness below her mind went back to her accident. In the space of a second the whole memory came crashing back and the rest of her courage fled. Her earlier fear was nothing compared to what she felt now.

"No...no," she said in a trance, backing up.

In her mind, she saw it all as if in a dream...the castle high above the river, the wind whistling, whipping and tearing at her cloak. Lars and Hayne stood on one side of her watching as the door at the other end began to splinter from the men battering it down. Herself, standing there in terror, looking out at nothing and Royce looking back towards the men as they rounded the corner and headed straight for them.

This was death for them all and even knowing that, she couldn't do it. She couldn't jump. It would be the end of everything.

But Royce wouldn't let her hesitate. He pulled her over to the edge and prepared to jump.

"I can't. I can't," she cried, suddenly finding her voice. "No, don't make me, you don't understand...no. *No.*" She had grabbed onto his arms holding her shoulders and was fighting to pull herself back to the safety of the wall.

What if she woke up in a hospital bed? What if she went somewhere else? What if she lost Royce forever? She wasn't even thinking about death in the normal sense. But the fear of making that jump into the darkness of a raging river was just too much for her.

Royce looked at her face and then his eyes went past her to the men running down the path.

"We have too." His words barely penetrated. Without hesitation he put his arms around her, picked her up and in one fluid movement, turned and jumped. Lars and Hayne followed straight behind.

Her scream echoed the whole way down.

The minute Royce stepped off that wall, the sky lit up with a streak of lightening illuminating their fall. Arrows swirled around them on their descent in a surreal dance. Her stomach dropped and she pushed away from Royce flailing her arms and legs in a feeble attempt to save herself.

"Go into the water straight," Royce yelled next to her.

But she barely heard him. Instead, she was flashing back to her accident...the man in the road, the men on the ramparts, Royce and Lars face as they were fighting and Louvain with his evil leer...everything that had happened to her in the past month flew through her mind in the space of seconds.

They both went in deep and were almost immediately caught by the current. She hit the water so hard and fast she forgot to take a breath. Disoriented she didn't know which way was up. In desperation she opened her mouth, inhaling water and her lungs rebelled.

If it weren't for Royce's hold on her cloak, she didn't think she would have made it. He pulled her to the surface as they were swept downstream. Arrows were still being fired from above landing around them, but the river quickly took them out of range.

"Don't fight it." Royce struggled with her cloak, holding her tighter to him. "Just let the river take us," he yelled.

She could hardly do anything. Her body was in severe pain. It felt as if she had hit concrete instead of water. Royce had managed to turn her around, facing them down river.

"Put your feet up like you are floating," he ordered.

At this point she couldn't respond. Her self-preservation had left her and she was too exhausted to fight. Her body was numb. She could feel Royce trying to swim over to the shore but couldn't help him.

The river seemed to open up a little and the roar of the water got louder. In one last effort Royce managed to grab onto something and began pulling them to safety.

It was a few minutes until her feet touched the sandy bottom and she was able to stumble out onto shore. Collapsing onto the bank, Royce made sure she was well out of the water before scrambling to his feet.

There was some yelling and then Royce, Hayne and Lars fell down next to her in a heap. They were all breathing hard and it was a few minutes before anyone could talk.

"That was close. We were almost part of the Severn," Lars gasped for breath next to her.

"I know. The river has to be at the highest I've ever seen. I don't think I've ever seen it move so fast," Royce agreed.

"Bloody Hell, I feel like I jumped off a cliff." Lars rolled over to cough up more water.

"Anna, you haven't spoken. Are you alright?" Royce put out a hand to touch her arm.

But she couldn't respond. Her chest was so tight it was hard for her to breathe. They had made it out and miraculously survived that fall. Putting her hand up to her eyes, she tried to hold back the sob that caught in her throat.

"Anna?" Royce asked worried. Rolling onto his arm, he pulled her hand away from her face. "Is it your throat?"

She shook her head. "No, that's fine now."

"Is it something else? Are you hurt?" Concerned, he began running his hands over her body looking for broken bones.

"No, I don't think so," she said a sob escaping. She pushed herself up into his arms.

Confused, he held her as her sobs grew louder. Crooning quietly in her ear, he tried to comfort her. "It's alright...we're alright, shh..."

"How could you?" Pushing back from him, she hit him angrily on the chest. "How c-could you jump off that wall?" she sputtered. "I've never been so sca-scared in my <u>li-li-fe</u>." Sniffling, she continued, "I've been so afraid, first Ro-Robert..."

Royce stiffened. Grabbing her shoulders, he tried looking into her face. "What did he do?"

"Who?" Confused, she stopped crying for a minute.

"Robert?"

"He *threatened* me," she exclaimed throwing her hands wide.

"Threatened you?"

"Yes. He threatened me a-and..." she sniffed louder. "And said horrible things and th-then...and then that horrible man...Lou-Louvain and then I didn't know who to trust and then Denny, or Hayne came in and... and... if it wasn't for him...I...I... you..."

Royce watched her gesture, pointing back and forth between them. Starting to hiccup, she tried to reprimand him between sobs before finally collapsing into his arms.

He was quiet, holding her tight to him.

"Did they touch you?" he asked. "Hurt you?"

"N-no-noo, but they were so mean and they said they were going to and if it wasn't for..." Looking up out of his arms, she gestured to Hayne again before burying her head again in his chest. "If it wasn't for Ha-Hayne...I d-don't know...I don't know what I would've d-done..."

Sighing, Royce held her, breathing into her hair. "Me either, love, me either."

"I was afraid I would ne-never see you again," she stammered into his chest, in a muffled voice.

"Not possible." With a rumble, and a grunt, he squeezed her tighter, "God would never do that to us." Finally, he bent, kissing her ear and whispered, "Does that mean you forgive me?"

A choked laugh escaped her and she pushed out of his arms again, before another sob erupted. "No, forgive *me*. I'm so sorry... I'm so sorry for what I said."

"There is nothing to forgive." Cupping her face with his hands, he pulled her forward. "It is I who am sorry, I let you down again."

"Never...never," she exclaimed, leaning into him. "Never..." She breathed into his mouth, kissing him gently. She still hadn't gotten control of her emotions. One minute she was sobbing, the next she was shaking with rage and then desire for Royce hit her deep in the gut.

Her mouth swirled over his urging him on, and for a moment they forgot where they were and who they were with. The desperation of the last few days, the fight for their lives still raw and the need for each other overrode everything else. He felt so good, solid and hard, she couldn't stop herself from touching him.

Groaning, Royce answered her kiss, his needs as raw and urgent as her own. He pulled her down on top of him, rolling to the side, crushing her to him. They were both lost in a moment of their own making.

"Christ." Lars muttered, still lying in the sand next to them and then grumbled, "We don't have time for this."

Royce ignored it, but she couldn't. Pulling away from him she peered over Royce's shoulder at Lars.

"I'm even happy to see you, Lars," she said, giddy just from being in Royce's arms.

Another sound of disgust made her giggle. Lars ignored her.

"Hayne, you alright?" Lars asked, rolling the boy over.

Retching up more water, Hayne tried to nod his head.

"Thank you, both of you." Giving the boy's shoulder a pat, Lars stood and his voice took on a serious note, "I don't know how you did it...God's toes, I don't know how you did it, but thank you."

Royce stood bringing Anna with him and flexed his shoulders, taking a better look at their surroundings. "Do you think you can walk?"

"I think so," she said with a groan.

"Aren't you going to ask me if I'm hurt?" Lars asked with humor in his voice.

"After that swordplay you displayed back there, you bloody well better be hurt." Royce grunted.

"It wasn't my idea to take the river. No, I said the gate, but nobody listened."

"If we'd have taken the gate, we'd all be hanging from it right now. You're just lucky Hayne and Anna saved your life, because I was getting damn well close to getting free just to strangle you," Royce said, peering out at the water.

"Your sweet words woo my heart." Lars grinned. "Now where, my Lord?"

"We've got to get out of here. We're far enough to give us an advantage, but not far enough to take our time. First things first, we need a boat. If we keep walking along the shore we should come across something and with the rain, by morning our trail will be tough to follow."

"Come on, boy." Lars leaned down giving Hayne a hand. "We need to get going."

Standing, Hayne took a deep breath, "Wait, we need to get to Canterbury."

"Canterbury?" Royce's attention shifted back to the boy.

"The rumor is true. There's to be an assassination attempt on the Prince."

"God's teeth." Lars whistled. "I knew it. When?"

"Early September..."

"That doesn't give us much time." Royce was quiet for a moment, his head down. "Then it looks like we need to split up. We'll go southeast and you two need to warn Ramsey...we meet in Hythe in three weeks."

CHAPTER

17

Thunder rolled across the sky and lightning lit up their path. Royce walked along the bank searching behind every nook and cranny. Suddenly darting behind a rock, he issued an excited aha, before appearing again, dragging a small boat.

"The fisherman just beach their skiffs and hide them in the brush." His smile flashed in the darkness conveying his good humor. "I knew I'd find one here somewhere, climb in."

With a grunt and a shove, they were floating. Taking up the oars Royce quickly steered the little boat out to the middle to catch the current. It wasn't long before the river opened up and they were officially in the rough waters of the Severn estuary.

The rain was steady now, a gentle drizzle. The chilly air and the dark skies gave off little light. Wrapping the soaked cloak around her, she tried to balance herself in the middle of the boat. For the first time in weeks they were alone.

Lars and Hayne had headed north, trying to get ahead of Louvain's men, while she and Royce were headed south across the Severn. If they were lucky, Royce said, they would be able to make it to Avonmouth or maybe Portishead before spotting the first fishermen of the morning.

She had no idea how long they traveled down river. It seemed impossible to tell where they were. A few times the boat almost capsized and she finally crouched down in the bow to give it better balance.

Royce had been steadily steering the boat to the opposite shore, keeping them far enough away that if somebody happened to be looking they wouldn't notice them, but close enough if their boat overturned they could make it to shore. Finally, he turned the boat inland. Jumping out, he pulled her with him, and then released the craft back into the current. It swirled away, bobbing in the white waves.

"Just in case?" she said from the safety of his arms.

His grip on her tightened. "Just in case," he agreed turning and making his way to the beach.

The shore line was sandy and he waited until they were on more stable ground before setting her down. His balance faltered for a moment and she put her hand up to steady him as she regained her footing. She was exhausted and he must be too.

"Royce?"

"We need to get farther inland before we stop." He said ignoring her question. He flexed his arms again and stretched his back grimacing. "I think I've got a few hours left in me, how about you?"

"Royce," when she put a hand up to his face, he felt cold and shaky. "When was the last time you had anything to eat?"

"It's been a few days." White teeth flashed as he covered her hand with his own. "I'll be fine. Come. We need to get inland and find a place to rest." He reached up taking her hand from his face and kissed her palm before turning and leading her into the brush.

Following behind him, she was amazed at his strength. After all they had been through tonight and who knows what he had to endure in the last few days, he was determined to reach safety. What that meant she wasn't sure, but she seriously doubted it meant a bed and a big meal. They needed to stop and soon. They were both exhausted and the sky was beginning to lighten. Either that, or her eyes were becoming so used to the dark, she was able to see.

The underbrush was light and the ground was fairly matted with mud from all the rain. Royce tried to keep them on the rocks or drier land to hide their tracks.

They got a few miles in before she simply couldn't walk anymore. They had entered a rather dense forest with tall trees and rolling hills. It reminded her a little of northeastern Vermont and the countryside she used to camp in every summer. The rain had stopped and morning was on its way, the birds alerting them with their busy chatter.

"Royce, I can't make it any farther."

When he turned to face her, she was startled by the fatigue on his face. His eyes were a hollowed-out shadow of their former brilliance. The beard she felt before hid a myriad of bruises.

"What?" he asked resting his hands on his hips at her startled gasp.

"Your face, it's all purple and green. I don't even want to know what it looks like in daylight." She gently cupped his jaw.

His lips curved up trying to smile, but it was obvious he was exhausted.

"You're right. We need to stop. I was hoping we could make it to the abbey. I think it's just beyond that hill.

"Abbey? As in a bed and food?"

"Yes, they'll take us in, but we need to hurry. Dawn is close and once they go to ablutions we'll have to wait for the Abbess before we'll be let in. Do you think you can make it? Just over that hill?"

Following his finger, she grimaced. It was a small hill, but she was sure it would take longer than he made it sound.

"Yes, I can make it." Taking a deep breath, she set her jaw.

Grabbing his hand, she forged ahead, this time leading him and he let her. It took the good part of an hour before they were at the abbey doors. If not for the cloudy skies she was sure dawn was about to make an appearance.

Voices lifted in song greeted them as the barrier opened and Royce stepped forward asking for a place to sleep and some food. The old nun who answered their knock hesitated, taking in their ragged appearance. Finally, she stepped back and let them in, leading them down a back hall and out to another building. Opening the door to a small room, she paused and looked back at them with a keen eye.

"You're married, right?"

"Yes, Sister, we are," Royce replied.

Nodding solemnly, she opened the door allowing them entrance.

"I'll bring fresh water and some food for you. It's small, but it's all we have." Muttering to herself she turned to leave. "Lots of people on the road, must be because of the storm, no room left." Then the door closed behind her.

Anna stripped off the cloak and dress, leaving them in a pile on the floor and fell into bed beside Royce. He was already asleep. She pulled the covers up and snuggled into him. In the back of her mind, she thought she heard a key turn in the lock. But it had to be her imagination...after all, they were safe now, right?

CHAPTER 18

"Thieves? You say they are thieves?"

Anna's eyes cracked open to see two women leaning over the bed holding a candle. Still in the thickness of sleep she was slow to react. Beside her the bed shook as Royce bolted up and reached behind his head for his sword. The ladies jumped back in alarm making the flame flicker and dance.

"See?" The smaller nun who had shown them in earlier gestured.

"Nay," the older woman relaxed. With gentle pat of her hand she said, "It means he's a soldier, Sister Marie." With a nod to Royce she went on, "It's not there, sir. No weapons in here. I'm sure you know that. You'll get it back at the gate."

Royce blinked and regarded them owlishly, his head swiveled taking in the room before returning to the nuns. She could feel the tension leave him and his shoulders relaxed. He gave them a respectful nod before reaching down to draw the blanket up to cover the two of them that his sudden movement had thrown off.

"Don't bother," the Abbess's face creased in a smile. "A woman my age has seen it all. Besides *you're* still dressed young man, if you can call those rags you're wearing clothes."

She headed to the door, "Feed them, bathe them and give them some new clothes then bring them to me. They must leave at once."

Sister Marie sniffed. Turning back to them she frowned, "Well?" her eyebrows shot up. "You heard her. Up with you. You've slept the day away."

Pointing to Anna, she lifted a robe off the bed and signaled for her to step into it. "Come now, we'll get you cleaned up and dressed, then you can eat. The Abbess has much to do before she lays her head down tonight and we don't want to keep her longer than possible."

Royce started to rise, but Sister Marie spun her face away holding out her hand. "Stop, sir. You are not to step out of that bed 'til we're gone."

Royce and Anna both froze. Royce covered himself back up and helped Anna crawl over him to get out of the bed. Obediently he leaned back and pulled the covers up to his neck.

Sister Marie scowled at him as she covered Anna with the robe and ushered her out. She pointed back to the bottom of the bed again in agitation. "Your robe is there, sir. One of the other sister's will be along to take you to a bathing chamber. Come along, my lady."

Anna's body protested each step. The sister moved at a swift clip and she could barely keep up. A groan escaped her lips as they descended a few stairs.

Sister Marie glared back without sympathy. Her frown deepened. "Shhhhhh, she hissed, "We don't want to alert the whole place."

Turning at the end of the hall, they came into the kitchen. A large fireplace was in use against the back wall. Counters lined one side of the room with only a few older women cleaning up with what looked like the last remnants of dinner. The smell of baking bread almost brought her to her knees. Automatically she reached for a roll on the table as they passed. Sister Marie's hand shot out like a whip and slapped it away.

"Ye cannot eat, filthy like ye are. Ye must bath first." Sister Marie tugged at her elbow, pulling her off to the side of the room closer to the fireplace. With a sweep of her arm she pulled back a curtain, revealing a small private nook and waved her forward. "Go on."

A barrel tub sat in the middle of the room, the smell of lavender and thyme filled the air.

Shaking the sting of the slap on her hand, she followed the nun into the room. A bath...her second real bath since she'd been here. She could barely contain her excitement. She stepped over and dipped her hand in. The water was hot. What a luxury. Without hesitation she stripped off her robe and eased in. A young novice stepped forward and poured a fresh bucket sending a fresh plume of steam into the air. She put her head back and relaxed into the heat. For a moment she couldn't move. Bliss was all she could think...This was bliss.

Twenty minutes later she was sitting at the table enjoying a simple meal. Dressed in sturdy brown wool with her hair plaited back and wearing the softest boots of calfskin leather that she'd ever thought she'd put on. The hot rye bread, cooked oats and meat pie were heaven and the potent red wine she washed it down with just added to the pleasure.

Sister Marie came back just as she was wiping up the last of the oats with her bread. She gave her a smile and sat back in her chair with a hand over her belly.

"Wonderful. Thank you so much."

Sister Marie gave her a stern frown that made Anna chuckle. She was by far not the friendliest nun, but she didn't care. She was clean, fed and rested and somewhere in this place was Royce.

She turned to the other two ladies and thanked them again. Coming to stand by Sister Marie, she raised one eyebrow at the old woman.

With a noisy sigh, the old woman blew out, "Come on with ye then."

The small parlor was off of the main hall. Royce was standing with the Abbess next to the fireplace. Anna smiled and quickened her step.

The beard was gone. His hair was still damp and swept off his face allowing her to see the damage. Both eyes still had more than a hint of blue shading around them. There was a fresh mark on his jaw and a cut across his right cheek that had turned purple and red. He looked terrible. He looked wonderful. She clasped him around the waste and leaned in for a kiss. When had she come to depend on him so much?

"Your husband seems much improved, does he not?" The Abbess walked over to her desk and sat. A simple habit covered her hair and warm blue eyes twinkled when she talked. Her manner suggested business, but the tone of her voice was gentle. Not knowing what to call her, Anna simply smiled and nodded back.

"You seem much improved too, my dear." Inclining her head, she went on, "I forgot to introduce myself. You may call me Sister Agatha,"

"Thank you, Sister Agatha, for your kindness," she said.

"You are welcome. Now-let us discuss what you are doing here. Sister Marie swears you are thieves who are here to rob us and take all our possessions." The Abbess held out her hands and looked around the bare room. "Which you can see we have very little of," she gave a chuckle. She turned her focus on Royce. "I know you, sir."

"Yes, Sister Agatha, you do."

"You may speak."

"I am Lord Royce Barrett De'Mark Sutton. My father was-."

"Your father was Lord Nicklaus Sutton. I knew him well. His mother was a good supporter of our work here. Yes, I can see the resemblance." Breathing in deeply through her narrow nose she took a moment, before turning her sharp gaze on Anna. "And you, my lady? From where do you hail?"

"May I introduce Lady Anna Harrington, my wife." Royce bowed, answering for her.

Nodding, her gaze came back to rest on Royce. "You seem to have come into some ill luck, my lord."

"Yes, Sister Agatha, we did."

"Are you still about our good Duke's business, my lord?"

"Yes. I strive to bring him to throne."

She frowned. "Is there a chance that could be challenged, sir?"

Royce hesitated. With a nod of ascension, he replied, "There is rumor..."

She accepted his answer without question. "Then you must be off. We'll supply you with a ride and food, but I can do no more for you."

She started to say something else and then stopped herself. Pushing herself up from the desk with both hands, she ended the conversation. "Well then, I bid you good journey. May God watch over you and keep you in safety."

CHAPTER
19

The nun's idea of a ride and Anna's were two completely different things. A young mule had been pressed into service for them, which the beast obviously didn't care for. His large brown eyes stared back resentful and he brayed announcing to one and all his displeasure. Loaded down with packs, at first, he'd refused to budge till Sister Marie came forward with a long stick and slapped him hard on the rump.

"This one's full of piss and vinegar. Ye'll have to use a stick for sure or you'll get nothing from him." She said handing the stick to Royce. "Ye might want to use it on her too if she gets too feisty." She nodded her head at Anna with what appeared to be a smile.

"Hey," Anna responded.

Royce just thanked the nun and grabbed the back of Anna's robe when she started to walk towards the old woman. He tucked her neatly under his arm and with another nod turned and started off leading the sullen mule into the dark.

The stars were out and the night was clear making it easy to see the path. Royce had chosen to stay off the main roads and they were taking what appeared to be a farmer's cart path. Deep trenches marked the trail making it easy to follow. The road, if one could call it that, was rocky and she was never more thankful for her shoes.

"It's a long walk," Royce whispered, "and needs to be a silent one as we go around Bristol."

Small huts dotted the countryside and fences barred their way on more than one occasion forcing them to go around the field. The heat from the day still hung in the air making the heavy cloak she wore feel stifling at times. But a cool wind was kicking up bringing clouds and the promise of more rain.

She kept quiet as she trailed along beside him. She'd never been so happy just walking next to somebody. It was amazing. Never in her life would she have thought she would feel so comfortable with somebody. Every small gesture, every small glance told her volumes and even though she was dying to talk to him...ask him what happened at Chepstow, she could tell he wasn't ready to talk about it yet.

He gazed at her with yearning in his eyes. His touch was soft and tender. Helping her over some of the deep ruts, his hands would brush just under her breast and he would hold on a little too long to her waist.

He wanted her, just as she wanted him and a few times he'd been close to speaking but held back. She was hoping there would be time to talk later. Right now, walking on the outskirts of these small villages, she knew they couldn't risk it.

The sky was beginning to turn pink by the time they stopped. They had been going through a particularly wooded area and Royce turned off the path and began walking towards a ridge some half a mile away. They found a cave big enough to keep the donkey while they rested.

Royce set up camp letting her sit for a minute while he built a fire. She laid down on the cold hard surface, closing her eyes for just a moment until a hand gently shook her.

Blinking awake she sat up, realizing she had dozed off. Royce had a fire going and was patiently waiting for her to take the well-cooked rabbit from his hands.

"Did I sleep?" she said, taking the rabbit and sinking her teeth into the juicy meat.

"Yes, you were out."

Anna looked towards the entrance. "What time is it?"

"Late morning." He followed her gaze.

When he turned to grab something from one of the packs, a ray of light shone across his back revealing dark stains on his tunic. Startled, she sucked in her breath.

"What?" Royce jumped up, grabbed his sword and faced the entrance.

"Your back." Leaning forward on her knees, she placed a hand on his arm pulling him back down. "What did they do to your back? Your face was bad enough, but are those whip marks?" she asked, turning him around and lifting his tunic.

Another gasp escaped her. "Good lord. What did they do? Oh, my God, how did you row the other night? How did you fight?" She gently touched the half dozen lash marks, half healed with a bloody crust, nearly reaching his waist.

"Not that I had a choice..."

"First, your face, and now your back? Did they hurt you anywhere else?" she pressed, easing him around slowly, examining his body for more wounds.

There was a dark purple bruise on his rib cage and numerous cuts and bruises marred his arms and legs. None were bleeding now, but they all looked like they hurt.

"Why? Why would they do this? Oh, baby, I'm so sorry. What did they do to you?" she crooned softly, choking back tears. Leaning forward, she placed a kiss on the bruise on his chest.

"Nothing. Nothing that my own foolishness didn't cause," he closed his eyes at her touch.

"I saw the bruises earlier on your face, but never in the light...but this...oh my God, does it hurt?" She tenderly touched the marks on his back.

"Not anymore...and when it did I was thankful for the pain."

"Why?"

"Because, then I knew I was alive."

"Royce," she said, gently holding his face. "What happened to you?"

Cupping her hand to his face, he kissed her palm. Tears entered his eyes and he measured his words. "Not me-you, Anna. It doesn't matter what they did to me, but you."

"Me? But they did nothing to me."

His eyes closed again and his jaw flexed. "Are you sure?" he asked, his voice a mere whisper.

"I'm sure. I told you, they talked about it...told me what they were going to do, but I was out for- I don't know how long, and then the old woman came in and told me it was time. That's when they came. It was supposed to be the other night, but..."

"But what?" he asked his voice full of emotion. "What happened?"

"Hayne came in and we worked out a plan." She shrugged her shoulders.

"A plan? "his brow puckered. "Tell me. What plan?"

"I gave Louvain some of my karate, self-defense moves," she replied, chopping at the air.

Watching her quick movements, the light came on in his eyes and he chuckled under his breath. "Karate, self-defense moves?"

"Yeah," she pretended to hit him in the nose softly with the heel of her hand. "Like this."

Playfully, he caught her hand and held her there. "You hit him in the nose?"

"And a few other places," she gave a him a grin.

"And what did he do?"

"He dropped like a stone," she said, warming to her story.

"A stone?"

"Yep, a stone."

"And where was Hayne?"

"He came in after."

"After you dropped Louvain like a stone?" His other hand came up and began drawing slow circles on her back, lazily moving downwards, easing her towards him.

"Oh yeah, like a stone," her voice a husky whisper as he caught her hip and pulled her forward.

"My Anna, so brave." His hand moved into her hair, gently hooking her neck. "Are you brave enough to finish what you started the other day on the beach?" he asked, his mouth an inch from her own.

"But you're hurt."

"Not as much as I will be if I don't have your healing touch."

"Oh really," she replied laughing. "My healing touch?"

"Yes, its magic. You touch me and I feel better. So, are you brave enough to finish what you started the other day at the beach?" he asked again.

She smiled and pushed him back softly, "Yes. Yes, I am."

Carefully they touched, gentle hands exploring bruises trying to heal, words of exclamation as they discovered what the last few days had wrought on their bodies. The fading pain was replaced with pleasure.

Royce eased her dress up and checked her body in the light, tenderly kissing each bruise. It wasn't until he got back up her body and saw the red scar on her neck that he stopped. For a moment he just stared at it, the dark slash bright on her neck.

Murmuring words of regret, he pulled back, hesitant to go on. But she needed him now and wouldn't let him.

"Don't. No more words of regret. We're here. Love me. Love me now," she said into his eyes.

His fingers brushed over the angry red welt.

"I don't want to hurt you."

"You won't," she answered her voice thick with desire. "It's your turn to heal me, Royce. Heal me." Letting her hand slip down, she took hold of him. He was hard velvet. His eyes glazed over and the regret was replaced with lust. Moving up onto her knees, she guided him in, gasping as he filled her. His hands stilled when their eyes met.

"No regrets," she said again beginning to move.

He lay still, letting her seek her pleasure until he could hold back no more. Grasping her hips, he plunged into her arching up and her head went back in surprise.

"Harder," she gasped.

He answered her thrust for thrust until they both cried out and she collapsed on top of him. His arms came around her and he hugged her to him.

"Never again will anyone take you from me," he whispered.

Barely able to respond, she moaned and agreed. He thrust one last time, sending spirals of pleasure through her.

"Never again," she whispered back letting him roll her to his side and tucking her in his arms.

Still breathing hard, he reached for the blankets covering them both up. "Sleep," he murmured. "I need sleep."

But she was already there.

They woke in the afternoon to the mule nosing through the packs rooting for food. Royce jumped up, smacking the animal on the rump to keep it away from the grain the sisters had given them.

"That's not for you."

With its ears back, the grumpy mule faced the wall, nose down and Anna started to laugh.

Never had Royce looked more charming. He was standing there naked in the half-light next to a hungry, moody mule. His hair was everywhere and the disgruntled looks he was exchanging with the animal amused her.

"You laugh, my lady?" Royce looked back at her and raised an eyebrow.

"Slaying dragons, my lord?" she returned.

"Yes," Royce smiled. "In fact, one who won't get up."

Taking up the switch the nun had given him, he walked boldly towards her.

"You wouldn't dare." She laughed, laying back down and covering herself with the blanket.

"I would dare if you disobey me." He dropped the switch and slide in behind her under the blanket.

"What?" she said playfully and turned to face him.

He smiled again, nuzzling her neck, one hand coming around to caress the tips of her breasts. "Remember? I had to do it before."

Stumped for a moment she tried to think what he was talking about, her mind being distracted by his caresses. "When? I don't re-," and then the memory filled in.

He *had* done it before.

"You mean when you lost your uncle's favorite hunting knife?"

"No," he raised his eyebrows. "When *you* lost my uncle's favorite hunting knife. I couldn't sit down for a week because you got mad and tossed it in the creek. I searched for that knife for hours until it got dark and I had to go home and face my uncle." Pausing for effect he slid his hand lower. "You got me in so much trouble that day and many after come to think of it…"

"Ha. You paid me back two-fold, chasing me around the meadow and then ripping my nightshirt."

"You were getting away. I had to do something."

"Talk about trouble. How do you explain a muddy handprint and a rip that goes all the way up the back of your nightshirt to your mother when you're nine?"

"Good question. We'll discuss it later." He rolled her over and took a nipple into his mouth.

"We should settle it now." She sighed, cupping his head intimately to her breast.

"Fine, you win." He moved her hips under him, effectively silencing her reply.

An hour later, the mule refused to be cowed by Royce anymore and started announcing his hunger to all. Royce got up and took the beast out to be tied to a nearby tree.

"Get dressed, and come out," he said coming back in, an undercurrent of excitement in his voice.

She was in the middle of eating a loaf of bread. Breaking off a piece, she passed some to him before grabbing up her dress and slipping it over her head. By the time she was done he had gathered up the blankets and packs and set them near the entrance of the cave. Taking up a jug of wine he grabbed her hand and pulled her out.

They left the mule munching on grass nearby the entrance of the cave and walked down the opposite way they'd come the night before. The late afternoon sun was starting to sink when he pushed aside some shrubs revealing a hot spring.

Royce pulled her forward to the edge of the warm water. "Bath, my lady?"

Poking her toe in, she gave an excited yelp and jumped back watching the small bubbles come up from the bottom of the clear pool. Without hesitation, she pulled her dress over her head and walked in. Royce was right behind her.

For a few minutes they floated next to each other reveling in the warmth. The water was coming up from a small hole in the ground near an outcropping of rocks. The closer she got to it the hotter the water. One could easily get burned, but here at the edge, the water was shallow and the perfect temperature.

Stretching out her legs, she enjoyed, breathing deep and letting her sore muscles relax. It would be another long night of walking. They needed to make it to Wiltshire if possible. But the ground would be marshy and difficult. Looking up at the trees swaying gently above her a strange sense of déjà vu washed over her.

"Have we been here before?" She asked.

Royce laid next to her, a hand casually around her waist his head thrown back in relaxation.

"No."

"How did you know about this place?"

"I didn't. But this area is riddled with hot springs. When I brought the mule out, I heard the stream and followed it. It shoots down right through there, you see." He pointed over to where the trees parted revealing the edges of a large stream surrounded by grassy stretches.

She sat up, hugging her knees. "I feel like I've been here before."

"Not here. This one's new to me." He pulled her close again.

Shaking off the feeling, she let Royce tease her with a story before he announced it was time to go. Getting out of the water he bent down for a kiss, and then playfully slapped her backside when she tried to escape his grasp swimming deeper into the pool.

Drying off, he donned his tunic and strapped his sword on before turning back to her. "I'll go and get our things. Come out now. It's too hot in there to stay too long and we have to get going."

"Yes, sir," she said playfully.

"I like that." He grinned back. "Sir. That should always be your response."

Sticking her tongue out at him, she lay back in the water and stared up at the sky darkening sky. It was beautiful here, a quiet, little out of the way spot, perfect for hidden rendezvous.

But no matter how hard she tried, she couldn't shake the feeling that she'd been here before. Getting out, she pulled her dress over her head and sat down to wait for Royce, squeezing the water from her hair.

A sudden feeling of being watched came over her. The hair on the back of her neck stood to attention. Her senses sharpened and a small noise behind her alerted her that someone was coming.

Getting up, she slipped over to where Royce had left her clothes and searched for the small knife he'd left for her. Shivers crept up her spine and, suddenly, she knew why this place seemed so familiar.

Turning to run after Royce, she came face to face with one of the men from her dreams.

"Hello dove."

"You." She backed up, hiding the small knife behind her back. "I knew I recognized you."

"Did ye now? You know me, ye say." He smiled, his voice taking on an exaggerated brogue.

Swallowing, she refused to answer. She'd said too much already.

"Ye know me?" he asked again. "Of course, you do, from the ale house. But then we didn't get a *proper* introduction." He bowed down to her with an eyebrow raised. "Allow me to introduce myself *properly*." Extending a leg, he made a motion with his hands, "I am Lord Edmund Mortimer of Gloucester, King Stephen's man of service." He smiled as though trying to be charming. Opening his simple black cloak, he dusted off the dirty dark blue vest and leggings. It was a far cry from the outfit he had worn when she met him the first time.

"Please pardon my appearance. I have been traveling for some time and have not yet had the chance to change my clothes. I had no idea I'd come across such a captivating lady as yourself in the middle of the wilds.

"Out here enjoying one of the many hot springs? Imagine my luck." His gaze turned wolfish, taking in the damp dress clinging to her figure. "But there's time for that later. My goodness, my dear, whatever are you doing here and where is your husband? Tis lucky I found him, I have news for him from the king." He finished casting his glance around the small area.

She didn't move, her mind trying so hard to place his face. Without a doubt she'd dreamed of him.

"You know it really is amazing," he said coming closer. "We happen to chance across each other, what? Two times in a fortnight?" Waving his own comments away, he took yet another step towards her. "Now where did you say your husband is?"

When she still didn't answer his gaze narrowed.

"Come, quick now, I don't have time. It's a very urgent message from the king."

He obviously didn't know that Robert had turned him in. He was standing nonchalantly pretending to be interested in the small pool, but when the only response was the quickening of her breath he turned and took a better look at her, his eyes focusing on her neck.

"What happened to your neck, my lady? Meet with some bad luck?"

Her hand went up to cover the scar. Instinctively, she tried to dart past him, but he jumped in her way and threw her back.

"Now why would you try to run?" His voice lowered and took on a more menacing tone. "I'm asking myself. A pretty thing like you would have nothing to fear from me...would you?"

She gripped the little knife tighter in her hand, trying to control her alarm. The sense of déjà vu grew. His touch sent a wave of revulsion down her spine and no matter how hard she tried, she couldn't calm her heart. She feared her panic showed on her face.

"It's the last time I'll ask nice. Where's your husband?" He advanced on her.

She backed away.

"You're awfully quiet. What is it you've got behind your back there? A rock perhaps? A small knife?" Taking the last step, he closed the gap, grabbing at her hand when she tried to strike out. The small knife glanced harmlessly off his shoulder. Squeezing her hand, he easily disarmed her, bringing her to heel.

"Now that wasn't nice," he growled giving her a shake. "Now was it, dove? Be nice now. I don't want to have to get mean. I'll ask one more time. Where is your husband? I know he's around here somewhere."

He gave a glance around. "Maybe one of my men has found him, eh? And is keeping him busy," he sneered bringing his face within an inch of hers.

Suddenly, she was able to place him. He'd given that same sneer to a group of women and children hiding in one of the villages. They were to live. Their lives had been spared by Lord Sutton, but Robert had given a separate order and Mortimer had carried it out.

She was with a woman and her three children crouching down behind a hidden door. Anna wanted to open the door and help the others, but the woman shook her head, no. She put her face against the cool stone and peered through a tiny hole into the bright, colorful room.

The sheers at the windows billowed in with the breeze, and the light danced across hopeful faces. Large pillows decorated the floor where children sat huddled together watching the knight advance.

The eldest woman had walked to meet him, bravely thanking him for sparing their lives, hushed voices, his answering smile and then the grate of his sword being drawn.

With one quick motion he sliced her head clean off. Her body crumpled to the floor. Sudden screams filled the small room. In horror, she watched as he began hacking at the children.

Nobody was spared.

The memory made her sick. Swallowing her terror, she returned her gaze to his. "You spared no one, not even the children," she choked out.

"What does that mean?" He narrowed his eyes.

"It was you. It was you that day, that day in Lisbon. You were supposed to spare the women and children but you slaughtered them instead. You tried to blame it on Royce, but Royce had been searching the southwest quadrant. "When you realized nobody would believe you, you set the fire, destroying the whole town. It's been you all along, you and Robert. Louvain is nothing more than a pawn. You're doing it for the Bishop, for money, all of this."

Halted by her words, his mouth turned unpleasant. His hand came up, choking her, silencing her words.

"How would you know that? Robert wouldn't talk." Bringing her face closer to his, he wrapped his other hand around her neck lifting her slightly off the ground, just enough so her toes could touch, but not enough to alleviate the pressure on her throat. Easing off on her throat, he growled, "Speak."

"The men from Flanders, their involved too," she bit out. She wanted him to know she knew. He wasn't going to get away with this.

His eyes flashed dangerously. "How could you know that? Nobody was there for that meeting but Robert and the Bishop. There's no way either would talk, so I ask you again, how would you know that? Are you a spy? How would you know me?" He shook her again and lifted her off the ground as she clawed at his hands.

He let her hang there, watching her fight for air before releasing her and throwing her back. "You know nothing, or at least you will soon."

Scooting backwards across the ground, she gasped for breath. He withdrew his sword with a hiss and stepped closer. Opening her eyes, she put up her hands to ward off his next blow.

"Robert wants you alive, but I think it's best if you have a little accident, my lady."

Gulping for air, she took one last breath and then screamed for Royce as loud as she could, her voice rising through the quiet glen.

"Yes, call for your lover. Bring him here to me. Though, I suspect he's got his hands full with my men," he said standing above her.

"Not anymore," Royce said from behind him.

Edmund whirled to face him, the surprise on his face quickly replaced with a smug smile as he took in Royce's torn and bloody clothes.

"It looks like you met up with some trouble Royce."

She scooted back, putting as much distance as possible between them.

"He's the one who did it in Lisbon." She cried trying to warn Royce. "He murdered all those women and children, killing them and then set fire to the village. He's in league with the Bishop. It's the Bishop that wants the throne, not Louvain. The men from Flanders, they're the real threat...He's tryi-."

"Shut up, you stupid whore." Edmund yelled back to her.

But she was already on her feet and running around the outer edge. When Edmund turned to face Royce again, he was ready.

The sound of swords clashing rang through the small clearing. Ducking down she scrambled under the thick brush at the side and raced back to the cave, praying the mule was still there with their packs. One thing she'd noticed the good ladies of the convent had gifted them with was a simple bow and a quiver full of arrows. She hadn't had time to examine them close, but for now hopefully, they would do.

The sight that greeted her near the cave chilled her blood. Royce had been busy. Six men lay at odd angles around the entrance. She clamped a hand over her mouth, swallowing back the bile and stepped carefully over the splayed bodies.

The mule's bridle was caught in a shrub nearby and he stood quiet at her approach. His ears flickered forward as she rummaged through the packs secured tight to his back. When she found what she sought and turned to leave, the animal called after her, unhappy to be left alone again.

Running back through the forest she slung the quiver over her shoulder, praying she wouldn't be too late. As she neared, she could hear Royce and Edmund still fighting. Ducking back under the brush, she peered into the glen, watching Royce defend himself against Edmund's onslaught. His movements were slower, his tunic revealing new blood-soaked slashes across his chest.

With no hesitation, she stood and fitted an arrow in place. Drawing back, she narrowed her gaze, gave a prayer and let it fly. The first one hit the back of Edmund's thigh and she quickly reloaded.

He cursed. Turning, he spotted her and took a step in her direction.

The next arrow hit his sword arm and Edmund's face turned purple with fury. Passing his sword from his right to his left hand, he ran at her, his sword raised ready to strike her down. Royce followed and took a thrust at his back.

"Turn around and fight you coward," he yelled.

The injuries only seemed to fuel Edmund's rage and he struck out violently at Royce, swinging his sword in a mad arc.

Royce jumped back, neatly missing the angry swing. Bringing his sword around in a large sweep, he cut deep into Edmund's wrist and hand. Edmund cried out dropping his sword, a few fingers falling to the ground with it. He cupped the bleeding hand in front of him, the surprise at the wound registering on his face.

Without waiting, Royce leaped forward again slicing him open across the stomach. Edmund dropped to his knees. Royce's chest was heaving with effort. He stood silent nearby, watching the realization grow on Edmund's face that he was dying. Bleeding from two arrow wounds, and with half his hand gone, he was clutching at his gut trying to stop his intestines from pouring out.

"He's in league with the Bishop to try and kill Prince Henry," she said gasping for breath. "The assassins are coming from Flanders."

Royce looked down at her and nodded the sweat and blood mingling to run down his chest. Crouching down in front of Edmund, he asked, "Who is your contact in Flanders?"

When Edmund didn't look at him, Royce took his sword and put it under the man's neck tipping his head back. "I said, who's your contact in Flanders? Who's your contact with the Bishop?"

Edmund's eyes had begun to glaze over and he lips twitched in a gruesome smile. Blood spilled out of his mouth staining his teeth. He grunted, "Go ahead kill me. Like I'd tell you, you dirty whoreson."

Royce stood and stepped away. Edmund leaned his head back fully expecting the final blow.

"I'll not kill you. That stomach wound will do it soon enough." Looking around, he listened to the call of a wolf before he brought his gaze back to Edmund. Picking up Edmund's sword, he tossed it deep into the hot spring. "Maybe an animal or two will help."

Turning, he reached for her hand and pulled her beside him leaving Edmund there on the ground. The surprise on Edmund's face showed his dismay at being left alone to die in the wilderness.

"Come back here, you bastard and finish the job." He called out to Royce, his voice growing more desperate and weaker with the distance.

As they drew away from the light infused glen, the hushed sounds of animals coming awake penetrated her haze. Anna took a good look around, her senses on high alert. Night was falling fast and the shadows lengthened in the woods.

The ringing in her ears from the sword fighting had dulled down and she could actually hear the noisy birds making their way home for the night. She found the eager twittering and calling soothing and let her mind blank out on everything that had just happened.

When they reached the cave, she didn't hesitate like she had before. She walked easily past the dead men littering the ground, her mind numb.

Royce picked his way through the grizzly scene pulling her behind him. A form of disembodied shock washed over her when they reached the braying mule.

Neither of them spoke. Royce stripped off his bloody tunic and threw it to the ground and then did the same with her ruined dress. Grabbing up the towel that he had used earlier, he began gently wiping away the blood on her body as one would a child who had fallen and hurt themselves.

Reaching into the pack, he pulled out the other dress, this one older and if possible uglier than the one she had worn earlier. Dark brown and itchy, it scratched her skin as he pulled it over her head. Without the soft linen of her slip underneath this one would soon grow uncomfortable and begin to chafe, and yet she hardly noticed.

She stood silent, watching him do the same for his own body. He pulled out a long tunic in the same mud color as her own. This one reached just past his knees and looked like a friar's robe. With the dried smeared blood on his face and neck he looked like a crazy man. She was sure she didn't look much better.

Gathering up his sword, he tied it to his waist and went about disarming the men he'd killed earlier. He didn't bother to explain. Anything of value he took. Anything that looked like it could identify him as their killer he left for the next passerby.

From one he pulled out a small bag of gold, another had an unadorned dagger that he tied to her thigh and the swords that were plain in appearance he loaded on the mule.

A horse nickered nearby as the call of the wolves sounded again. Night was full upon them. The smell of blood hung thick and heavy in the air. It was time to go or fight off the predators that would soon be roaming these forests.

Royce grabbed the mules lead rope and her hand and pulled them both back through the forest until they found where the men had left their mounts. Seven horses were prancing around, pulling nervously at their reins.

Royce undid three of the saddles and bridles freeing the smaller horses. They jumped back and quickly took off away from the sound of the encroaching wolves. Throwing her up on one, he passed her the lead of the mule, then jumped up on another and tied the reins of the two remaining animals to the back.

Kicking his horse forward, she listened to the renewed screams coming from the glen just behind the small hill. The wolves had found their first meal for the night.

CHAPTER
20

"How did you know about Edmund?" Royce slowed his horse and waited for Anna to come up beside him.

Anna peered into the darkness at his profile. They'd been riding for hours now and this was the first words he had spoken.

They'd taken wide berths around any town they came across and kept to the trees as much as possible. Royce had released the extra horses and the mule near a quiet village knowing they would be well taken care of by a local. He'd even traveled north about an hour to do it just in case. Now they were back tracking south to Trowbridge.

"I recognized him from my dreams." She kept her voice low. In the softness of the night, her voice seemed to echo through the trees.

"You've had them since you've been here?"

"I had them when I was at the castle. The old woman who tended to me told me she gave me something that would give me the 'dreams'. When I woke, it was like I had all the answers...suddenly, I knew everything. So, when she came in later and asked if I'd had the 'dreams' it kind of threw me a little and..."

"And then what?"

"And then she said, if I paid attention they would tell me the answers."

"Did you pay attention?"

"I think so, but after that, everything got kind of crazy and I lost my focus. They all became a little hazy again."

Pausing, she let the intimacy of the dark fill her. "You know, for the past year I've feared my dreams...feared the night, but here I am riding through a forest on a moonless night and I'm not afraid." Her voice was a quiet whisper surrounding them. With a chuckle she went on, "Maybe I should be, but after so much fear-fear about who I was, why this was happening to me, why I couldn't control it. It feels good to let it go. Just like at the castle, I was afraid the other night, but I fought through my fear. I fought back and it felt amazing."

Turning to face him, she could see his outline. He was just a shadow beside her, and yet his presence filled her with a sense of contentment and peace the likes of which she hadn't felt since her childhood.

"I'd forgotten about you...all this...I'd buried you along with my sister. Now I realize you've been with me all along. Somewhere, somehow, deep inside, I guess I've always known you where there with me."

Royce reached over and pulled her from her saddle, onto his horse. Settling her sideways on his lap in front of him, he wrapped his arms loosely around her. "Tell me more."

"When I first came back, I didn't want to know. I didn't want to remember. I fought it. And then I was afraid too, because the last year they've been horrible, my dreams. And I thought they were all you.

"But when I woke up, I realized they weren't. They were just a part of your life. It's just so bizarre. If I think about it too hard it hurts my brain." She shook her head, bewildered. "I don't know how any of it's possible, but I know it's happened and been happening to me, to us, since we met. Did you know Robert saw me? He knew who I was. He recognized me. He kept calling me the white lady."

Royce stiffened.

"He told me all the men could see me, that I was their white lady, *your* white lady. What does that mean?"

He didn't answer right away. She went on needing to share it with him.

"Sometimes I could feel the heat from the fires. I would wake up and my hands would be singed, my nails dirty. One time I was running so fast and I was so scared, I tripped and fell over a body and when I woke up, my knees were skinned and I had cuts and scrapes all over me...dirty feet, hands, face. I didn't go outside for two days."

"You were here." He cleared throat. "I saw you. So many times, I saw you. Other men saw you too. I just couldn't get to you in time."

"I thought so, but I couldn't be sure. It was all so different. Everyone was covered up in armor and there was always so much smoke and fear. I wouldn't be able to remember the details, just the feelings of violence and danger. You live such a dangerous life."

"Yes."

"Was it so horrible over there?"

He didn't answer. Had she over-stepped her bounds? She turned back to him and put her hands up to his face until he looked down at her.

"I'm sorry you had to go through that," she said gently.

His smile radiated even in the darkness. He leaned down to kiss her softly before settling her forward again.

"What of the white lady?" she asked, remembering their conversation. "What does that mean?"

"It's an old legend. The white lady will come and lead her men to victory. You were always in white." He met her gaze. "Every time I saw you, you were always in white."

Turning his eyes back to the road, he swallowed, "I think that's how the story got started, I don't really know. I never spoke of you. The men would ask right before battle, 'Do you think she'll come today?' It started as a joke, and then, well...you kept showing up. "So often I would only get a glance, or I would see a hint of white from far away and I would try to get to you, but I never could. A few times there at the end I was close, so close. The last time I had your hand, but then you slipped away."

Clearing his throat again, he shook his head before continuing,

"It was maddening. I would dream of you. I knew you were coming, and still it took me a year to find you. Every day waiting, every night dreaming and then you came." He smiled down at her.

She returned his smile, enjoying this talk.

"Tell me about the legend."

He grimaced and drew in a deep breath. "The legend, hm? I don't know it really, and there are many versions, something about a lady who was captured by a warring lord. It was a family fight for the right of the throne, an old story but not an uncommon one.

"The old king died and he had no sons, so the kingdom was up for grabs. Two men of equal birth and rank were fighting for the kingdom when one took the other's wife. She was considered to be quite a beauty and of royal blood. It was said they married for love not money, which is unusual in most marriages.

"When the lord came to get his wife, the other stood her atop the highest wall in a simple white shift to show his rival that his wife was unharmed. He told the lord, for her to live, he would have to give up the throne or she would die right there in front of him.

"While she was standing there, she took down her hair and dropped the white cloth that was holding it back. Her husband's army took it as a signal and attacked, surprising the opposing lord and overpowering the castle."

"Hmm, I like that story."

"I don't."

"Why not? It's a wonderful story of love and-"

"She died that day. It was said her sacrifice to her country earned her the right to still walk among her people and she will return when they need her again."

"Ick." Goosebumps broke out on her arms and she shivered. "I can see why you don't like that story."

"Now you understand why I don't encourage talk about you being the white lady. It's also the reason I don't want you wearing white. Never wear white...promise me," he said with a shake.

"I promise," she laughed prompting another kiss from him.

"It is interesting." She faced forward, growing thoughtful.

He changed the subject. "Now tell me about the men from Flanders. What of them?"

She sat up straight, eager to talk of something else. "I saw him with a bishop, I think, or somebody in the church. They were all well dressed-Edmund, Robert and this guy in heavy robes and they were planning the assassination. They kept talking about the men from Flanders. I'm not sure who they are, but they kept mentioning them."

Royce fired off one question after the other trying to help her recall every detail. What did the man in robes look like? Was he young, old-did he have a beard. What color was his hair? The more he asked the better her memory. Finally, he fell silent after she had described the older Bishop in as much detail as she could.

"I didn't want to believe it," he said after a moment.

"Believe what?"

"Remember the man who attacked us by the river."

"When I first got here?"

"Yes. Do you remember the tunic he was wearing? It was a red tunic under a mail coat, but it had a small insignia on the sleeve. Do you remember it?"

Anna thought for a minute. "I didn't look that closely at him. But the Bishop I can see clearly. He was in a dark blue robe with a coat of arms on the front. It was a red shield pierced with two swords. Does that help?"

"Yes," Royce said, taking a deep breath. "And no, the man by the river had a white shield pierced by three swords, but it's similar. His brother is the third sword, the third house, you see? The Bishop is the second house, his brother is the third. The first brother died a few years ago. I don't know the circumstance, but it was nasty business.

"Since then the Bishop has kept a rather low profile or, at least, I thought he did. I've not heard much of him in France. The Bishop's a very powerful man here and if he's involved...his whole family...then it's worse than I thought. There's no love between the Bishop and myself, so I'll get no quarter there. But it's going to be hard to convince Henry that he is against him. He's practically a father to him." Royce finished quietly.

"Does Henry know him that well?"

"Yes, the Bishop visited on numerous occasions and both Henry and his mother have been guests of his at Dover." Clicking to his horse he turned east. "We need to go to Dover, but first we have a few stops to make."

"Where to?"

"Brighton."

Two weeks later they came to Saltwood and were immediately given entrance to the castle there. Anna watched with mixed emotions as the drawbridge was lowered and voices called out in greeting from above. It had been wonderful spending the last two weeks just with Royce. She wasn't sure if she was ready to give that up.

They had gone from town to town casually making inquiries about a few people, never sleeping in a bed, but every night finding a place to camp out under the stars. No word had been heard from Gordon Ramsey, and Royce had mentioned on several occasions his worry about the man. Gordon, or Keefe as she had been told, had left them weeks ago when they had slipped away in the middle of the night and boarded a boat from the beach.

Hopefully, Lars and Hayne had reached him by now to let them know of the conspiracy or the peace that Henry promised would be at risk. At Brighton, they had sent a message to Henry through one of Royce's friends warning him of the Bishop's deception.

Anna stared at Royce's back as he waited patiently. His teeth flashed in a grin when a familiar head peered over the wall from above.

"Where the hell have you been? We've been waiting here for a week for you," Lars called down.

"Have you now? I doubt that since we've been following your trail for three days back."

"Well, why didn't you just catch up?"

"We weren't looking for your company, man."

Lars laughed and his head disappeared. The drawbridge finished its descent and they started their horses forward over the large moat.

Trepidation filled her and she questioned it. She should be happy. They would have a bed again and food they wouldn't have to catch and cook, but even as these thoughts flashed through her mind, she knew she would miss the last two weeks.

For the first time since she had been here, they had had some measure of peace. Yes, they had to be cautious. Every time soldiers were spotted they would turn away and quickly leave the area. They'd been careful to keep to themselves and not draw attention to their actions. Trying to blend in, they'd taken on the guise of traders which would help explain the horses they were riding.

Whenever a curious villager would ask, Royce would say they were on their way east to catch the boats coming in from France for trade. But few had asked. Most didn't care, and Anna had found the friendly easy banter that had accompanied them from town to town enjoyable.

On the few times they had been invited to eat at a table, she had enjoyed herself immensely listening to the stories passed around. The villagers were uncomplicated people, easy going and humorous with frank talk. For the first time in her life she felt like she belonged.

She had enjoyed her status as a married woman and took pride in the interested looks thrown Royce's way and the easy jests given to her.

On one such occasion, the woman voicing her opinion had to be well into her seventies with barely a tooth in sight. She winked at Royce and promptly informed Anna and the whole table how lucky she was to have such a strapping young man to dance between her thighs every night. Royce had laughed and hugged her close. Anna had joined him, burying her head in his shoulder.

The threats they faced seemed farther away with each mile they had gone. With that had come a sense of calm and happiness in the simple acts of picking berries warm from the sun to catching fish for dinner or skinning her first rabbit.

She felt different, and she wasn't ready to give that up yet. But yesterday when Royce told her they were almost to their destination;

her heart had picked up its beat and unease had settled over her with the realization that their time alone together was coming to a close.

Going under the large gate, she checked the urge to turn and run. The drawbridge wheel groaned. She watched the dusty road behind them disappear behind the heavy wooden door.

"About time you got here." Lars called out, coming down off the ramparts towards them.

Royce grinned, but she could tell from the set of his shoulders he was eager to talk to his friend alone. He clapped Lars on the back before turning to swing her down.

Leaning in, pretending to pull something from the sacks strapped to the back of the horse Royce whispered, "Did you reach Gordon?"

"Yes, all's well. Come. Come. Fitzhugh is waiting for you in the keep," Lars nodded to her.

Relief flooded her system as she viewed Lars. He did look hale and hearty. He was dressed again in a heavy tunic and leggings, simple but well-made and vastly different from the clothing they were wearing.

For the first time in weeks she thought about her clothes. A quick look up to the wall revealed several ladies sitting and watching their entrance and her concern about her appearance blossomed.

Those were definitely ladies. Bright gowns swayed in the wind and their hair was swept back and contained with lace, ribbon or some kind of headpiece. Even from this distance, she could see jewels winking from all angles.

She ran her hands over the unshapely dress she was wearing. It had been creek washed yesterday, but it was the same one from two weeks ago and had to look seriously worse for the wear.

Ignoring the twittering from above, she set her jaw. Let them look. Putting her head up and shoulders back, she followed her husband inside.

Entering the four story keep, she was amazed at how large and new it was. Thick stone walls held a decoration of lethal looking swords, maces and lances next to beautiful tapestries. The wide stairs led up to the great room and a few men still enjoying breakfast at the tables scattered around the room. The smell of fresh bread permeated the room making her mouth water. Women and boys ran from table to table with jugs of ale and porridge.

The man at the head table stood and ushered them forward, wiping his chin before coming around to shake Royce's hand.

"Food," he called in a booming voice. "Tell Mistress Marks to bring more food. We have guests."

Turning back to Royce, he clapped him on the back, and motioned for them to sit. "Lord Sutton, Lars told me you were on your way. And you've brought your lovely wife. I am Lord Fitzhugh, my lady, and you honor me with your presence."

She curtsied to the man and held her tongue. She felt completely self-conscious. She tried not to fumble with her hair which hadn't seen a comb since the abbey. No doubt she looked awful.

Once they were seated and served, he started in on Royce as to the developments of the last few weeks. He wanted to know where they had been, who they had seen, and what they had discovered about Louvain's plot. He expressed horror over the Bishop's involvement, and then grew silent.

Anna listened with half an ear, the food on the table taking much of her attention. Breakfast was warm bread and porridge which she ate without complaint. The ale was cool and the best she'd had in weeks.

When she'd had her fill she finally looked up. The men were waiting for her to finish. Coloring slightly, she bobbed her head and nodded again in agreement when Fitzhugh offered her the use of his daughter's room to change and rest.

"My daughter is in London. She's to be married at the end of the month. You just caught me. I'm to leave in the morning for the ceremony." Standing, he called to one of the maids. With a last look at Royce, she curtsied to the men and turned to leave the room following the small maid up the stairs.

CHAPTER

21

Upstairs the young maid turned down a hall and let Anna into a large room that overlooked the back garden. The lovely room was cool with a nice breeze coming in through the open windows. More tapestries hung on the walls and there was even a rug on the floor near the bed. The bed wasn't huge but certainly big enough for her and Royce.

"My lady's wardrobe is at your disposal. There's some water to refresh yourself." The girl pointed to a pitcher and bowl on a small stand in one corner. "I've laid some clothes out for you. If you need help getting dressed I can come back." The young maid hovered near the door.

"I think I need a little more than a change of clothes, a bath maybe?" she asked, hopeful.

"Of course, my lady." The girl nodded. "It will be a few minutes to heat the water." With a curtsey she left, closing the door behind her.

Anna went and stood at the window, leaning out to view the vast flower garden below. Taking a deep breath, she let the sweet scent of summer blossoms fill her senses. At the sound of voices, she looked down. Right below her the pretty women she'd seen earlier were walking out to the garden. She jerked back in the room so they wouldn't see her.

Their words floated up to her like the smell of the flowers. They were talking about Royce or Lord Sutton as they called him. Their excitement over his arrival was palpable, just as their dismay when one of them told the others that the woman he'd arrived with was his wife.

"His wife? That was a woman? Hardly. I think you are mistaken, Beth. That was his servant," one voice said above the others.

Anna took a chance and peered down at them, wanting to know who was speaking.

It was the small blonde with the elaborate head gear that she'd seen earlier. Taking a good look, she assessed the ladies. They looked more like girls. They couldn't be more than eighteen. Each was dressed in heavy brocaded gowns despite the summer heat.

"Oh no," the taller brunette retorted. "I just heard it from one of the kitchen maids. She's his wife alright."

"Even if they are married, that doesn't mean anything," the woman with the light brown hair commented. Putting her hand on the blonde's arm, she said, "I'm sure they'll have separate rooms."

All the women started to laugh as they continued their stroll down the path and out of her hearing range. She watched them go, whispering and laughing behind ringed fingers until they disappeared around a hedge.

Disappointment settled in her. Oh, well, nothing she could do about it now, she thought turning back to her room.

Going over to the large wardrobe the young maid had mentioned, she opened it and was startled at the brightly colored gowns and cloaks that spilled forth.

Maybe there was something she could do about it after all. She ran her hands over a few of the gowns. Fine silk slid through her fingers.

"Perfect," she said out loud.

On the other side of the wardrobe in front of the fireplace, two chairs were placed next to it to catch the warmth. Unfinished needlepoint lay in baskets beside the chairs.

She bent down for a closer look at the fine stitching on the sampler, when a movement from behind the wardrobe door caught her eye. Turning back, she froze at her own reflection shining back at her. Startled, her first thought was a stranger in the room with her. It took a moment to recognize herself.

She stared at the image in the long mirror. It wasn't a mirror like she used to have, giving back a perfect reflection, but a tall looking glass of shiny metal. Her reflection was distorted slightly with the bumps and valleys of the metal. Still it was her, but not the way she used to look.

Putting her hand up, she touched the rough surface of the metal, running her hands over the image of her face.

Her hair was long and sun-kissed and hung around her face in a mass of soft curls. She was definitely thinner and her cheekbones stood out stark in her face. Her eyes seemed huge in the sunburned cheeks and she smiled in spite of herself.

Gone was the pale girl with a vacant stare who had lived her life like she was half alive. How often had she wondered if this was it? The life she'd lived seemed so empty. She'd never worried about money or her next meal, always being able to afford whatever she needed when she needed. Fashion hadn't been important. She'd worn what was comfortable, but the clothes had always been expensive. She'd kept up with her skin and religiously applied sunscreen. She'd worn makeup... not a lot but taken care with her appearance.

Now, her face looked older, more alive, the vivid green of her eyes bright. Her dark hair was streaked with red and gold. It was a natural, wild beauty that one couldn't get in a salon and a far cry above those primped, pale girls from the garden.

She started to undress, curious about the ways the rest of her body had changed. Undoing the ties on her dress, she pulled it open revealing her breasts and stomach. A dark tan covered her face, chest and arms leaving the rest of her a milky white. She had new muscles everywhere.

The last few months of hard living had been that-living. She had been living since she got here, instead of just existing like she had in her past. Her body was hard and soft at the same time, long, thin well-developed arms, and full, soft breasts led to a well-developed belly and trim hips. A confidence that had eluded her all her life breathed through her. This was a woman's body, a woman who knew what it was like to be well loved and to love in return.

"Anna." A soft rap announced Royce's arrival. Her name died on his lips as he stopped in the doorway. Surprise flashed across his face seeing her half-naked in front of the mirror.

She didn't turn. She just watched him in the reflection, continuing to run her hands leisurely over her body. Her skin started to tingle and excitement shivered up her spine. Did Royce see what she saw? A woman in all her glory possessed of herself and her sexuality.

He stood poised on the threshold as if unsure what to do, his eyes traveled down her body and back up again. It felt like forever since they had a room to call their own. They'd been living on the fringe of society for so long, always on the run, sleeping where they could. Now to be in a room alone together...

He closed the door and came forward to stand behind her, his fists clenched. He was clearly captivated by her image.

Turning her gaze back onto herself, she let a smile play across her lips and edged the dress slowly off her hips, enjoying the delicious wave of heat that settled in her belly. Breathing through her nose, she let it fall to the floor.

She had never felt so sexy in her life. Running her hands back up her hips, she gently cupped her breasts.

Royce's nostrils flared and his mouth flattened. Flexing his fingers, he reached out and touched the small of her back.

She arched into his touch.

"You're so beautiful Anna," he said, his voice a low guttural whisper.

Not ready to break the spell, she reached behind her without talking and pulled his hand around to join hers in cupping her breast. His hand cradled the weight and began running his thumb over her taut nipple ever so gently. Still watching in the mirror, Royce took a step, closing the gap between them. His other hand came around and slid down her hip.

She pushed back into him. Reaching down, she guided his hand up her thigh to nestle in her curls. Groaning, he began to move behind her, watching her body gyrate in the mirror.

She couldn't seem to stop herself. She felt provocative and free at the same time. She put her hands on top of his, guiding him where she wanted him to be, squeezing slowly, teasing madly, rubbing and thrusting. Her body melded like fluid in his hands and she used him to bring herself to a full orgasm. Wave after wave crashed over her as he held her, one finger deep inside her, the other hand upon her breast. With her body open and head thrown back in complete abandonment, it took a moment for her to return to reality.

Her eyes met his in the mirror and, instead of embarrassment, a thrill of fulfillment rushed through her. Her body was flush with excitement, her eyes lazy and seductive. The heat of him behind her spurred her on. She reached for him. He was hard as a rock, his body vibrating with want and need.

Without a word Royce swept her into his arms and carried her to the bed.

They hadn't made love in a bed since that first night. Instead, it had been in the middle of the forest or in a cave. Once he'd taken her against a tree so great was their hunger. She never said no, always welcomed him with open arms, hard and fast or long and slow, she was ready for him.

But this, this was beyond her expectations. Throwing her on the bed, his eyes feasted on her naked body. She scooted back to allow room for him. Her hair fell over one breast, and she left it there.

Pushing her back fully on the bed, he lay down on top of her and began a leisure exploration with his mouth, suckling first one breast and then the other. She tried to force his mouth up for a kiss but he captured her wrists in one hand, pinning them above her head. Moving down her body, he released her wrists and his hands fastened on her breasts gently teasing the hard peaks.

He kissed her belly, her hips and the inside of each thigh before he found her center. She arched off the bed and twined her hands in his hair, his tongue exploring her intimately. With infinite slowness he took his time, bringing her to another full climax. Still shaking, she watched him come above her and enter her, pulling her legs up to allow deeper access. Holding her hips, he thrust into her fully. Again, she arched off the bed, her body so taut and sensitive. With continued slowness he entered her again and again, until he began to tremble in her arms.

With a final cry, he thrust harder one last time before sinking into her spent. For a moment he just laid there on top of her, his breath coming in ragged bursts. His weight bore down on her in the straw covered mattress. Gradually, the sound of birds twittering from outside permeated her hearing and the beat of her heart lessened, reality intruding on her bliss. Royce rolled to the side, allowing the cool breeze to sweep over their sweat drenched bodies. She dragged air deep into her lungs and let out a sigh.

It was then that she heard the movement's coming from the other side of the door. Royce must have heard it too, because his head came off the pillow at the same time.

"Who goes there?" he yelled in a hoarse voice. Jumping up he pulled on his hose and moved towards the door a heavy frown on his face.

She covered herself with one of the sheets, the delightful fog from their lovemaking quickly evaporating. Getting up from the bed, she followed him to the doorway just as he turned away leaving it open.

"It's the maid," he said stumbling back to throw himself across the bed. "She has brought a tub for you. I'm going to lie down for a minute while you bathe. My God, woman, you have taken my reserves," he muttered closing his eyes.

She smiled at the maid whose heavy blush told her that she had heard more than she probably should have. A few more women filed in, filling the tub with bucket after bucket of steaming water. She waited for the embarrassment to hit her, but it wouldn't come. Instead, an odd sense of pleasure washed over her knowing that these maids would most likely carry tales back to the kitchen about their lovemaking.

Looking back at Royce who was splayed on the bed, one arm thrown over his eyes, his mouth open emitting a soft snore, satisfaction filled her. Yes, she could please her man, but more importantly he could please her.

"Anything else, my lady?" The first maid cleared her throat as the others cast envious glances at the sight of Royce passed out on the bed.

She dismissed the rest and smiled at the young girl. Dropping the sheet, she walked towards the tub.

"Yes, please help with me with my hair," she said sinking into the tub.

CHAPTER 22

"Out with you." Anna flicked her hands at Royce who was lying across the bed behind her. His arms were behind his head and he kept flexing his muscles and smiling at her in the reflection of the mirror. White teeth flashed in a brazen smile and a slow wink sent her pulse racing while Thea, the maid, tried to braid her hair.

"I'm not coming back to bed with you," she said exasperated as the maid dropped the comb in her lap...again. Standing, she handed it back to Thea and went over to the bed.

"Up." She laughed. "You're making the girl nervous."

"Come here." He ignored her comment and reached up, pulling her down. "Just one more time," he whispered in her ear rolling her under him and nipping at her neck.

Out of the corner of her eye, she saw Thea start for the door, embarrassment coloring her face.

"No, wait Thea," she called out, pushing up out of his arms. "He's going, not you."

After Royce left the little maid worked quickly, pulling the curls back from her face and braiding it down her back. She tried to convince Anna to wear an elaborate, ugly brown headdress, but she refused, only allowing a sheer piece of lace to be woven into her hair.

The first gown Thea brought in matched the brown headdress and she asked for another. While Thea went to get a different dress, Anna fingered through the gowns on display in the armoire and came across one in a beautiful shade of pale blue silk. When the maid returned with another gown in an atrocious shade of gray, she became suspicious.

"Where are you getting these gowns?"

Thea averted her eyes and went to busy herself near the table before answering. "It's what I've been told to give you, my lady."

"By Barron Fitzhugh?"

"No, by-" The maid stopped and turned back around.

She didn't push any further. So that was how it was going to be. Changing tactics, she pulled out the blue gown and laid it over the chair.

"I would like to wear this one, please."

"Oh, no, my lady, I can't. That's one of Mistress Beth's."

"Barron Fitzhugh invited me to wear anything in his daughter's wardrobe and it's obvious she has more than enough gowns. So, either you help me with this or you may be excused," she said catching the girl's eye.

Thea swallowed and began backing out of the room.

"I realize you answer to another lady here, but do you really think Barron Fitzhugh will be pleased to know you refused to help me?"

Stopping at the door, the girl's owlish expression stared back at her.

"I'll make you a deal. Help me get started and I'll finish dressing myself. You can say I kicked you out before the end." She paused and waited for the maid's reaction.

Uncertainty flew across the young face and she felt bad for putting the girl in this predicament, but she wasn't wearing either one of those ridiculous dresses she'd brought in.

Finally, Thea nodded her assent and stepped forward going over to a small alcove. Pushing aside the curtain she opened a narrow chest and pulled out a soft pair of leather shoes. Placing them on the floor next to

Anna, she then went and got another slip, this one a light cream with large bell sleeves and helped her into it. The girl motioned to the dress and then went over and opened a box on the floor to display an array of jeweled belts. Without saying anything, she pointed to a narrow silver chain that would match the dress perfectly. Tiny blue stones decorated the length of the darkened silver. The style was simple and elegant.

"Thank you," Anna whispered sincerely. "It will look beautiful together."

Thea bowed her head, picked up the discarded dresses and left the room without another word.

The rest was easy. Anna slipped the dress over her head and tied the front before putting on the soft slippers and adding the belt as a last touch. Surveying the results in the mirror, she was pleased. She did look pretty, just as pretty as those women in the garden.

Whoever had tried to sabotage her clothes she would meet soon at dinner.

When Royce came back she was ready for him. She turned from the mirror just as the door opened and laughed at his expression.

"Come in, it's me," she teased. "I won't bite."

Heat entered his eyes and the surprise on his face was replaced with a smoldering look and a wolfish grin.

"Don't you like it?" She twirled, letting the dress bell out at her feet.

"My lady," he winked and bowed low over her hand. "Nothing could compare to your beauty."

"Why thank you, kind sir," she nodded regally and fluttered her eyelashes up at him. "The same goes for you, husband." She walked around him, letting her finger linger at his belt. "Where did you get these clothes? They fit you so well they could be yours."

"They are mine." He puffed out his chest, showing off the black tunic he wore. It was simply cut, but of a heavy brocade material and had silver stitching around the open neck. He wore a new belt around his waist of dark leather with a dagger at his side and dark hose. "One of my ships docked yesterday and Lars had a couple of my trunks delivered here. Do you like them?" He turned in a circle for her.

"Very much," she laughed, "One of your ships?"

"Didn't I tell you about my ships?" He grabbed her around the waist and pulled her into his arms.

"No." She arched an eyebrow, glancing at him from under her lashes. "Tell me about your ships, how many do you have and what do you use them for?"

"I have four. Most are used for trade. These are coming from my property in France." He bent to nibble on her neck as he spoke.

"I thought you gave up your property there?" She asked pushing him back.

"I did. My father's estate, but my mother had some deeded to her from her grandmother. Henry let me keep it."

"There's still so much I don't know about you." She shook her head amazed.

"Ask and I shall tell you, my sweet." He bent down and growled in her ear, "Besides, we have plenty of time to talk later."

"Stop that. I'm asking you a question." She tried to ignore his mouth swirling up her neck. "So, Henry, you mean Prince Henry? He let you keep property your grandmother left you?"

"Yes," he rasped. "You smell good."

Laughing, she pushed him away again and took a step to the window. "How kind of him."

"It was," he agreed.

"Is it big?" She asked.

"You mean am I rich?" He raised his eyebrows and took a step towards her, clasping his hands innocently behind his back. "No. Not by any means. It's a small property on the water. While the keep is nothing now, the land is rich and fertile and there's enough of it to work someday. Right now, I'm not there enough, but I have somebody overseeing it. I visit when I can. I hope that doesn't disappoint you."

"Of course not, I'll be excited to see it someday. How did you get your boats?"

"Ships, Anna. There's a big difference between a ship and a boat. And that kind of happened by accident. We can talk about it later. What is this you're wearing under here?" He fingered the thin material at the top of her dress.

"That is none of your business, sir." She playfully slapped his hand away from her bosom. "Now back to your boats..."

His smile broadened and then turned wolfish again at her flirtatious refusal. Pushing her against the wall he said, "The *ships* can wait, I cannot." Casually, he lifted her skirts and began drawing lazy circles up her thigh until a loud knock on the door stopped him.

"Royce. Come on, man. It's time to go down," Lars called from the hall.

With a groan he dropped her skirts and leaned into the wall resting his forehead on hers. "Go away, Lars," he yelled.

"For God's sake man, you're expected to supper. You're the honored guest. You can't keep the man waiting."

Unable to suppress a giggle, she slipped under his arm and opened the door for Lars. Raising her shoulders, she gave him her best 'I'm innocent' look before returning her gaze to Royce. Lars raised his eyebrows at the dark frown on his friend's face, which only sent her into a fit of laughter.

"I knew if I didn't catch you now, you would be late." Lars shook his head with pretend disgust before turning to Anna. "My lady, you steal the sun with your shine." He offered his arm. "May I escort you down to dine?"

She took it graciously letting Royce follow behind. Casting a glance over her shoulder, she caught his admiring focus on her bottom. She gave it a saucy shake and his eyes traveled up to her face to give her a promising wink.

"Lars, I have a question for you. Royce was just telling me about his boats."

"Do you mean his fleet of ships?" Lars cocked his head to the side.

"He has a fleet? How many ships do you need for a fleet?"

"It is a modest fleet, my lady. One he acquired in the Middle East. It was how he decided to come into the business of trade. Did he not tell you of his riches?"

"Riches? He has riches?"

"Well, of course. You must know. I mean, why else would you marry him. He's such an ugly fellow." Lars paused on the stairs to look back at Royce who just raised an eyebrow. "I mean," Lars went on in mock disgust. "That face is surely one only a mother could love. Just wait till we get to supper. All the ladies will be cowering away from his ugly form," Lars whispered as they rounded the corner, coming into the great hall.

The conversation in the room died at their entrance. People stopped and stared, their curiosity palpable. Right away Anna spotted the petite blonde that she'd seen earlier from her window. The girl couldn't be more than sixteen. The blonde frowned and began whispering behind her hand to the brunette next to her.

Anna's smile grew at the blonde's obvious jealousy and at the same time was amazed at her own confidence. She was buoyant in her self-assurance. Peace stole over her as she walked forward.

"See." Lars tugged at her hand and bent to whisper. "They shrink from him like a dark cloud, my lady. But it is you, the sun, who will bring them all back with your beauty."

"Oh, nicely done, kind sir." She gave him an elegant nod.

The room was full of people she didn't recognize and didn't care to meet. Only one face stood out among them. Hayne came forward hesitantly, stopping in front of her and offering a leg.

"My lady."

"Hayne, you made it." She went forward, grabbing both his hands. "I had no doubt."

The rest of the night passed slowly. Dinner was a loud, festive and yet formal affair. Mediocre wine was passed in abundance. Vegetables and bread were served first and followed by two types of meat. One of the courses looked to be peacock and the other was pork. The last course to arrive was a selection of cheeses and fruits.

She shared a platter with Royce to her left, while Lars sat at her right. Everyone ate with their fingers or a two-pronged fork and a little dagger.

Royce cut her meat for her while talking to the Barron on his left.

When the blonde, who was sitting two down on the other side of Lars claimed she needed help, Lars happily leaned over to accommodate her. The pucker on her face told Anna that was not what she had planned.

But nothing could ruin this. She found humor in the whole situation. The room was full of beautiful, well dressed people. Bright colors caught the eye and the richness of dress left no doubt they were in the company of wealth.

The women she had observed earlier sat at the same table with them in between the men. Lars had gone over and requested the blonde's company at dinner and the brunette sat at on the other side of the Baron. They entertained the company with stories and peppered the men with questions about their journeys.

A few times the blonde coyly asked Royce questions about France and the Middle East. He answered politely in bored tones before going back to his conversation with the Barron.

Anna was content to just sit back and observe. She understood there was power in silence. Besides, she knew there was a lot to learn and she needed to keep her eyes open.

The whole affair lasted over two hours and just when she thought it was over, the lower tables were pushed back and entertainment came in the form of jugglers and a troubadour.

The music was soft and playful. A few ballads about love were sung as the man went from table to table with a man on a lute following behind.

Anna was relieved when the Barron finally stood, signaling the end of the night. She was more than happy to seek her bed, and for the first time in weeks, she floated easily off to sleep in a bed next to her husband.

Voices penetrated Anna's conscious. Warm hands lifted her and covered her with a soft blanket. She couldn't tell where she was, but it had to be important. Try as she might, she couldn't open her eyes and a sense of flying came over her. Calm voices and warm hands rubbed at her arms and legs creating a tingling sensation that rippled up her spine.

Bright lights and then noise. She was being moved. Louder now, people around her talking, but she couldn't seem to respond to what they were saying.

"What's her name?"

"I don't know. We found her near the river. We thought she was dead, but then we noticed she was breathing. We got her here as soon as possible. She hasn't opened her eyes once."

"Her pulse is slow, and she's lost a lot of blood. It looks like she's broken a few ribs here and the cut on her head looks pretty serious. Admit her into ER under Jane Doe till we have an ID. Let's see if we can stop that bleeding first and then I want some x-rays. Let's *move* people."

What were they saying? She couldn't understand. She knew the words, but somehow, they wouldn't translate. More voices, a pin prick in her arm and then nothing.

She came awake suddenly, sitting straight up in bed, her hand going to her arm in a protective manner. A cold sweat washed over her and chills went down her spine as the dream faded.

Please no. Don't let that be real...not now.

It took a moment for her eyes to adjust to the soft morning light coming in through the windows. Her hand automatically reached for Royce on the bed and came up empty. Panic filled her as her gaze swept the room.

Royce was standing in the corner getting dressed. He turned at the small noise she made and came over to her, crouching by the bed in the half light.

"Is everything alright?" Concern laced his voice. He stroked the hair away from her face. "You're so cold. Did I steal all the blankets?"

Relief flooded her system. She closed her eyes and leaned into his touch, shaking her head.

"Is everything alright?" he asked again. Taking a seat on the bed, she lay back down and he covered her up with the blankets.

"Now it is," she nodded. Clearing her throat, she put her hands up to his face and looked at him tenderly, "Come back to bed and warm me up."

"Bad dream?" He frowned.

She gave a faint laugh and put her hand over her eyes. "Sort of...I don't know, I can't even remember it now."

"Liar..."

Choked laughter escaped, but she didn't say anything else.

"You want to talk about it?"

"Not now. Come back to bed and hold me." She peered at him from between her fingers.

"I can't my love." Taking up her hand, he kissed her palm and laid it on his cheek. "The Duke's landed in Dover and we need to leave to meet him."

"Then I'll get up." She started to swing her legs over the side of the bed.

"No. You stay. We'll not leave for a few hours yet and I want you well rested. Sleep for a while longer. Laze about in bed until I send the maid in with water. It's early yet." He stopped her, pushing her legs back under the heavy coverlet. "You sleep and I'll send someone to get you."

Kissing her on the mouth, he tucked the blanket up under her chin, grabbed up his sword and left, quietly shutting the door behind him. Outside the birds started their early morning chatter and she worried over what the dream meant.

A faint noise started echoing in her head. A quiet beep, monotonous in tone kept pace with her breathing. It was so faint she could barely make it out. She got up and went over to the window to see if it was coming from outside. But the noise of the birds in the garden overshadowed the slight sound and she shook it off, going back to bed and lying down.

Snuggling under the covers, she allowed herself a moment to think about her dream but everything had vanished. Coldness swept over her and she got up to pile more blankets on the bed, curling into a ball and rubbing her arms. Even without the images, she knew what it meant and it scared the hell out of her. Sleep would be impossible now.

A few hours later a new maid came in to help her dress. She introduced herself as Maddie. When Anna asked about the other girl, she was told that Thea was busy and the Baron had asked specifically for someone else.

"The Baron has given leave for you to take as many gowns as you like for the trip. You must be well dressed to meet the Duke and it would fall on the Baron's house if he did not take care of his guest in that matter."

The maid went to the door of the armoire and waited for Anna to join her before pulling out two richly colored garments. "I would recommend the green silk and the jade blue would suit your coloring."

"That would be lovely." Anna smiled fingering a white and cream-colored silk with gold trim. "This one's beautiful. Do you think I-"

"Your husband asked you not be dressed in anything white, my lady," Maddie interrupted.

"He did? Oh, yes, I forgot."

"And these, my lady?" She held up a scarlet cloak and another dress in navy.

"Yes," she smiled. "Those will be wonderful. I'll be happy to have them."

She met Royce in the courtyard less than an hour later. The horses were saddled and most of the Baron's men were ready to go with them. The Baron, already on his horse, came over to greet her, eyeing her with approval.

"Good morning, Madam. I trust you slept well?"

"I did indeed, sir," she replied, dropping into a deep curtsey.

"I see Maddie was able to attend to you. Were you able to pick some gowns for our journey?"

"Yes, thank you for your generosity. It is most welcome. I'm sorry for the delay on your daughter's wedding, sir."

"Yes, well, not for too long, I hope. It is my wish to see my daughter good and wedded before I die. Better yet, if it is to the tune of an England on the mend. Enough with this damn feuding. I've a desire to see the Duke come to throne. For too long now England has lived in fear of a few men."

Stopping as if he'd said too much, he smiled down into her upturned face, nodded again and turned his horse away.

Royce came over to help her into her saddle.

"How many gowns did you take? Surely, we don't need that many," he whispered into her ear with a teasing tone watching the two large satchels be loaded onto a mule.

"It's not the gowns. It's everything else she insisted I take. Shoes, slips, cloaks-that woman knew her stuff."

"She should. It's his daughter's maid and he sent her to you after he heard the other women talking. He came and apologized to me this morning swearing he didn't know. I wasn't sure what he was talking about. Do you know?"

"I have some idea." With a laugh she mounted up, her eyes sparkling down at him.

He was so handsome just now standing there beside her. One hand was on her ankle and the other was holding the horse's bridle and he seemed in no hurry to release her. Her breath caught as she gazed at his rugged profile.

Her earlier dream had created a seed of doubt in her mind and she was desperate to release it. No, she wouldn't think about it. She needed to be here, be with him. Taking a mental snapshot, she let her smile widen. He was so confident, self-assured and, right now, so happy. It was such an intimate moment in the crowd of the courtyard with horses and people stirring around them. Cocooned by his warmth, she wished fervently-*let this be real...please, God, let this be real. Let him be real.*

CHAPTER
23

The day grew hot. Anna was glad she had worn the lighter of the dresses they'd selected. Even with the thick dust from the road settling on her, she counted herself lucky. She had a mount and she was at the beginning of the long train of soldiers and knights as they made their journey east. About an hour into their trip, they'd been intercepted by a young knight on horseback who brought news that the Duke's army was moving to Medway Valley. They were to meet up there.

The Duke had landed in Dover and left immediately for Canterbury when they'd gotten word of Louvain and the bishop being holed up in a stronghold in West Malling. The ride that was to take half the morning would now be a two-day journey, especially with all these people. There had to be at least fifty knights along with Baron Fitzhugh. He said he'd sent for soldiers from two other estates and more were to join throughout the day.

She was grateful for the time, anything that would keep her mind off her earlier dream. She had yet to tell Royce and wasn't sure she wanted to...at least not yet. Nervously, she touched the new bruise at the bend in her elbow. She didn't need to see it to know what it looked like. Earlier today when she was getting dressed the blooming bruise had given her a start. Even the maid had commented on it, the bright purple and blue standing out on her delicate skin.

She knew what it was. She had felt it earlier as the needle had gone in.

"Anna?" Royce said from beside her.

"Hmm, yes?"

"Are you sure you're alright? I've called you three times."

"Yes, I'm sorry I-I was lost in thought."

The frown of worry on Royce's face deepened and the silence stretched between them.

"I'm fine," she said again meeting his look with a smile.

Giving a snort of disbelief, he turned and waved to the man calling his name. "I need to ride ahead," he said, turning back to her. Stay with Hayne and Lars and I'll catch up with you later. We'll talk tonight," he finished bluntly. He gave her a meaningful look before kicking his horse forward to catch up with the group breaking away heading west from their caravan.

The panicky feeling watching of him go made her almost cry out. She wanted to tell him to stop, yell his name, anything to make him come back. She was afraid to be without him now.

Stop it, she told herself. She couldn't think about that. Putting her face up to the sun, she let the heat beat down on her. This was where she belonged.

By the end of the day she was relieved to stop. They'd been riding since morning; the pace was slow and plodding and the heat and flies had been merciless.

Lars and Hayne helped her down and quickly set up a make shift cover beneath the trees, just far enough for privacy and yet still within sight of the camp. She went down to a nearby stream to wash some of the dust from her throat.

Man, and beast seemed to have the same idea as one man after another led their horses to the water. There would be no privacy here for a bath so she did the best she could by just rinsing her face and wading in, letting the cool water wrap around her dirty feet and legs.

When she turned around Lars and Hayne were both standing there with their backs turned, keeping the curious men away. She almost laughed at how they protected her.

"I'm done," she called out wiping at her face with a cloth and then wrapping it around her neck.

Lars glanced back over his shoulder at her and scowled. "You're indecent now. Go and change your dress."

"What are you, my father?" she snapped. "It's hotter than blazes out here. This dress will be dry in a minute."

His scowl deepened and he came down, grabbed her arm and half led, half pulled her to the tent and pushed her inside, closing the flap behind her.

"Change your dress," his voice came through the tent clipped and clear.

She was half inclined to defy him.

"You can see the white of your undergarment," he went on.

"So?" she said exasperated until she looked down and noticed that the white linen slip wasn't really the problem. It was the outline of her nipples that bled clearly through the soft silk of the dress.

"Oh," she mumbled. "Fine," she called to him. She pulled out another dress from the bag they had brought to the tent and began the process of changing, which wasn't easy in the small confinement.

Emerging later, she hooked back the flap and walked over to Lars. "Better?" she asked unable to keep the sarcasm out of her voice.

His smile turned charming and he led her to where food was being doled out at one of the other fires.

The meal was simple with hard bread and venison. The men around the fire talked amongst themselves. For the most part they left her alone.

She ate silently, listening to the stories that rolled around the campfire. Royce still wasn't back and the later it got the more she worried. The sun set in a blaze of glory and darkness was settling over the camp. Finally, she quit pretending, got up and went over to the edge of camp, scanning the horizon.

"He'll be back soon," Lars said from her side.

"How did you know I was thinking that?"

"Because you haven't spoken since he left. Your eyes keep searching the road and you've worn that perpetual frown for hours now. Rest easy, Anna. He'll be back soon."

"How do you know?"

"Because the man's too stubborn to die now," he said with a shrug of his shoulders. Turning, he started to walk back to the fire.

"Lars," she called out after him. "You're not fooling me. You worry for him too."

"Worry about what?" He stopped and shook his head before snorting. "The man being a damn fool? Now that is something I cannot worry about, because there's nothing I can do about it."

She smiled at the man's bluster and pretend indifference before turning back to scan the horizon one more time.

He said he'd be here tonight, so, where was he?

Retiring to her tent, Anna thought to keep a vigil inside. But the tiny beeping in her head grew in the silence. Just the fact that it was still there worried her. During the chaos of the day with the other noise around, she hadn't been able to hear it. Now, it echoed in the darkness.

Unable to stand it anymore, she threw back the flap of the tent just in time to see Royce coming down the road with a long train of men moving silently behind him. She recognized his silhouette immediately and, choking back a sound, took off at a dead run for him.

Like a rag tag army, the men filed in to the campsite and the murmurs of greetings started. Voices called out as men renewed acquaintances with one another.

Royce had silently gotten off his horse and enfolded her in his arms before directing the men where to bed down for the night. When at last he turned to her, he eyed her form up and down.

"I thought you'd be asleep."

"No, you didn't."

"No, I didn't," the end of his mouth quirked up. "But you should be. It's late."

"Just as late for you. You must be exhausted." She took his arm and pulled him over to the fire.

But he stopped her from sitting down with the men, instead calling to Hayne.

"Bring food and wine to my tent. Lars, make sure the men get settled." With a last glance around, he motioned her forward.

"I have need of a bath. It's too hot. Come with me to the stream while I clean up." He took her hand and pulled her along.

Walking in silence, she took a deep breath. Should she tell him? But tell him what? That she had a dream about them finding her and now she knew she wasn't dead. If she wasn't dead, what was she? In between worlds? Covering her elbow with her hand, she pressed gently on the colorful bruise. Not yet. She couldn't tell him yet.

"Who are all those men you came with?" she asked. "Did you pick up more from another lord?"

"Those are my men. I sent for them weeks ago and they've been growing fat around the ports waiting for me," he said distracted.

"How many are there? It seems a lot."

"A little over a hundred-"

"A hundred? Oh, my goodness, that's a lot of men."

"Oh, my goodness?" He stopped and turned to face her. "Enough, Anna. I know you are trying to divert me and you're not very good at it. So tell me. Tell me now what you dreamed."

Sputtering for a moment, she searched for something to say.

"You're not good at it, trust me." Catching her chin in his hands, he held her face up to the light coming from the moon. "No lies. If we don't have honesty between us, then we have nothing. Now tell me. I've been thinking about it all day and it's not going away until you tell me."

She sighed, the air going out of her and she looked down, still hesitating.

"The truth." Tipping her chin up again, he stared into her eyes which filled with unshed tears. "Tell me the truth."

"I dreamed I was found," the words escaped in a rush.

"Found? Found where? By whom?"

"Found in my own time. I don't know who. Just found."

"That's it? Just found?"

"The thing is, I thought I was dead in that time. Now I don't know. I don't know what I am or who I am or where I'm supposed to be."

"You're my wife." The worry on Royce's face deepened. His other arm came around and pulled her to him in a bone crushing hug. "You're where you are supposed to be," he said fiercely into her ear.

"Ya'r supposed to be here." A heavy voice confirmed from behind them. Royce whirled around and pushed her back, pulling his sword from his belt as a man stepped from the shadows of the trees.

"Tis true, you're supposed to be here, my lady. I knew you from before. I recognized the name." The cloaked figure stepped towards them.

"Who are you?" Royce demanded.

"Rest easy, my lord. I've come to bear blessings on your journey and see the prophecy fulfilled."

"What prophecy? What are you talking about? Show yourself, man." Royce advanced on the shadowy figure.

Gnarled fingers pushed back the heavy hood revealing the smelly, little friar who had married them. His face leered at her in the pale moonlight. The light reflecting on what little was left of his teeth. His eyes bore into hers with rapt attention.

"The prophecy, my lord. Surely ye know it. She comes in white to lead the army to victory. Annaysis Whit-"

Royce's sword stretched out, catching the man under his neck.

"Ye know it," he choked out. "Tis true." The old man's eyes widened and his focus turned to Royce. "I've heard all these years she was coming, the angel in white will walk again. Now tis true. She walks among us. She lives to return England to the rightful throne. Her name, my lord. Tis the same name of the white la-"

His voice faltered again when Royce stepped forward and dug the tip of his sword farther into his neck.

"Now listen here, old man," Royce said in a low, guttural voice. "I've never killed a man of God before, but there's always a first time. I know what her name is and what it means, but you're wrong. Breathe one word of this and I'll find you. I'll cut your tongue out and choke you with it. Bid me well. She's not who you think she is." He shoved the old man back. "Get out of here before I change my mind and kill you now."

The old monk fell over a log as he scrambled away. He disappeared into the forest, but not before saying, "She comes, my lord. She comes."

Royce stood there for a minute his body, stiff as stone. He took a step, appearing to waver between chasing the man or letting him go.

Swallowing the lump in her throat, Anna shook off the chill the friar's words had brought and went over, putting her arms around Royce and kissing his shoulder.

"Let him go. He doesn't matter. He's crazy," she said, quietly.

"But your dreams-" The tension eased out of him as he turned to face her.

"They're nothing. They mean nothing, truly. It's you. I was always meant to be here with you. I know it. In my heart, my soul, I know it."

His frown became one of sadness and she ached to make it right for him. No matter what happened, now she was his, only his.

"But, what of th-."

"Shhh." Putting her fingers up to his lips, she silenced him. "It will be alright," she whispered. Even as she said it, she knew it had to be true. Somehow it would be true.

The look in his eyes faltered, indecision wavering there. With one last glance out to the forest, he turned back to her.

"I have something for you." He pulled a thick chain up out of his tunic and off his neck. A heavy ring dangled at the end.

She recognized it immediately. Her eyes brimmed with tears. She nodded and smiled. It was one of the ring's her grandmother had always worn. Set in sterling silver with an emerald the size of a large pearl nestled in the middle, she had always admired it as a child and often asked to wear it. Her grandmother had always said, "No, not yet."

There had been two of them, one in gold filigree with a large sapphire and the emerald in silver. She'd worn one on each hand. The emerald was to be hers one day and the sapphire her sister's.

The day they buried her sister she had watched her grandmother slip the sapphire ring off her finger and onto her sister's cold hand. When she had asked her grandmother why she did that, she raised her tear stained face and smiled sadly. "It's her ring now."

The memory of that moment filled her head as Royce raised her hand and slid the emerald on. Joy filled her. But as the heavy weight settled there the crazy sense of déjà vu she kept experiencing ran through her again.

It would be alright, she told herself. It had to be.

That night she clung to Royce, her head on his chest trying to dispel the feeling of dread that threatened to rise up in her. Sleep was impossible for both of them. Neither had spoken of the monk, both not wanting to acknowledge it. Instead, Royce had led her to a sheltered spot in the creek, stripped her bare and made love to her in the cool water letting the dark of the night cloak their fears and misgivings.

CHAPTER 24

The day promised to be as hot as the one before and Anna was never so excited to reach their destination. Now, with an added entourage of over a hundred men, they moved at a snail's pace and being surrounded on all sides by Royce's men made the dust worse than before.

Instead of feeling protected, she felt claustrophobic and begged Royce more than once to clear the men away. But he was adamant about keeping her as shielded as possible, the grim line of his mouth not breaking into a smile once all day.

The closer they got to their destination the more bear like he became. Insisting she wear a heavy robe that hid her hair and dress. Insisting she ride in the middle of a circle of men, men she didn't know or from their appearance or attitude care to know.

Lars and Hayne had disappeared and the faces around her stared straight ahead ignoring her very presence, never once talking to her or making eye contact. They were in full battle armor and even with their visors up they had to be ten times hotter than she was. But she wasn't in the mood to be charitable.

She felt invisible. With the heat and the flies, she was close to fainting at the day's end. Whatever was going on it seemed to have affected everyone. Yesterday, there had been friendly chatter passed along as the rode. Last night when the men joined them, easy banter over the fires filled the night air.

But this morning she had awoken to a different attitude. The men had stayed away from her and either averted their eyes in her presence or stared openly. It wasn't lust. It was curiosity. Voices whispered as she walked by, but she couldn't quite catch what they were saying.

This morning when Lars and Hayne had come to get her, they had been gruff and business like. Standing rigid by her, their normally open, friendly faces were closed off for all to see. Not a joke or a laugh crossed the stiff lips of the men and she knew the little monk had not held his tongue.

When Royce first left her this morning, he had leaned down and kissed her playfully. But when he returned a few minutes later with breakfast, he had stopped her from going out, his mouth grim and his shoulders set in a way that scared her.

"I was just coming out," she said as he entered with some water and a tray of food.

"It's best you eat in here this morning," his voice hard and serious.

"But I want to come and see your men. I didn't get to meet anybody last night and I-"

"You can't, Anna. It's best you eat in here," he stated firm.

"Royce, it's hot in here and I just wanted to wash up and-"

"No, Anna," he said again, "You can't. Do you understand? You can't."

"What is it?" she asked going over to him and enfolding his arms about her.

He squeezed her tightly and held onto her, his forehead pressed into hers. Taking a deep breath, he had just stood there holding her for a moment before taking her shoulders and looking her straight in the eye.

"Anna, the next few days could...they could be hard on you. I need you to be strong and not listen to all the gossip around the campfire.

Be strong and stay silent. Do you understand me? Whatever is asked of you, *stay silent.* Tell no one of your delivery from the river."

"Royce, you're scaring me. What is it? Did that old man talk?"

"I don't know, but I should have seen this coming. Prince Henry's not pleased with me at the moment and I don't know what he'll ask. We must be prepared for anything." Kissing her hard on the lips he said, "Stay with Lars and Hayne. They'll protect you no matter what." And then he had left.

After that, she'd seen little of him. He'd spent the day riding up and down the line of men, barely glancing at her when he went by.

When she'd called out, he'd simply ignored her request or bid her silent. At this point in the day, she was hardly feeling generous to any of the men right now.

It was late afternoon when they crested the hill of Medway Valley. Below them the Duke's army was spread out in front of a four story keep, surrounded by a stone wall. Water bordered the west wall and the town sat to the east of it. Crofter's huts had been burned and continued to cast smoke up to the sky, giving an eerie feeling to the landscape. Men rode up to greet them and Royce, Lars, Baron Fitzhugh and a few others were quickly ushered to the Duke's side.

Anna had thought she would meet the Duke, but Royce had sent her on with Hayne and a few other knights to set up camp.

At first disappointed when Lars and Royce rode away, her frustration was soon replaced with relief when she approached the tent where she was to be.

Nestled under a canopy of trees, the large pavilion had bedding already in place. Cool water was waiting for her when she got there. Three large chests sat at the back with an unlit candle placed on one of them.

Closing the flap behind her, she striped off her gown and ran a wet cloth over her face and arms. With a groan she collapsed on the makeshift bed and drifted off, lulled by the noise of the men working outside.

Sleep came easily in the cool darkness of the tent and just as easily came the dreams.

She was searching for something. No matter how hard she tried, she couldn't find it. In the background, someone was crying. The weeping grew with each passing moment and the desperation in her matched the urgency of the cry. Now, she needed to do it now or it would be too late. Men all around her, she had to hurry, not much time. Someone was calling to her. It was time to go. *You don't belong here* reverberated through her head.

Her father called to her, her sister by his side and then Royce, his hand out, waiting for her. She reached for him, but he was gone and she was falling.

She awoke with a start, sitting up straight, she gasped for breath. The tent flap pushed open and a strange face peered in. Anna instinctively cowered back, pulling a blanket over her form. The guard didn't smile. His eyes searched the tent before coming back to her.

"Is everything well, my lady?"

Still disoriented, she needed a moment to remember where she was. The noise outside slowly replaced the voices in her head. Turning away from him, she ran her hands over her face and wiped at the sweat that gathered on her brow.

"Yes, yes, I'm okay. I just dozed off. A bad dream, that's all." She gave him a shaky smile, trying to pretend it was nothing.

Wordlessly, he exited the tent. She lay back down and ran her hands through her hair trying to quiet her breathing. The noise in her head had increased slightly and now the chilling sound of somebody crying was added to it.

She checked the bruise on her arm...still there, as bright as ever. Pressing the heels of her hands into her eyes, she swore she wasn't going to cry. That would do no good now, but damn, it would make her feel better. Choking back a sob, she tamped down her panic and froze as words were exchanged outside her tent by two soldiers walking by.

"Do you think she'll come?"

"I don't know. She hasn't been seen for months."

Getting up, she slipped over to the canvas wall to capture more of their conversation.

The tent flap opened and Lars stood at the threshold with a jug of wine and some food wrapped in cloth just as words of the white lady came from the men on the opposite side of the tent. Lars took in her posture and what the men were saying within her hearing range, the smile dying on his face.

Closing the flap abruptly, she heard his hurried step around to the back where the men were standing and started yelling at them to move on.

"My lord, we were just wondering if you think the white lady will make an appearance for the duke, sir. You know the story. The white lady will appear on the wall and let down her hai-"

"I know the tale. And fable is all it is. It's Prince Henry here. Now begone. You're disturbing Lady Sutton with your talk."

"But, sir..."

"And don't repeat that tale to anyone. It's nothing more than myth."

"But you saw her, sir. At Lisbon. Everyone did that day."

"I remember Lisbon well enough." Changing his tactics, Anna could hear Lars voice soften and knew he was drawing the men away from her tent. "Yes, I saw something, what I'm not sure. Maybe it was the heat, I don't know. But enough of this talk. You know how Lord Sutton feels about it. Do not go about spreading rumors."

"'Tis all over camp, sir...some say it is the Lord Sutton's own wife and she's returned from the dead to lead the men to victory."

For a moment, they were quiet. Anna could almost feel Lars displeasure through the tent, but if she had any doubt, the chill in his voice confirmed her thoughts.

"Do *not* repeat that to anyone," Lars said firmly, the hiss of his blade accompanying his words. A few seconds later, Lars appeared again at the entrance, a fake smile adorning his face.

"Oh Lars, really," she gave him a harsh chuckle and waved him in. "You don't have to pretend for me. I heard them."

"Eat, Anna." Blowing out heavily, he set the food in front of her. "It's been hours and you must be hungry. The prince requires your audience and I've come to fetch you for him."

"Oh, so it's the prince now, is it?" She tried to joke.

"No more need for secrecy." Lars looked bleak. "So yes, it is the prince."

"Why are you standing there so grim, Lars? Do you have some bad news? Where's Royce? Is everything alright?"

"Yes, Royce is fine," he said distractedly. "The battle's to be tomorrow morning and the prince has sent him to Chatham. He should be back by morning before the battle."

"By morning? My God, he'll be exhausted."

"He's a soldier. He does as he's told," Lars said with bitterness, giving Anna a start.

At the confusion on her face, he frowned again. Then nodding his head, he turned to go. "Eat something and then prepare yourself, my lady. The prince is waiting and I assure you, that's not something he's good at."

"Lars, please...don't go. What's going on? It feels like I'm being kept prisoner here. All day everything's been so tense and everyone is so unfriendly. Is it really that bad out there?"

He wavered.

"I have barely seen Royce at all today," she continued when he didn't answer. "And, now I have these men whispering about me. What is it? What isn't anyone telling me?"

He stopped just short of the tent flap, and then hesitated before coming back in with a sigh. "My lady, it's nothing." He forced a smile.

"Stop, Lars. Wow, that's the weakest smile I've seen from you yet and we've been in tighter places than this, haven't we? At least I think we have." When he didn't laugh she searched his closed expression. Then with a sigh, she turned away to take a seat.

"I'm too tired for games and I can tell by your face you are too. Just tell me what's going on...please."

Defeated, he took a seat across from her. "Eat quickly. We don't have much time, I'll talk. It's time you knew."

She took a deep breath and prepared herself.

"It's a myth, a story told long ago about a fight for the crown…an old legend, one passed around the fire the night before the battles. The white lady will come and lead the way for the rightful monarch."

"I know it."

"You do?"

"Yes, Royce told me."

"He did? Hmph, I never thought he would," Lars said with surprise. Shaking his head, he stared at the ground. "All these years he's discouraged the talk. No matter what was said about him, he would never talk about it. Always said it was the men's imagination and they saw what they wanted to see. I can't believe he told you."

"Those men aren't the first time I've heard somebody say something. I wanted to know, so I asked."

"Who else told you about the white lady?"

Shrugging, she wasn't sure how to answer. She took a bite of food before replying, "It doesn't matter. Nobody really, I've just heard people mention her."

"I didn't think it had reached that point here. He took only his most trusted men, but it's understandable now that the rest of his men have come."

"He was reluctant to tell me," she admitted. "It's such a sad story, but I don't see how this has anything to do with me."

Lars was staring at her intently, as if unsure what to say. Finally taking a deep breath, he just started talking. "It began years ago, long before I met Royce. I'd heard of a young knight who had the luck of the white lady and I wanted to meet him. You see, men flocked to him. They all wanted her protection. They all wanted to be under his command. It was said, he saved the young Duke during an attack in Spain and that was the first sighting of the white lady.

"It wasn't much, I think, just a flash of white, probably nothing. After that, it grew with each battle. A woman in white would appear running among the people. And then someone would try to reach her," he snapped his fingers. "And just like that she would disappear."

He waited for her to look up from her meal.

"Some say they could hear her screaming. That's how the rumors started about the myth coming to life."

Shivers ran up her back. She was trying to keep all emotion off her face. It felt like Lars was testing her, like her friend had become an enemy and she wasn't sure how to react. She pulled the blanket up over her shoulders, trying to cover the goosebumps rising on her arms.

"But weren't a lot of women in white? Couldn't this be a mistake?"

"No. Not there and not white like this. The women wear bright colors or muted dark colors, but not white and their faces and hair are covered up, wrapped. You could never see a women's face there, not like here. She was different from the other women, which is why the men noticed her. The prophecy has come, they would say."

"Who would say?"

"Land in any port and ask after the white lady and you'll hear a different tale." He slid his eyes to her. "Some say she has come for the Duke, our Prince Henry. Others say she has forsaken England and come back for her lover."

"Her lover? But I thought he was her husband?"

"Husband, lover-does it really matter?"

"Lars, you're talking in riddles. What are you saying? What? Everyone thinks I'm this white lady?"

Clearly uncomfortable, he got up and paced the tent a few times.

"They think I'm the white lady, don't they?" she answered for him.

Stopping in front of her suddenly, he met her eyes and the chill reflected back froze her heart.

"Yes."

"And the prince? What does he think?"

"The prince is not as superstitious as the men. I think he's not sure what to believe, but if the men believe it, he will support it. Anything to help his cause."

"How convenient. Is that why he wants to meet me? See if I'm this mythical creature?"

"I would imagine."

"And that's why Royce didn't want me to meet him, right? Why he's tried to hide me all day?"

Lars didn't say anything, but his silence told her all she needed to know.

"I thought as much." She got up and wiped her hands. Coming to stand in front of Lars, she asked him quietly, "What do you think? Do you think I'm this white lady? This ghost?"

"My lady," he shook his head, his eyes narrowing again. "I don't know what to think."

"Yes, you do." She smiled at him in sadness. "You just don't want to say it." Meeting his gaze, she stared at him for a moment before asking, "Who are you Lars? Who are you really?"

"What do you mean?"

"I know you're Royce's friend, but what is your role in all this? Who do you serve?"

His mouth tightened and his eyes narrowed. "I serve the rightful King of England, my lady, Prince Henry-as does your husband. I am Prince Henry's vassal first, Royce's friend second."

"So I thought. Does Royce know that?"

"He knows it." His face growing flushed, Lars spoke harshly. "Trust me, he's no different. We must *fight now*. It's what we've worked for. What *we've* all worked for."

His stance was rigid. He put his hands on his hips and tilted his head. "Do you have any idea what Royce gave up to come and find you? Do you? Do you know how, even now, his life is in danger? The men that hunt him, hunt you. The price on his head has tripled since he's come back here. His allegiance to the prince, what he's done for France, England, his people...everything, he's put on the line for you and now he must do as his prince bids or he dies here, tonight...maybe under my blade. Do you understand what's at stake?"

Anna blanched at Lars' words and stepped back from the storm on his face.

Lars followed and bent his face close to hers, meeting her gaze. "He is my friend Anna, make no mistake," he said slowly, "but there is nothing more I can do for him."

Tears clouded her vision as she jutted out her chin and responded, "How can you be his friend?"

"I would have followed him to the ends of the earth if he asked. His wounds have been mine. I love him as a brother, but just as a brother, I cannot stop him from destroying himself." He turned to leave.

"What? Wait-" She tugged on his arm. "What are you talking about? I don't understand? Why is he in danger?"

He rounded on her again, his eyes glittering. "He gave up everything to come back and search for you. There is nothing for him here now or in France unless Prince Henry takes the throne."

"But earlier you said he was rich? You said he had a fleet of ships. How can you say he has nothing?"

"He has them. For now. Don't you understand? Our wealth depends on who we follow. He defied the orders of the prince to come and find you. Yes, we did it under the guise of getting Gordon back safe to his father, but that would have been an easy matter.

"Instead we crisscrossed the countryside waiting for you. Searching, for you. Every day in danger of being discovered by either King Stephen's men or Prince Henry's, let alone that bastard Louvain and the Bishop.

"Now, the prince has welcomed him back with open arms because he was successful in getting Gordon back to Scotland and uncovering the assassination plot. But we must finish this-here and now-or it will all be for naught. "Then, and only then, can he live in peace and get his precious Okehampton back. He risked his life. *We* all risked our lives to help him come and find you, his white lady."

"He said that?"

"He didn't have to. I saw you, Anna. I *saw* you. Me, who doesn't believe in anything anymore-not love, not God-not life...After the horrors in the Holy Land, I couldn't believe anymore. I thought God had forsaken me...and then I saw you. I saw Royce and I knew who you were and what you were.

"Do you know you saved my life one day? It was you who shouted at me, warned me of a sword coming at my back. By the time I turned around, Royce had almost reached you and then you just disappeared. Vanished into thin air.

"I couldn't believe it. I swore then and there that day that I would do everything in my power to help him. Serve him, thereby serving you, my lady."

He inhaled deeply through his nose and pointed at her. "Let me ask you, Anna, from where do you come?"

She didn't say anything, just widened her eyes. Her breath was coming in shallow pulls making her heart hammer in her ears.

"You can't answer that, can you? And, truthfully, I don't know if I want the answer."

"Lars, it's not what you think. I'm not who you think I am. Truly, I'm not." But she had trouble speaking, her mouth going dry and her words fell on deaf ears.

Turning from Lars, she tried to walk away but he grabbed her wrist stopping her. Slowly, he eased her hand over exposing the old scar at the base of her left thumb. His finger slid along the raised welt.

The wound was from one of her most violent dreams last year. It was the first time she had woken up with blood on the sheets, but it hadn't been the last.

His eyes met hers again, and he said in a harsh whisper, "I saw you, Anna."

Gasping, she pulled her hand away as angry tears emptied onto her face. She tucked the evidence in her skirts.

"It doesn't matter who I think you are." Almost gently now, he shook his head. "It matters who *they* think you are and what you can do. I know you don't understand any of this, but England has shed enough blood under King Stephen."

"I understand that, Lars. I do. But I can't help them," she replied trying to keep her voice even.

"Yes. You. Can. These men are here because they fight for freedom in their homeland. For twenty years they've been under King Stephen's rule and he's let this country go to men who don't deserve it. Do you have any idea what life has been like for the people here? *My people.*

"England's riches have been hoarded by few, men with no honor, no value on life or land. It's time for the bleeding to stop. These men believe in you and Royce. They need to see him tomorrow leading them into battle.

"As for whether or not you're truly the white lady, it doesn't matter. They'll believe what they want no matter what I tell them. I can't discourage them anymore than I just did. These men out there, they will fight and die for England. For you, if you let them. Whether you like it or not, this is your role. You *are* the prophecy," he finished, his voice cold and hard.

"I'm not. I'm *not* Lars. Even if I could help-what is it you expect me to do?"

"You know the answer to that, my lady. You know the tale," he said with meaning. "If you don't appear tomorrow it will be on Royce's shoulders. If you want any measure of peace for him, or you, you must do this."

"You don't understand. I don't think I can do it," she called out to him as he turned to leave.

Looking back at her, he took in her pale shaking form but didn't bend. "I'm not asking, Anna. It's not a choice, for me or for you. Now wipe your tears and change your dress. The prince is waiting. He'll keep Royce busy until this is through, you understand? He's afraid if he finds out, he'll run with you. If that happens, it will be me who'll have to hunt you down and God help us all then."

CHAPTER 25

Meeting a prince was not quite the experience Anna thought it would be. There was no pomp and circumstance. Jewels didn't glitter from his clothes and no crown decorated his head. Instead, a rather ordinary gentleman with light brown hair that brushed his shoulders, a prominent nose and sun browned skin greeted her as she entered.

The smile he gave her was bright enough and he seemed sincere in welcoming her with the offer of refreshments, however his eyes missed nothing. She was instantly on guard. He walked around her like she was a horse he was sizing up at auction.

Only a few men remained in his tent but stood back and were not introduced upon her entrance. Empty compliments were thrown about before he got down to business.

"Mistress Sutton, so nice to finally meet the woman Lord Sutton left France for. I was beginning to think you didn't exist. He found you in Spain, they say?"

"Yes, my lord, in Madrid," she replied smoothly.

"Ah, wonderful." The Prince's eyebrows raised and he smiled again nodding. "Your mother and father?" he asked in fluent Spanish, "How do they fare?"

So that was how he wanted it. Two could play at that game.

"My father and mother died last year, your highness," she replied matching his fluid Spanish with her own.

"I'm sorry for your loss. How did they pass?"

"Their ship went down off the coast of Africa. It was one of Royce's ships. When he came to offer his respects, we were introduced."

"Your parents were?"

"Lord and Lady Harrington, your Highness."

His eyes narrowed and he looked behind him at one of his men, who gave a slight shrug of the shoulders before turning back to her.

"I am not familiar with them, my lady, so you see my confusion."

"You would not be, sir. They did not move in the highest of circles. It was my grandfather who passed on the title."

"His name?"

"Robert de Halverson of Flemby, sir." The name popped into her head and slipped out of her mouth without hesitation.

The prince's eyebrows shot up and again he turned to face the man behind him. This time the man nodded back.

"I have heard of him." The Prince's face eased into a smile. "He left England. "Yes, I remember my father talking of him. A good man. Interesting...and fortunate that our good servant has found a jewel like you."

Going over to a seat, he eased himself down. He didn't invite her to sit. Instead, he motioned one of his men forward.

"Truly, I am thrilled then to know our Sutton has found one of such value, my lady, and I shall allow the marriage to stand." Taking a parchment offered to him he stared down at it, seeming to forget her presence.

Nobody moved around him and she found herself swaying at the heat in the tent. Just when she feared she might faint, the prince raised his head as if surprised to see her still there. With a flick of his wrist and a glance at Lars, he dismissed her.

But as she exited the tent he spoke again.

"I've sent your husband on to Chatham on an errand for me. He'll not be back until morning. I don't know if Lord Thomas has told you, but you'll be my comfortable guest until this battle has ended. You, and your husband, my lady."

She didn't let the chill his words gave her reach her eyes. With as much meekness as she could muster, she bowed low. "Of course, Your Highness," she murmured before exiting the tent.

"Was I too bold?" Anna couldn't resist the one barb.

Lars snorted, refusing to answer the reference she'd made to one of his earlier comments. On the way there, Lars had told her to keep her eyes downcast and play a proper wife of a lord. Lars true assessment of her character had been the one time today she'd been hard put not to burst into laughter. For a moment, he had sounded just like her uncle John and she had to look at him twice to make sure this all wasn't a great trick God was playing on her.

"Don't look him in the eye like you do every man," Lars had said. "It's disconcerting and Prince Henry will think you too bold. Since I've met you, you have yet to keep your damn tongue in your mouth when you should and you stare at everybody like you own the world. Didn't your mother ever teach you modesty or meekness? I'll take a switch to my daughter if she goes about as you have done."

She hadn't known whether to be offended or proud and had almost commented back but could tell from the set of his mouth he was serious. It wasn't the time to pick a fight about women's rights. That was far in the future.

Now he was staring straight ahead, his grip on her arm bruising as he pulled her along back to her tent. Night was falling fast, and she matched his long stride to keep up. The men fell back as they walked by, Lars' heavy scowl discouraging anyone from approaching.

"I'll pull all but one guard in the morning and your horse will be saddled and ready for you," he gritted out.

His words left her feeling cold and hollow.

"You realize they'll kill me, don't you?" She turned to face him as he opened her tent.

"No, they won't. They'll be too busy with us to worry about you."

"Does Royce know?"

"No. No one does and you can't tell him. You won't be doing him any good if you tell him."

"How lucky he is to have such a friend. I'm sure it will give him such comfort in the night to know his truest friend is willing to sacrifice his wife for England's honor."

"To use your words, Anna, I'm not who you think I am." Pausing on the threshold, he looked down. "I truly am his friend, and yours."

"This is what you call friendship?"

In the pale light coming from the open flap, he stood for a moment staring at something outside before giving his head a little shake.

"Yes." He turned back to her.

"Say what you want if it will help you sleep tonight." Spinning away from him, she regarded the dark wall of her tent. "But I wouldn't want to be you when Royce finds out what you've done."

He sighed heavily and then was gone.

Another night with little sleep. Another night when the dreams became more of a reality. Vivid dreams of faces old and new. The monk made an appearance asking her to deliver the prophecy. Her father was there again and the images of the hospital became clearer. People working over her, calling her name and then they were gone.

The soft muffled sounds of someone crying pierced her dream and she awoke with a start. Cold, she was so cold. Leaning over, she tightened her grip on Royce desperate to share some of his heat. He'd come to her in the early morning when pink was just touching the sky and made love to her gently, before curling her in his arms and falling asleep.

After Lars had left, she'd had a lot to think about. She'd paced the tent for hours trying to think of a way out of this situation, but the more she attempted to focus, the louder the noise grew in her head. With it a headache had bloomed, causing her to finally give in to her body's demands and lie down.

Morning brought exchanged words of love before Royce departed. She hadn't been able to stop touching him, and tears kept cresting threatening to spill over. He wiped them away and frowned down at her.

"Don't worry. I'll be back." He caressed her face. "Then we can go home."

"Where's home?" An emotional laugh escaped and she beamed up at him.

"Okehampton," he said returning her smile. "It's promised to me. It's our home and I want to go back there with you. It's what I've been fighting for, you and our home."

"You just want to go back to the cherry trees, I think."

"Yes," he confessed, "Back to the cherry trees." He bent to give her a kiss that began tender but turned into one of fierce possession.

He gave her one last look, worry still on his face. Then with a nod, he grabbed up his sword and left, leaving her alone once again.

As the morning wore on the beeping in her head became louder and more insistent and her headache grew. The incessant noise matched the beat of her heart, making it hard for her to hear beyond it. Her breath began coming in deep, ragged pulls.

There wasn't much time left. She was dying. She was sure of it.

She could barely feel her feet and she had moments when things began to look soft and hazy around her. If she was going to do anything in this world it had to be now.

Leaving Royce had become a reality not a choice. It was just in the how. Whispers near their tent throughout the night had let her know the men's thoughts. And after what Lars had told her yesterday, she really didn't have much choice.

Rolling the heavy ring around her finger, she watched the emerald dance in the light.

For England.

No, for Royce she would do this.

Making up her mind, she put on a heavy red cloak, tying it with a sash. Grabbing up one of Royce's white tunics, she ripped it down the middle. Stuffing a strip in her sleeve just in case and used the other to bind her hair back. Pulling up the hood of her cloak, she opened the tent flap and went over to the horses.

"My lady." The young guard followed her. "Lord Sutton bid you to stay in the tent."

Mounting easily into the saddle, she took up the reins, but he moved in place to stop her.

"My lady, Lord Sutton bid's you stay," he said again louder.

"I heard you, soldier." She glanced down at him taking a deep breath. Then looked past him to where the army was beginning to gather.

"Now step aside, please. I don't want to run you over, but I will." Her voice was soft steel as she returned her gaze to his.

Confused, he put a hand up to grab the bridle, but she pulled back tight on the reins, forcing the horse's head up. The animal reared, whinnying loudly, announcing its displeasure to both of them.

"But, my lady-" the man stuttered, side stepping the dancing hooves.

"Get the men ready." She brought the animal down with control and held him steady.

"Ready for what?"

"Tell them their white lady is here."

She kicked her heels in the horse's soft sides and the animal jumped forward, sending the guard reeling back.

"Lord Sutton. Lord Sutton." The young guard burst into the royal tent.

Royce turned irritated at being interrupted, but when he saw the man's face, his stomach dropped.

Pushing the prince's guards out of the way, he grabbed the young soldier by the shoulders.

"What is it?" he demanded, already knowing somehow what the lad was going to say but needing to hear it anyway.

"It's Mistress Sutton. She's left. She's-"

Royce pushed past the soldier and ran from the tent. How could she do this? How could she leave him? Doesn't she know what it will do to him? Reaching their tent, he pushed the flap open.

"*Anna*".

Silence greeted him. He picked up his torn tunic from the ground, his mind churning. What was she doing? Running back outside, he encountered Lars and the young guard with the Prince and his entourage behind them.

"What did she say?" Losing his temper, he grabbed the young guard's tunic and hoisted him off the ground. "By God, answer me or I'll-"

"You'll choke him to death before he can speak, Royce." Lars grabbed his arm, forcing him to stop.

Pushing the young guard back, Lars stood between them and addressed the young man.

"Tell him. Where did she go?"

Fear clouded the young face as he stared at Royce. Swallowing and coughing he choked out, "She said to get the men ready."

"Ready?" Royce reached past Lars and grabbed both of the young man's shoulders, giving him an effective shake. "Ready for what?"

"She said to tell them our white lady is here," the guard finished quietly, wincing as Royce's hold on his shoulders tightened.

For a moment nobody spoke. Glances were exchanged between Prince Henry and his men. Then people came alive. Weapons and horses were called for.

"*Stop*," Royce yelled as Prince Henry turned away and began talking strategy. "She's *not* the white lady. This will do no good."

Prince Henry turned to face him, the excitement leaving his face. "She does great sacrifice for-"

"There is *no* sacrifice." He slashed angrily at the air with his hand going to stand in front of Prince Henry. "She's not the white lady. Don't you see? It's all myth. All of it. None of it's true."

Prince Henry's eyes narrowed dangerously. "I'll excuse your behavior because of the honorable sacrifice your wife does for this country. I know you are grieving for her, but do not push me, Royce. Friend or not, no one takes such liberties with the rightful King of England."

He glared back at Prince Henry until the guards moved in and pushed him away. Lars held onto his arm trying to reason with him.

"She's not the white lady," Royce yelled again. "Don't you see? There is no such thing."

"Nevertheless," Prince Henry said, watching his face. "We will take it as a sign, Sutton." Turning away, the future King signaled to his men and headed back to his tent, leaving Royce and Lars alone.

Going over to one of the horses Royce grabbed the reins and started to saddle up, before Lars pulled him down.

"You can't go after her."

"Leave me." Royce pushed at his friend.

"Royce..." Lars grabbed at him again. "Let her go, man."

Staring at his friend, Royce hesitated in shocked realization. "You believe it, too. You believe she's the white lady."

Lars mouth hardened and he dropped his grip on Royce. Turning, he ran a hand through his hair. "I was there. I saw, Royce."

"What have you done?" He grabbed Lars by his tunic.

"Royce...I... the men...they believe..."

"Believe what? That my wife is some ghost sent to guide them to victory?"

Lars shook his head. "Don't go their friend. I saw her too many times on crusade. At first, I didn't believe it, couldn't believe it, and denied it even. But then the men, there's no mistaking what happened in Damascus and then again in Jerusalem, Lisbon...she was *there*. I saw. Others did too."

Royce shook his head with disbelief. "No," he said softly.

"She *is* the white lady, Royce. She doesn't belong to you. She never did. This was always her destiny."

"No-You don't know what you *do*." He shoved Lars back.

"She *is*," Lars yelled, letting his voice carry to the men nearby, watching their fight. "I saw her come that night. I saw the magic. You did too and you've known this from the first."

Royce glanced around. The soldiers edged nearer, pretending not to listen. Their conversation would be spread throughout the troops in minutes. Nothing he could do now would persuade these men otherwise.

"The white lady is myth," his voice rang out trying to discredit Lars statement. "It's *not* true. It's a legend. Nothing more. Anna is not the white lady. My *wife* is *not* the white lady."

"You're wrong," Lars shook his head and lowered his voice. "And she's about to prove it to you. She's about to become legend. She belongs to the king, not you."

"She *never* belonged to the king. She's mine. She's *my* lady," he spat out before walking away.

"You can't help her, Royce," Lars called out behind him. "The only way to get her back is to win the battle. That's the best you can do, man."

Royce froze. Turning back to Lars, he grabbed him by his tunic. "I'll win your precious battle and get her back, but you, you Judas. You are my friend no more. I wonder now if you ever were."

"I *am* your friend. And we will get her back. I swear it to you."

"No. *I* will get her back. You stay away from me. From us."

CHAPTER 26

en dove out of the way as her horse tore through the field towards the castle. Soldiers scattered on both sides. The other army called out for her to stop, but she ignored them galloping right up to the gate. As she neared the castle wall Louvain's men rode up next to her taking her horse's reins. Ripping her out of the saddle, they half dragged, half carried her through a small door next to the gate and into the courtyard.

"Bring her here. Bring her to Lord Robert."

Anna walked silently beside them, barely hearing the excited murmur that rose up among the men.

"Who is she?"

"Lord Sutton's wife."

"Why is she here?"

"The white lady?"

"If she's here, that means we will win," men whispered behind their hands. "She has come to us, hasn't she?"

She focused on keeping her heart steady. The beeping in her head grew with every passing moment.

When she arrived in the great hall, Robert was waiting for her near the large fireplace at the back. Off to the left soldiers were coming down a wall of stairs that she hoped led up to the ramparts.

"My lady," he said surprise in his voice. "Such a pleasure to see you again. Decided to choose the winning side, did you?" He reached up and grabbed her hair forcing her head back. "Or did your bastard husband send you to talk peace?"

"Nobody sent me. I came of my own accord."

His brow puckered, puzzlement filling his face as though he didn't know what to do with this good fortune.

"Grown tired of him already, eh?" A cocky smile twisted his lips and he let his hands roam over her body, pulling her tight against him.

"Get your hands off me," she hissed meeting his eyes with a glare of her own.

His hands stilled and he eyed her levelly before smirking. "You are mine now," his lip curled, "To do with at my pleasure. When this is all over I will be your master."

"You have no govern over this body-now or ever," her voice slow and strong, she punctuated each word.

Fury entered his eyes. In one quick motion, he backhanded her, causing her to cry out. Reaching forward, he grabbed her again and shook her. "I own you now." He gritted out. "I will do as I please or you will meet your death on this day like your husband is about too."

"I'm already dead," she hissed. Spitting out the blood filling her mouth before going on, "There's nothing more you can do to me. Now release me."

He frowned down at her, seeming astounded at her boldness. Her headache reached a new level making her grimace. She cried out softly. Putting her hands up to her ears, she tried to stop the pain. He released her when she cringed backwards. Robert's eyes raked her form, no doubt thinking her injured.

"Did you hurt her? Did you have to use force?" he barked at his men.

"No, my Lord." The man who had brought her in backed away. "She met us at the gate and gave us no fight."

Reaching out, he grabbed her arm again and shook her. "What's the matter with you?"

But she was already beyond him. The tempo of her heart was steadily increasing, making it hard to breathe. People from far away were now speaking excitedly and cool hands touched her body. She didn't have much time. Forcing herself to focus, she reached into her gown and gripped her knife. With one quick move, she whipped the knife out, aiming for Robert's face. A long thin cut opened across his cheek, just missing his eye.

He jumped back in shock, then furious that he'd underestimated her. "*You bitch,*" he yelled staring at the blood on his hand.

She was already up the stairs, leaving men bleeding in her wake. Grabbing up a fallen soldier's weapon, she slashed her way through using every defense move she'd ever learned. Her quick actions startled the soldiers and a few fell back with limbs cut open.

Robert was yelling for them to stop her, but her reputation as the white lady preceded her and other than a few feeble attempts, none got in her way.

Her heart was beating so fast now the sound in her ears was almost unbearable. Pushing open the door, she paused on the landing the sunlight caressing her face. She couldn't feel its warmth.

Focus, Anna.

She needed to go to the left. Somehow, she knew the army was to the left. Running over to the wall, she looked down, her eyes searching the battlefield. Both armies were already assembled and lined up. She recognized Royce easily. His armor showed bright in the sunlight. Even from here the insignia was clear. He would live today. The same armor she had watched him don this morning was the one that had graced her grandparent's front hall.

When she had seen it this morning, she'd not been able to disguise her surprise.

"Oh, my God. Where did you get that?" She asked walking over to where Hayne was helping him into his armor.

"I had it made in France." He rolled his shoulders around as he tested his sword reach. "It's a good fit, yes?"

She smiled in disbelief, tears spilling forth.

"Why do you cry?" he asked confused. Coming over to her, he paused letting her run her hands over the fine engraving on the chest.

"It is beautiful," she nodded her head. "It will serve you well today."

"Anna?"

"I just wanted you to know," she stared into his eyes, her face earnest. "You've always been my hero," she whispered.

His face grew serious and he stared back before pulling her close for a kiss. As gently as he could he wound his arms around her, lifting her off the ground. It was the soft kiss of promised passion.

The memory warmed her as she looked at him. It would bore the dent of a hatchet to the shoulder and countless marks would crisscross the front and the back, but he would live today. She was sure of it.

He was holding his helmet, sitting on his stallion beside Prince Henry who had met Louvain and the bishop in the middle of the field to discuss terms. Immediately, his eyes found hers and just as before she knew he saw her. Pain slammed in her chest as she looked at him. She gave herself a moment to remember forever what he was to her. Smiling bravely at him, she came forward.

Almost at once the army on the ground focused on her. It was time. Jumping up on the wall, she threw off her cloak letting it fall. Her white slip billowed around her. A murmur sounded below and she waited, making sure she had everyone's attention.

The sudden silence from the field alerted Louvain there was a problem. Slowly, he turned to gaze up to her in complete disbelief. Even from this distance, she could see his expression go from one of smugness to panic.

The beeping was so loud now and the pain in her head increased. She struggled to breathe. Her heart was beating so fast and erratic...

She was almost out of time.

Suddenly, everything slowed down. She watched her gown twist and turn in the air, falling to the ground below, the bright red satin a stain in the green grass. She could hear Robert coming. Satisfaction filled her as she looked back. He was steps away from her. She knew he would never reach her in time.

Now. Do it now.

Her heart gave a lurch and the beeping in her head became one long continuous sound.

"She's having a heart attack." More voices filtered in.

"How is that possible?"

"She's flat lined. I don't know, just get the paddles. Anna, stay with us, dammit. Stay with us, Anna."

Not yet, she wasn't ready to go yet. Gasping for breath, she reached up, releasing her hair and shook it out, letting the wind catch the simple white linen strip that had bound it back. It floated there in front of her, the white standing out against the brilliant blue sky, before fluttering downward. A roar from below reached her ears and she turned her attention back to the field.

She saw it all. She was there...the prince's army, weapons raised ready for attack, surged forward with a resounding battle cry catching Louvain's men by surprise. Louvain's men struggled helplessly caught in the power of Prince Henry's army.

Royce's voice rose above the others and her eyes sought his for the last time. Her heart lurched again and everything around her began to spin. He was there, yelling for her, anguish on his face as he watched her from below. Her vision blurred and black crept around its edges blocking out the bright sun. A hand grabbed her foot, yanking her back. Clutching her chest wordlessly she fell, the world around her coming to a crashing halt.

Floating, weightlessness and bright light, then a flash and noise...so much noise. The monitor had gone flat announcing to one and all that her heart had given out. Voices were calling to her again, telling her not to give up and to hang on. Another bright light and then she could see.

The room was crowded with people and machines. Everything surrounding the small form on the bed that she knew instinctively was her. Doctors and nurses worked desperately on her motionless figure. Paddles were applied to her chest. Her body jumped and the monitor flickered before resuming its straight line and the monotonous tone continued.

She stepped forward, gazing down at her lifeless body. So many tubes were coming out of her she barely recognized herself. Her face was pale and drawn as if it had never seen the sun. Limp hair clung to her forehead and a body with muscles so thin, they were a shadow of what they once were.

That wasn't her. Not even a shell of her.

She wanted to tell them to stop. She'd lived more in the last few months than most people do in a lifetime. To live now, here with them, was not what she wanted-a numb monotonous existence in a fake world.

No. She had lived, finally. She had lived, maybe not in this life but in Royce's. With Royce she had experienced more love and passion then anybody could ever hope for. Here, everything seemed so sterile and artificial-shades of gray. This wasn't life. Not for her anyway.

A cry reached her ears as the doctors applied the paddles again. Someone was in the corner. It was the same cry she'd been hearing in her dreams the last few nights.

Kate sat shivering on a chair pressed against the wall, her face full of shock and horror. Poor Kate. The guilt she felt was reflected in her expression. Her friend's thoughts were as clear to her as if they were her own.

"If only I hadn't let her leave that night this wouldn't have happened. My fault-it's all my fault."

Going over, she sat beside Kate and laid a hand on her knee trying to comfort her. Almost immediately Kate stopped crying and froze as if she could feel Anna.

"Kate, please don't cry," she whispered. "I don't belong here."

"Anna?" a voice called from the door.

Her father stood there with his hands in his pockets looking young and boyish.

"Dad?"

"It's time to go, honey." A serene smile graced his face. He motioned with his head for her to come. "You need to choose." His eyes flicked back to her body lying on the bed.

"I don't belong here," she said softly staring down at her lifeless figure.

"You never did, sweetheart." He nodded in agreement.

"How could you know?" She asked walking over to him.

The smile that graced his face was a beam of light. "You've always belonged with him." He shrugged his shoulders. "I didn't know. But you always did. In your heart you've always known it. You've just ignored it these last years."

When he moved aside at the door, the hall opened up to reveal Royce fighting to get to her. His face was a mask of concentration terrifying to behold. It hid the sheer panic that she knew was in his heart. Lars fought beside him clearing his path. Together they worked as a team. They had beat back Louvain's men and the castle had surrendered, but Robert and a few men were still fighting on the ramparts. Her crumpled body lay thrown into a corner.

"He's waiting for you," her father said quietly beside her.

She shared a smile with her father and with one last glance at her unresponsive body she was ready to go. Peace stole over her. She wasn't afraid. Royce was waiting for her.

"Anna?" A small voice filled the corridor.

She looked down as Kate's daughter, Lily, came running up.

"She's not dead, Mommy. She's right here," the little girl said over her shoulder. Kate had just come out of the room and collapsed into her husband's arms.

Kate turned her tear stained face to her daughter confused at what she was saying. She glanced beyond her at the empty hall.

"Honey, Anna is-" Kate started to say, walking soothingly towards her daughter.

But Lily turned away from her mother and just stood there holding her stuffed puppy, stroking its head, waiting for Anna to speak.

"You've got to go, Anna. He's waiting for you," her dad said from beside her. She looked through the light at Royce as he reached her on the ramparts. Anguish pulsed through him. He picked her up and crushed her to him, calling angrily to the heavens. His voice echoed through her and her body answered.

It was time to go. Leaning down, she whispered in Lily's ear and the little girl nodded in response and then ran back to her mother who was calling her.

As she left, Lily's little voice rang out behind her. "She's not dead, Mommy. She said to tell you not to be sad. She's happy now."

But Kate's response was lost as the sound of battle rang out around her.

As she walked through the light, the air around her changed. Electricity surged through her and a searing pain filled her chest as her heart resumed its beat.

"Anna-Anna," Royce called her name over and over again.

Gasping for breath she came to, letting the air fill her lungs.

Clutching Royce's arm, she squeezed letting him know she could hear him. He pulled back and peered into her face. She smiled weakly back. A strangled moan escaped him and he looked up as though thanking the heavens.

"Don't you ever do that again," he growled, hugging her to his chest. "What the hell did you think you were doing? By God, woman, I don't know what to do with you."

Laughing weakly, she closed her eyes. "Ow."

"What?" He released her a little.

"Your armor hurts."

"That's not all that's going to hurt, madam." Cursing loudly, he stood with her in his arms, forcing the men around them back.

"She's alright? But I thought...we thought she-wait. Royce, where are you going?" Lars said from beside him. "Prince Henry wants to congrat-"

"Prince Henry can be damned. He got his battle and his win."

"But where are you going?"

"Home...Anna and I are going home."

About the Author

Announcing Jennifer Lynn in her first breakout novel sharing a timeless story of love, loss and discovering your destiny. Jennifer is an OSU buckeye native, currently residing in Ohio with her two children but can sometimes be found hitting the trails of Colorado and Utah. Now a widow after 20 years of marriage to the love of her life she understands how quickly life can change and the power of moving forward. Travel into the past with her heroine Anna, as she struggles with grief, love and finding her path in life.